P9-DEN-430

CONTEMPORARY AMERICAN FICTION

IF THE RIVER WAS WHISKEY

T. Coraghessan Boyle is a native of Peekskill, New York. He is the author of five previous works of fiction—*Descent of Man* (1979), *Water Music* (1982), *Budding Prospects* (1984), *Greasy Lake* (1985), and *World's End* (1987), winner of the PEN Faulkner Award—and his stories have appeared in most of the major American magazines, including *Esquire*, *Harper's*, *The Atlantic*, and *The Paris Review*. He lives in Los Angeles.

*I*F THE *R*IVER *W*AS *W*HISKEY

STORIES BY

T. CORAGHESSAN BOYLE

PENGUIN BOOKS

PENGUIN BOOKS
Published by the Penguin Group
Viking Penguin, a division of Penguin Books USA Inc.,
375 Hudson Street, New York, New York 10014, U.S.A.
Penguin Books Ltd, 27 Wrights Lane,
London W8 5TZ, England
Penguin Books Australia Ltd, Ringwood,
Victoria, Australia
Penguin Books Canada Ltd, 2801 John Street,
Markham, Ontario, Canada L3R 1B4
Penguin Books (N.Z.) Ltd, 182–190 Wairau Road,
Auckland 10, New Zealand
Penguin Books Ltd, Registered Offices:
Harmondsworth, Middlesex, England

First published in the United States of America by
Viking Penguin, a division of Penguin Books USA Inc., 1989
Published in Penguin Books 1990

3 5 7 9 10 8 6 4

Copyright © T. Coraghessan Boyle, 1989
All rights reserved

Acknowledgment is made to the following, in whose pages these stories first
appeared: *The Atlantic*, "Sinking House"; *Antaeus*, "The Hat"; *The Antioch
Review*, "The Devil and Irv Cherniske"; *Gentleman's Quarterly*, "If the River
Was Whiskey" and "Thawing Out"; *Granta*, "The Miracle at Ballinspittle";
Harper's, "Hard Sell," "Peace of Mind," "Sorry Fugu," and "Zapatos"; *Inter-
view*, "Me Cago en la Leche (Robert Jordan in Nicaragua)"; *The Paris Review*,
"The Ape Lady in Retirement"; *PEN Syndicated Fiction Project*, "The Little
Chill"; and *Playboy*, "The Human Fly," "King Bee," and "Modern Love."

"Sinking House" also appeared in *Prize Stories*, *The O. Henry Awards, 1989*,
edited by William Abrahams.

Excerpt from "King Bee" by Slim Harpo reprinted by permission of Excel-
lorec Music.

LIBRARY OF CONGRESS CATALOGING IN PUBLICATION DATA
Boyle, T. Coraghessan.
If the river was whiskey: stories/by T. Coraghessan Boyle.
p.   cm.—(Contemporary American fiction)
"First published in the United States of America by Viking Penguin . . .
1989"—T.p. verso.
ISBN 0 14 01.1950 7
I. Title.   II. Series.
[PS3552.O932I34   1990]
813'.54—dc20   89-29956

Printed in the United States of America
Set in Bembo
Designed by Fritz Metsch

For Kerrie, Milo, and Spencer

You know that the best you can
expect is to avoid the worst.

Italo Calvino,
If on a Winter's Night a Traveler

CONTENTS

IF THE RIVER WAS WHISKEY

Sorry Fugu

"Limp radicchio."

"Sorry fugu."

"A blasphemy of baby lamb's lettuce, frisee, endive."

"A coulibiac made in hell."

For six months he knew her only by her by-line—Willa Frank—and by the sting of her adjectives, the derisive thrust of her metaphors, the cold precision of her substantives. Regardless of the dish, despite the sincerity and ingenuity of the chef and the freshness or rarity of the ingredients, she seemed always to find it wanting. "The duck had been reduced to the state of the residue one might expect to find in the nether depths of a funerary urn"; "For all its rather testy piquancy, the orange sauce might just as well have been citron preserved in pickling brine"; "Paste and pasta. Are they synonymous? Hardly. But one wouldn't have known the difference at Udolpho's. The 'fresh' angel hair had all the taste and consistency of mucilage."

Albert quailed before those caustic pronouncements, he shuddered and blanched and felt his stomach drop like a croquette into a vat of hot grease. On the morning she skewered Udolpho's, he was sitting over a cup of reheated espresso and nibbling at a wedge of hazelnut dacquoise that had survived the previous night's crush. As was his habit on Fridays, he'd retrieved the paper from the mat, got himself a bite, and then, with the reckless abandon of a diver plunging into an icy lake, turned to

1

the "Dining Out" column. On alternate weeks, Willa Frank yielded to the paper's other regular reviewer, a big-hearted, appreciative woman by the name of Leonora Merganser, who approached every restaurant like a mother of eight feted by her children on Mother's Day, and whose praise gushed forth in a breathless salivating stream that washed the reader out of his chair and up against the telephone stand, where he would dial frantically for a reservation. But this was Willa Frank's week. And Willa Frank never liked anything.

With trembling fingers—it was only a matter of time before she slipped like a spy, like a murderess, into D'Angelo's and filleted him like all the others—he smoothed out the paper and focused on the bold black letters of the headline:

UDOLPHO'S: TROGLODYTIC CUISINE
IN A CAVELIKE ATMOSPHERE

He read on, heart in mouth. She'd visited the restaurant on three occasions, once in the company of an abstract artist from Detroit, and twice with her regular companion, a young man so discerning she referred to him only as "The Palate." On all three occasions, she'd been—sniff—disappointed. The turn-of-the-century gas lamps Udolpho's grandfather had brought over from Naples hadn't appealed to her ("so dark we joked that it was like dining among Neanderthals in the sub-basement of their cave"), nor had the open fire in the massive stone fireplace that dominated the room ("smoky, and stinking of incinerated chestnuts"). And then there was the food. When Albert got to the line about the pasta, he couldn't go on. He folded the paper as carefully as he might have folded the winding sheet over Udolpho's broken body and set it aside.

It was then that Marie stepped through the swinging doors to the kitchen, the wet cloth napkin she'd been using as a dishrag clutched in her hand. "Albert?" she gasped, darting an uneasy glance from his stricken face to the newspaper. "Is anything wrong? Did she—? Today?"

She assumed the worst, and now he corrected her in a drawl so lugubrious it might have been his expiring breath: "Udolpho's."

"Udolpho's?" Relief flooded her voice, but almost immediately it gave way to disbelief and outrage. "Udolpho's?" she repeated.

He shook his head sadly. For thirty years Udolpho's had reigned supreme among West Side restaurants, a place impervious to fads and trends, never chic but steady—classy in a way no nouvelle mangerie with its pastel walls and Breuer chairs could ever hope to be. Cagney had eaten here, Durante, Roy Rogers, Anna Maria Alberghetti. It was a shrine, an institution.

Albert himself, a pudgy sorrowful boy of twelve, ridiculed for his flab and the great insatiable fist of his appetite, had experienced the grand epiphany of his life in one of Udolpho's dark, smoky, and—for him, at least—forever exotic banquettes. Sampling the vermicelli with oil, garlic, olives, and forest mushrooms, the osso buco with the little twists of bow-tie pasta that drank up its buttery juices, he knew just as certainly as Alexander must have known he was born to conquer, that he, Albert D'Angelo, was born to eat. And that far from being something to be ashamed of, it was glorious, avocation and vocation both, the highest pinnacle to which he could aspire. Other boys had their Snider, their Mays, their Reese and Mantle, but for Albert the magical names were Pellaprat, Escoffier, Udolpho Melanzane.

Yes. And now Udolpho was nothing. Willa Frank had seen to that.

Marie was bent over the table now, reading, her piping girlish voice hot with indignation.

"Where does she come off, anyway?" Albert shrugged. Since he'd opened D'Angelo's eighteen months ago the press had all but ignored him. Yes, he'd had a little paragraph in *Barbed Wire*, the alternative press weekly handed out on street corners by greasy characters with straight pins through their noses, but you could hardly count that. There was only one paper that really mattered—Willa Frank's paper—and while word of mouth was all right, without a review in *the* paper, you were dead. Problem was, if Willa Frank wrote you up, you were dead anyway.

"Maybe you'll get the other one," Marie said suddenly. "What's her name—the good one."

Albert's lips barely moved. "Leonora Merganser."

"Well, you could."

"I want Willa Frank," he growled.

Marie's brow lifted. She closed the paper and came to him, rocked back from his belly, and pecked a kiss to his beard. "You can't be serious?"

Albert glanced bitterly around the restaurant, the simple pine tables, whitewashed walls, potted palms soft in the filtered morning light. "Leonora Merganser would faint over the Hamburger Hamlet on the corner, Long John Silver's, anything. Where's the challenge in that?"

"Challenge? But we don't want a challenge, honey—we want business. Don't we? I mean if we're going to get married and all—"

Albert sat heavily, took a miserable sip of his stone-cold espresso. "I'm a great chef, aren't I?" There was something in his tone that told her it wasn't exactly a rhetorical question.

"Honey, baby," she was in his lap now, fluffing his hair, peering into his ear, "of course you are. The best. The very best. But—"

"Willa Frank," he rumbled. "Willa Frank. I want her."

There are nights when it all comes together, when the monkfish is so fresh it flakes on the grill, when the pesto tastes like the wind through the pines and the party of eight gets their seven appetizers and six entrées in palettes of rising steam and delicate colors so perfect they might have been a single diner sitting down to a single dish. This night, however, was not such a night. This was a night when everything went wrong.

First of all, there was the aggravating fact that Eduardo—the Chilean waiter who'd learned, à la Chico Marx, to sprinkle superfluous "ahs" through his speech and thus pass for Italian—was late. This put Marie off her pace vis-à-vis the desserts, for which she was solely responsible, since she had to seat and serve the first half-dozen customers. Next, in rapid succession, Albert found that he was out of mesquite for the grill, sun-dried tomatoes for the fusilli with funghi, capers, black olives, and, yes, sun-dried tomatoes, and that the fresh cream for the frittata piemontese had mysteriously gone sour. And then, just when he'd managed to recover his equilibrium and was working in that translated state where mind and body are one, Roque went berserk.

Of the restaurant's five employees—Marie, Eduardo, Torrey, who did day-cleanup, Albert himself, and Roque—Roque operated on perhaps the most elemental level. He was the dishwasher. The Yucatano dishwasher. Whose responsibility it was to see that D'Angelo's pink and gray sets of heavy Syracuse china were kept in constant circulation through the mid-evening dinner rush. On this particular night, however, Roque was slow to accept the challenge of that responsibility, scraping plates and wielding the nozzle of his supersprayer as if in a dream. And not only was he moving slowly, the dishes, with their spatters of red and white sauce and dribbles of grease piling up beside him like the Watts Towers, but he was muttering to himself. Darkly. In a dialect so arcane even Eduardo couldn't fathom it.

When Albert questioned him—a bit too sharply, perhaps: he was overwrought himself—Roque exploded. All Albert had said was, "Roque—you all right?" But he might just as well have reviled his mother, his fourteen sisters, and his birthplace. Cursing, Roque danced back from the stainless-steel sink, tore the apron from his chest, and began scaling dishes against the wall. It took all of Albert's 220 pounds, together with Eduardo's 180, to get Roque, who couldn't have weighed more than 120 in hip boots, out the door and into the alley. Together they slammed the door on him—the door on which he continued to beat with a shoe for half an hour or more—while Marie took up the dishrag with a sigh.

A disaster. Pure, unalloyed, unmitigated. The night was a disaster.

Albert had just begun to catch up when Torrey slouched through the alley door and into the kitchen, her bony hand raised in greeting. Torrey was pale and shrunken, a nineteen-year-old with a red butch cut who spoke with the rising inflection and oblate vowels of the Valley Girl, born and bred. She wanted an advance on her salary.

"Momento, momento," Albert said, flashing past her with a pan of béarnaise in one hand, a mayonnaise jar of vivid orange sea-urchin roe in the other. He liked to use his rudimentary Italian when he was cooking. It made him feel impregnable.

Meanwhile, Torrey shuffled halfheartedly across the floor and positioned herself behind the porthole in the "out" door, where, for lack of anything better to do, she could watch the customers eat, drink, smoke, and finger their pastry. The béarnaise was puddling up beautifully on a plate of grilled baby summer squash, the roe dolloped on a fillet of monkfish nestled snug in its cruet, and Albert was thinking of offering Torrey battle pay if she'd stay and wash dishes, when she let out a low whistle. This was no cab or encore whistle, but the sort of whistle that expresses surprise or shock—a "Holy cow!" sort of whistle. It stopped Albert cold. Something bad was about to happen, he knew it, just as surely as he knew that the tiny hairs rimming his bald spot had suddenly stiffened up like hackles.

"What?" he demanded. "What is it?"

Torrey turned to him, slow as an executioner. "I see you got Willa Frank out there tonight—everything going okay?"

The monkfish burst into flame, the béarnaise turned to water,

Marie dropped two cups of coffee and a plate of homemade millefoglie.

No matter. In an instant, all three of them were pressed up against the little round window, as intent as torpedoers peering through a periscope. "Which one?" Albert hissed, his heart doing paradiddles.

"Over there?" Torrey said, making it a question. "With Jock—Jock McNamee? The one with the blond wig?"

Albert looked, but he couldn't see. "Where? Where?" he cried.

"There? In the corner?"

In the corner, in the corner. Albert was looking at a young woman, a girl, a blonde in a black cocktail dress and no brassiere, seated across from a hulking giant with a peroxide-streaked flattop. "Where?" he repeated.

Torrey pointed.

"The blonde?" He could feel Marie go slack beside him. "But that can't be—" Words failed him. *This* was Willa Frank, doyenne of taste, grande dame of haute cuisine, ferreter out of the incorrect, the underachieved, and the unfortunate? And this clod beside her, with the great smooth-working jaw and forearms like pillars, *this* was the possessor of the fussiest, pickiest, most sophisticated and fastidious palate in town? No, it was impossible.

"Like I know him, you know?" Torrey was saying. "Jock? Like from the Anti-Club and all that scene?"

But Albert wasn't listening. He was watching her—Willa Frank—as transfixed as the tailorbird that dares look into the cobra's eye. She was slim, pretty, eyes dark as a houri's, a lot of jewelry—not at all what he'd expected. He'd pictured a veiny elegant woman in her fifties, starchy, patrician, from Boston or Newport or some such place. But wait, wait: Eduardo was just setting the plates down—she was the Florentine tripe, of course—a good dish, a dish he'd stand by any day, even a bad one like . . . but the Palate, what was he having? Albert strained forward, and he could feel Marie's lost and limp hand feebly pressing his own. There: the veal piccata, yes, a very good dish, an outstanding dish. Yes. Yes.

Eduardo bowed gracefully away. The big man in the punk hairdo bent to his plate and sniffed. Willa Frank—blonde, delicious, lethal—cut into the tripe, and raised the fork to her lips.

"She hated it. I know it. I know it." Albert rocked back and forth in his chair, his face buried in his hands, the toque clinging to his brow like a carrion bird. It was past midnight, the restaurant was closed. He sat amidst the wreckage of the kitchen, the waste, the slop, the smell of congealed grease and dead spices, and his breath came in ragged sobbing gasps.

Marie got up to rub the back of his neck. Sweet, honey-completed Marie, with her firm heavy arms and graceful wrists, the spill and generosity of her flesh—his consolation in a world of Willa Franks. "It's okay," she kept saying, over and over, her voice a soothing murmur, "it's okay, it was good, it was."

He'd failed and he knew it. Of all nights, why this one? Why couldn't she have come when the structure was there, when he was on, when the dishwasher was sober, the cream fresh, and the mesquite knots piled high against the wall, when he could concentrate, for christ's sake? "She didn't finish her tripe," he said, disconsolate. "Or the grilled vegetables. I saw the plate."

"She'll be back," Marie said. "Three visits minimum, right?"

Albert fished out a handkerchief and sorrowfully blew his nose. "Yeah," he said, "three strikes and you're out." He twisted his neck to look up at her. "The Palate, Jock, whatever the jerk's name is, he didn't touch the veal. One bite maybe. Same with the pasta. Eduardo said the only thing he ate was the bread. And a bottle of beer."

"What does he know," Marie said. "Or her either."

Albert shrugged. He pushed himself up wearily, impaled on the stake of his defeat, and helped himself to a glass of Orvieto and a plate of leftover sweetbreads. "Everything," he said miserably, the meat like butter in his mouth, fragrant, nutty, inexpressibly right. He shrugged again. "Or nothing. What does it matter? Either way we get screwed."

"And 'Frank'? What kind of name is that, anyhow? German? Is that it?" Marie was on the attack now, pacing the linoleum like a field marshal probing for a weakness in the enemy lines, looking for a way in. "The Franks—weren't they those barbarians in high school that sacked Rome? Or was it Paris?"

Willa Frank. The name was bitter on his tongue. Willa, Willa, Willa. It was a bony name, scant and lean, stripped of sensuality, the antithesis of the round, full-bodied Leonora. It spoke of a knotty Puritan toughness, a denying of the flesh, no compromise in the face of temptation. Willa. How could he ever hope to seduce a Willa? And Frank. That was even worse. A man's name. Cold, forbidding, German, French. It was the name of a woman who wouldn't complicate her task with notions of charity or the sparing of feelings. No, it was the name of a woman who would wield her adjectives like a club.

Stewing in these sour reflections, eating and no longer tasting, Albert was suddenly startled by a noise outside the alley door. He picked up a saucepan and stalked across the room—What next? Were they planning to rob him now too, was that it?— and flung open the door.

In the dim light of the alleyway stood two small dark men, the smaller of whom looked so much like Roque he might have been a clone. "Hello," said the larger man, swiping a greasy Dodgers' cap from his head, "I am called Raul, and this"—indicating his companion—"is called Fulgencio, cousin of Roque." At the mention of his name, Fulgencio smiled. "Roque is gone to Albuquerque," Raul continued, "and he is sorry. But he sends you his cousin, Fulgencio, to wash for you."

Albert stood back from the door, and Fulgencio, grinning and nodding, mimed the motion of washing a plate as he stepped into the kitchen. Still grinning, still miming, he sambaed across the floor, lifted the supersprayer from its receptacle as he might have drawn a rapier from its scabbard, and started in on the dishes with a vigor that would have prostrated his mercurial cousin.

For a long moment Albert merely stood there watching, barely conscious of Marie at his back and Raul's parting gesture as he gently shut the door. All of a sudden he felt redeemed, reborn, capable of anything. There was Fulgencio, a total stranger not two minutes ago, washing dishes as if he were born to it. And there was Marie, who'd stand by him if he had to cook cactus and lizard for the saints in the desert. And here he was himself, in all the vigor of his manhood, accomplished, knowledgeable, inspired, potentially one of the great culinary artists of his time. What was the matter with him? What was he crying about?

He'd wanted Willa Frank. All right: he'd gotten her. But on an off-night, the kind of night anyone could have. Out of mesquite. The cream gone sour, the dishwasher mad. Even Puck, even Soltner, couldn't have contended with that.

She'd be back. Twice more. And he would be ready for her.

All that week, a cloud of anticipation hung over the restaurant. Albert outdid himself, redefining the bounds of his nouvelle Northern Italian cuisine with a dozen new creations, including a very nice black pasta with grilled shrimp, a pungent jugged hare, and an absolutely devastating meadowlark marinated in shallots, white wine, and mint. He worked like a man possessed, a man inspired. Each night he offered seven appetizers and six entrées, and each night they were different. He outdid himself, and outdid himself again.

Friday came and went. The morning paper found Leonora Merganser puffing some Greek place in North Hollywood, heralding spanakopita as if it had been invented yesterday and discovering evidence of divine intervention in the folds of a grape leaf. Fulgencio scrubbed dishes with a passion, Eduardo worked on his accent and threw out his chest, Marie's desserts positively floated on air. And day by day, Albert rose to new heights.

It was on Tuesday of the following week—a quiet Tuesday, one of the quietest Albert could remember—that Willa Frank appeared again. There were only two other parties in the restaurant, a skeletal septuagenarian with a professorial air and his granddaughter—at least Albert hoped she was his granddaughter—and a Beverly Hills couple who'd been coming in once a week since the place opened.

Her presence was announced by Eduardo, who slammed into the kitchen with a drawn face and a shakily scrawled cocktail order. "She's here," he whispered, and the kitchen fell silent. Fulgencio paused, sprayer in hand. Marie looked up from a plate of tortes. Albert, who'd been putting the finishing touches to a dish of sauteed scallops al pesto for the professor and a breast of duck with wild mushrooms for his granddaughter, staggered back from the table as if he'd been shot. Dropping everything, he rushed to the porthole for a glimpse of her.

It was his moment of truth, the moment in which his courage very nearly failed him. She was stunning. Glowing. As perfect and unapproachable as the plucked and haughty girls who looked out at him from the covers of magazines at the supermarket, icily elegant in a clingy silk chemise the color of béchamel. How could he, Albert D'Angelo, for all his talent and greatness of heart, ever hope to touch her, to move such perfection, to pique such jaded taste buds?

Wounded, he looked to her companions. Beside her, grinning hugely, as hearty, handsome, and bland as ever, was the Palate— he could expect no help from that quarter. And then he turned his eyes on the couple they'd brought with them, looking for signs of sympathy. He looked in vain. They were middle-aged, silver-haired, dressed to the nines, thin and stringy in the way of those who exercise inflexible control over their appetites, about as sympathetic as vigilantes. Albert understood then that it was going to be an uphill battle. He turned back to the grill, girded himself in a clean apron, and awaited the worst.

Marie fixed the drinks—two martinis, a Glenlivet neat for

Willa, and a beer for the Palate. For appetizers they ordered mozzarella di buffala marinara, the caponata D'Angelo, the octopus salad, and the veal medallions with onion marmalade. Albert put his soul into each dish, arranged and garnished the plates with all the patient care and shimmering inspiration of a Toulouse-Lautrec bent over a canvas, and watched, defeated, as each came back to the kitchen half eaten. And then came the entrées. They ordered a selection—five different dishes—and Albert, after delivering them up to Eduardo with a face of stone, pressed himself to the porthole like a voyeur.

Riveted, he watched as they sat back so that Eduardo could present the dishes. He waited, but nothing happened. They barely glanced at the food. And then, as if by signal, they began passing the plates around the table. He was stunned: what did they think this was—the Imperial Dinner at Chow Foo Luck's? But then he understood: each dish had to suffer the scrutiny of the big man with the brutal jaw before they would deign to touch it. No one ate, no one spoke, no one lifted a glass of the Château Bellegrave, 1966, to his lips, until Jock had sniffed, finger-licked, and then gingerly tasted each of Albert's creations. Willa sat rigid, her black eyes open wide, as the great-jawed, brush-headed giant leaned intently over the plate and rolled a bit of scallop or duck over his tongue. Finally, when all the dishes had circulated, the écrevisses Alberto came to rest, like a roulette ball, in front of the Palate. But he'd already snuffed it, already dirtied his fork in it. And now, with a grand gesture, he pushed the plate aside and called out in a hoarse voice for beer.

The next day was the blackest of Albert's life. There were two strikes against him, and the third was coming down the pike. He didn't know what to do. His dreams had been feverish, a nightmare of mincing truffles and reanimated pigs' feet, and he awoke with the wildest combinations on his lips—chopped pickles and shad roe, an onion-cinnamon mousse, black-eyed peas vinaigrette. He even, half-seriously, drew up a fantasy menu, a list of dishes no one had ever tasted, not sheiks or presidents. La Cuisine des Espèces en Danger, he would call it. Breast of California condor aux chanterelles; snail darter à la meunière; medallions of panda alla campagnola. Marie laughed out loud when he presented her with the menu that afternoon—"I've invented a new cuisine!" he shouted—and for a moment, the pall lifted.

But just as quickly, it descended again. He knew what he had to do. He had to speak to her, his severest critic, through the medium of his food. He had to translate for her, awaken her with a kiss. But how? How could he even begin to rouse her from her slumber when that clod stood between them like a watchdog?

As it turned out, the answer was closer at hand than he could have imagined.

It was late the next afternoon—Thursday, the day before Willa Frank's next hatchet job was due to appear in the paper—and Albert sat at a table in the back of the darkened restaurant, brooding over his menu. He was almost certain she'd be in for her final visit that night, and yet he still hadn't a clue as to how he was going to redeem himself. For a long while he sat there in his misery, absently watching Torrey as she probed beneath the front tables with the wand of her vacuum. Behind him, in the kitchen, sauces were simmering, a veal loin roasting; Marie was baking bread and Fulgencio stacking wood. He must have watched Torrey for a full five minutes before he called out to her. "Torrey!" he shouted over the roar of the vacuum. "Torrey, shut that thing off a minute, will you?"

The roar died to a wheeze, then silence. Torrey looked up.

"This guy, what's his name, Jock—what do you know about him?" He glanced down at the scrawled-over menu and then up again. "I mean, you don't know what he likes to eat, by any chance, do you?"

Torrey shambled across the floor, scratching the stubble of

her head. She was wearing a torn flannel shirt three sizes too big for her. There was a smear of grease under her left eye. It took her a moment, tongue caught in the corner of her mouth, her brow furrowed in deliberation. "Plain stuff, I guess," she said finally, with a shrug of her shoulders. "Burned steak, potatoes with the skins on, boiled peas, and that—the kind of stuff his mother used to make. You know, like shanty Irish?"

Albert was busy that night—terrifically busy, the place packed— but when Willa Frank and her Palate sauntered in at nine-fifteen, he was ready for them. They had reservations (under an assumed name, of course—M. Cavil, party of two), and Eduardo was able to seat them immediately. In he came, breathless, the familiar phrase like a tocsin on his lips—"She's here!"—and out he fluttered again, with the drinks: one Glenlivet neat, one beer. Albert never glanced up.

On the stove, however, was a smallish pot. And in the pot were three tough scarred potatoes, eyes and dirt-flecked skin intact, boiling furiously; in and amongst them, dancing in the roiling water, were the contents of a sixteen-ounce can of Mother Hubbard's discount peas. Albert hummed to himself as he worked, searing chunks of grouper with shrimp, crab, and scallops in a big pan, chopping garlic and leeks, patting a scoop of foie gras into place atop a tournedo of beef. When, some twenty minutes later, a still-breathless Eduardo rocked through the door with their order, Albert took the yellow slip from him and tore it in two without giving it a second glance. Zero hour had arrived.

"Marie!" he called, "Marie, quick!" He put on his most frantic face for her, the face of a man clutching at a wisp of grass at the very edge of a precipice.

Marie went numb. She set down her cocktail shaker and wiped her hands on her apron. There was catastrophe in the air. "What is it?" she gasped.

He was out of sea-urchin roe. And fish fumet. And Willa

Frank had ordered the fillet of grouper oursinade. There wasn't a moment to lose—she had to rush over to the Edo Sushi House and borrow enough from Greg Takesue to last out the night. Albert had called ahead. It was okay. "Go, go," he said, wringing his big pale hands.

For the briefest moment, she hesitated. "But that's all the way across town—if it takes me an hour, I'll be lucky."

And now the matter-of-life-and-death look came into his eyes. "Go," he said. "I'll stall her."

No sooner had the door slammed behind Marie, than Albert took Fulgencio by the arm. "I want you to take a break," he shouted over the hiss of the sprayer. "Forty-five minutes. No, an hour."

Fulgencio looked up at him out of the dark Aztecan slashes of his eyes. Then he broke into a broad grin. "No entiendo," he said.

Albert mimed it for him. Then he pointed at the clock, and after a flurry of nodding back and forth, Fulgencio was gone. Whistling ("Core 'ngrato," one of his late mother's favorites), Albert glided to the meat locker and extracted the hard-frozen lump of gray gristle and fat he'd purchased that afternoon at the local Safeway. Round steak, they called it, $2.39 a pound. He tore the thing from its plastic wrapping, selected his largest skillet, turned the heat up high beneath it, and unceremoniously dropped the frozen lump into the searing black depths of the pan.

Eduardo hustled in and out, no time to question the twin absences of Marie and Fulgencio. Out went the tournedos Rossini, the fillet of grouper oursinade, the veal loin rubbed with sage and coriander, the anguille alla veneziana, and the zuppa di datteri Alberto; in came the dirty plates, the congested forks, the wineglasses smeared with butter and lipstick. A great plume of smoke rose from the pan on the front burner. Albert went on whistling.

And then, on one of Eduardo's mad dashes through the kitchen, Albert caught him by the arm. "Here," he said, shoving a plate into his hand. "For the gentleman with Miss Frank."

Eduardo stared bewildered at the plate in his hand. On it, arranged with all the finesse of a blue-plate special, lay three boiled potatoes, a splatter of reduced peas, and what could only be described as a plank of meat, stiff and flat as the chopping block, black as the bottom of the pan.

"Trust me," Albert said, guiding the stunned waiter toward the door. "Oh, and here," thrusting a bottle of ketchup into his hand, "serve it with this."

Still, Albert didn't yield to the temptation to go to the porthole. Instead, he turned the flame down low beneath his saucepans, smoothed back the hair at his temples, and began counting—as slowly as in a schoolyard game—to fifty.

He hadn't reached twenty when Willa Frank, scintillating in a tomato-red Italian knit, burst through the door. Eduardo was right behind her, a martyred look on his face, his hands spread in supplication. Albert lifted his head, swelled his chest, and adjusted the great ball of his gut beneath the pristine field of his apron. He dismissed Eduardo with a flick of his hand, and turned to Willa Frank with the tight composed smile of a man running for office. "Excuse me," she was saying, her voice toneless and shrill, as Eduardo ducked out the door, "but are you the chef here?"

He was still counting: twenty-eight, twenty-nine.

"Because I just wanted to tell you"—she was so wrought up she could barely go on—"I never, never in my life . . ."

"Shhhhh," he said, pressing a finger to his lips. "It's all right," he murmured, his voice as soothing and deep as a backrub. Then he took her gently by the elbow and led her to a table he'd set up between the stove and chopping block. The table was draped with a snowy cloth, set with fine crystal, china, and sterling borrowed from his mother. There was a single chair, a single napkin. "Sit," he said.

She tore away from him. "I don't want to sit," she protested, her black eyes lit with suspicion. The knit dress clung to her like a leotard. Her heels clicked on the linoleum. "You know, don't you?" she said, backing away from him. "You know who I am."

Huge, ursine, serene, Albert moved with her as if they were dancing. He nodded.

"But why—?" He could see the appalling vision of that desecrated steak dancing before her eyes. "It's, it's like suicide."

A saucepan had appeared in his hand. He was so close to her he could feel the grid of her dress through the thin yielding cloth of his apron. "Hush," he purred, "don't think about it. Don't think at all. Here," he said, lifting the cover from the pan, "smell this."

She looked at him as if she didn't know where she was. She gazed down into the steaming pan and then looked back up into his eyes. He saw the gentle, involuntary movement of her throat.

"Squid rings in aioli sauce," he whispered. "Try one."

Gently, never taking his eyes from her, he set the pan down on the table, plucked a ring from the sauce, and held it up before her face. Her lips—full, sensuous lips, he saw now, not at all the thin stingy flaps of skin he'd imagined—began to tremble. Then she tilted her chin ever so slightly, and her mouth dropped open. He fed her like a nestling.

First the squid: one, two, three pieces. Then a pan of lobster tortellini in a thick, buttery saffron sauce. She practically licked the sauce from his fingers. This time, when he asked her to sit, when he put his big hand on her elbow and guided her forward, she obeyed.

He glanced through the porthole and out into the dining room as he removed from the oven the little toast rounds with sundried tomatoes and baked Atascadero goat cheese. Jock's head was down over his plate, the beer half gone, a great wedge of incinerated meat impaled on the tines of his fork. His massive jaw was working, his cheek distended as if with a plug of tobacco. "Here," Albert murmured, turning to Willa Frank and laying his warm, redolent hand over her eyes, "a surprise."

It was after she'd finished the taglierini alla pizzaiola, with its homemade fennel sausage and chopped tomatoes, and was experiencing the first rush of his glacé of grapefruit and Meyer lemon, that he asked about Jock. "Why him?" he said.

She scooped ice with a tiny silver spoon, licked a dollop of it from the corner of her mouth. "I don't know," she said, shrugging. "I guess I don't trust my own taste, that's all."

He lifted his eyebrows. He was leaning over her, solicitous, warm, the pan of Russian coulibiac of salmon, en brioche, with its rich sturgeon marrow and egg, held out in offering.

She watched his hands as he whisked the ice away and replaced it with the gleaming coulibiac. "I mean," she said, pausing as he broke off a morsel and fed it into her mouth, "half the time I just can't seem to taste anything, really," chewing now, her lovely throat dipping and rising as she swallowed, "and Jock— well, he hates *everything*. At least I know he'll be consistent." She took another bite, paused, considered. "Besides, to like something, to really like it and come out and say so, is taking a terrible risk. I mean, what if I'm wrong? What if it's really no good?"

Albert hovered over her. Outside it had begun to rain. He could hear it sizzling like grease in the alley. "Try this," he said, setting a plate of spiedino before her.

She was warm. He was warm. The oven glowed, the grill hissed, the scents of his creations rose about them, ambrosia and manna. "Um, good," she said, unconsciously nibbling at prosciutto and mozzarella. "I don't know," she said after a moment, her fingers dark with anchovy sauce, "I guess that's why I like fugu."

"Fugu?" Albert had heard of it somewhere. "Japanese, isn't it?"

She nodded. "It's a blowfish. They do it sushi or in little fried strips. But it's the liver you want. It's illegal here, did you know that?"

Albert didn't know.

"It can kill you. Paralyze you. But if you just nibble, just a little bit, it numbs your lips, your teeth, your whole mouth."

"What do you mean—like at the dentist's?" Albert was horrified. Numbs your lips, your mouth? It was sacrilege. "That's awful," he said.

She looked sheepish, looked chastised.

He swung to the stove and then back again, yet another pan in his hand. "Just a bite more," he coaxed.

She patted her stomach and gave him a great, wide, blooming smile. "Oh, no, no, Albert—can I call you Albert?—no, no, I couldn't."

"Here," he said, "here," his voice soft as a lover's. "Open up."

MODERN LOVE

THERE WAS NO EXCHANGE of body fluids on the first date, and that suited both of us just fine. I picked her up at seven, took her to Mee Grop, where she meticulously separated each sliver of meat from her Phat Thai, watched her down four bottles of Singha at three dollars per, and then gently stroked her balsam-smelling hair while she snoozed through *The Terminator* at the Circle Shopping Center theater. We had a late-night drink at Rigoletto's Pizza Bar (and two slices, plain cheese), and I dropped her off. The moment we pulled up in front of her apartment she had the door open. She turned to me with the long, elegant, mournful face of her Puritan ancestors and held out her hand.

"It's been fun," she said.

"Yes," I said, taking her hand.

She was wearing gloves.

"I'll call you," she said.

"Good," I said, giving her my richest smile. "And I'll call you."

On the second date we got acquainted.

"I can't tell you what a strain it was for me the other night," she said, staring down into her chocolate-mocha-fudge sundae. It was early afternoon, we were in Helmut's Olde Tyme Ice Cream Parlor in Mamaroneck, and the sun streamed through the thick frosted windows and lit the place like a convalescent home. The fixtures glowed behind the counter, the brass rail was buffed to a reflective sheen, and everything smelled of disinfectant. We were the only people in the place.

"What do you mean?" I said, my mouth glutinous with melted marshmallow and caramel.

"I mean Thai food, the seats in the movie theater, the *ladies' room* in that place for god's sake . . ."

"Thai food?" I wasn't following her. I recalled the maneuver with the strips of pork and the fastidious dissection of the glass noodles. "You're a vegetarian?"

She looked away in exasperation, and then gave me the full, wide-eyed shock of her ice-blue eyes. "Have you seen the Health Department statistics on sanitary conditions in ethnic restaurants?"

I hadn't.

Her eyebrows leapt up. She was earnest. She was lecturing. "These people are refugees. They have—well, different standards. They haven't even been inoculated." I watched her dig the tiny spoon into the recesses of the dish and part her lips for a neat, foursquare morsel of ice cream and fudge.

"The illegals, anyway. And that's half of them." She swallowed with an almost imperceptible movement, a shudder, her throat dipping and rising like a gazelle's. "I got drunk from fear," she said. "Blind panic. I couldn't help thinking I'd wind up with hepatitis or dysentery or dengue fever or something."

"Dengue fever?"

"I usually bring a disposable sanitary sheet for public theaters—just think of who might have been in that seat before you, and how many times, and what sort of nasty festering little cultures of this and that there must be in all those ancient dribbles of taffy and Coke and extra-butter popcorn—but I didn't want you to think I was too extreme or anything on the first date, so I didn't. And then the *ladies' room* . . . You don't think I'm overreacting, do you?"

As a matter of fact, I did. Of course I did. I liked Thai food—
and sushi and ginger crab and greasy souvlaki at the corner stand
too. There was the look of the mad saint in her eye, the obsessive, the mortifier of the flesh, but I didn't care. She was lovely,
wilting, clear-eyed, and pure, as cool and matchless as if she'd
stepped out of a Pre-Raphaelite painting, and I was in love.
Besides, I tended a little that way myself. Hypochondria. Anal
retentiveness. The ordered environment and alphabetized books.
I was a thirty-three-year-old bachelor, I carried some scars and
I read the newspapers—herpes, AIDS, the Asian clap that foiled
every antibiotic in the book. I was willing to take it slow. "No,"
I said, "I don't think you're overreacting at all."

I paused to draw in a breath so deep it might have been a
sigh. "I'm sorry," I whispered, giving her a doglike look of
contrition. "I didn't know."

She reached out then and touched my hand—touched it, skin
to skin—and murmured that it was all right, she'd been through
worse. "If you want to know," she breathed, "I like places like
this."

I glanced around. The place was still empty, but for Helmut,
in a blinding white jumpsuit and toque, studiously polishing the
tile walls. "I know what you mean," I said.

We dated for a month—museums, drives in the country, French
and German restaurants, ice-cream emporia, fern bars—before
we kissed. And when we kissed, after a showing of *David and
Lisa* at a revival house all the way up in Rhinebeck and on a
night so cold no run-of-the-mill bacterium or commonplace
virus could have survived it, it was the merest brushing of the
lips. She was wearing a big-shouldered coat of synthetic fur and
a knit hat pulled down over her brow and she hugged my arm
as we stepped out of the theater and into the blast of the night.
"God," she said, "did you see him when he screamed 'You
touched me!'? Wasn't that priceless?" Her eyes were big and she
seemed weirdly excited. "Sure," I said, "yeah, it was great,"

and then she pulled me close and kissed me. I felt the soft flicker of her lips against mine. "I love you," she said, "I think."

A month of dating and one dry fluttering kiss. At this point you might begin to wonder about me, but really, I didn't mind. As I say, I was willing to wait—I had the patience of Sisyphus—and it was enough just to be with her. Why rush things? I thought. This is good, this is charming, like the slow sweet unfolding of the romance in a Frank Capra movie, where sweetness and light always prevail. Sure, she had her idiosyncrasies, but who didn't? Frankly, I'd never been comfortable with the three-drinks-dinner-and-bed sort of thing, the girls who come on like they've been in prison for six years and just got out in time to put on their makeup and jump into the passenger seat of your car. Breda—that was her name, Breda Drumhill, and the very sound and syllabification of it made me melt—was different.

Finally, two weeks after the trek to Rhinebeck, she invited me to her apartment. Cocktails, she said. Dinner. A quiet evening in front of the tube.

She lived in Croton, on the ground floor of a restored Victorian, half a mile from the Harmon station, where she caught the train each morning for Manhattan and her job as an editor of *Anthropology Today*. She'd held the job since graduating from Barnard six years earlier (with a double major in Rhetoric and Alien Cultures), and it suited her temperament perfectly. Field anthropologists living among the River Dayak of Borneo or the Kurds of Kurdistan would send her rough and grammatically tortured accounts of their observations and she would whip them into shape for popular consumption. Naturally, filth and exotic disease, as well as outlandish customs and revolting habits, played a leading role in her rewrites. Every other day or so she'd call me from work and in a voice that could barely contain its joy give me the details of some new and horrific disease she'd discovered.

She met me at the door in a silk kimono that featured a plunging neckline and a pair of dragons with intertwined tails. Her hair was pinned up as if she'd just stepped out of the bath and she smelled of Noxzema and pHisoHex. She pecked my cheek, took the bottle of Vouvray I held out in offering, and led me into the front room. "Chagas' disease," she said, grinning wide to show off her perfect, outsized teeth.

"Chagas' disease?" I echoed, not quite knowing what to do with myself. The room was as spare as a monk's cell. Two chairs, a loveseat, and a coffee table, in glass, chrome, and hard black plastic. No plants ("God knows what sort of insects might live on them—and the *dirt*, the dirt has got to be crawling with bacteria, not to mention spiders and worms and things") and no rug ("A breeding ground for fleas and ticks and chiggers").

Still grinning, she steered me to the hard black plastic loveseat and sat down beside me, the Vouvray cradled in her lap. "South America," she whispered, her eyes leaping with excitement. "In the jungle. These bugs—assassin bugs, they're called—isn't that wild? These bugs bite you and then, after they've sucked on you awhile, they go potty next to the wound. When you scratch, it gets into your bloodstream, and anywhere from one to twenty years later you get a disease that's like a cross between malaria and AIDS."

"And then you die," I said.

"And then you die."

Her voice had turned somber. She wasn't grinning any longer. What could I say? I patted her hand and flashed a smile. "Yum," I said, mugging for her. "What's for dinner?"

She served a cold cream-of-tofu-carrot soup and little lentil-paste sandwiches for an appetizer and a garlic soufflé with biologically controlled vegetables for the entrée. Then it was snifters of cognac, the big-screen TV, and a movie called *The Boy in the Bubble,* about a kid raised in a totally antiseptic environment because he was born without an immune system. No one could touch him. Even the slightest sneeze would have killed him. Breda sniffled through the first half-hour, then pressed my hand and sobbed openly as the boy finally crawled out of the bubble, caught about thirty-seven different diseases, and died before the commercial break. "I've seen this movie six times now," she said, fighting to control her voice, "and it gets to me every time. What a life," she said, waving her snifter at the screen, "what a perfect life. Don't you envy him?"

I didn't envy him. I envied the jade pendant that dangled between her breasts and I told her so.

She might have giggled or gasped or lowered her eyes, but she didn't. She gave me a long slow look, as if she were deciding something, and then she allowed herself to blush, the color suffusing her throat in a delicious mottle of pink and white. "Give me a minute," she said mysteriously, and disappeared into the bathroom.

I was electrified. This was it. Finally. After all the avowals, the pressed hands, the little jokes and routines, after all the miles driven, meals consumed, museums paced, and movies watched, we were finally, naturally, gracefully going to come together in the ultimate act of intimacy and love.

I felt hot. There were beads of sweat on my forehead. I didn't know whether to stand or sit. And then the lights dimmed, and there she was at the rheostat.

She was still in her kimono, but her hair was pinned up more severely, wound in a tight coil to the crown of her head, as if she'd girded herself for battle. And she held something in her hand—a slim package, wrapped in plastic. It rustled as she crossed the room.

"When you're in love, you make love," she said, easing down beside me on the rocklike settee, "—it's only natural." She handed me the package. "I don't want to give you the wrong impression," she said, her voice throaty and raw, "just because I'm careful and modest and because there's so much, well, filth in the world, but I have my passionate side too. I do. And I love you. I think."

"Yes," I said, groping for her, the package all but forgotten.

We kissed. I rubbed the back of her neck, felt something strange, an odd sag and ripple, as if her skin had suddenly turned to Saran Wrap, and then she had her hand on my chest. "Wait," she breathed, "the, the thing."

I sat up. "Thing?"

The light was dim but I could see the blush invade her face now. She was sweet. Oh, she was sweet, my Little Em'ly, my Victorian princess. "It's Swedish," she said.

I looked down at the package in my lap. It was a clear, skinlike sheet of plastic, folded up in its transparent package like a heavy-duty garbage bag. I held it up to her huge, trembling eyes. A crazy idea darted in and out of my head. No, I thought.

"It's the newest thing," she said, the words coming in a rush, "the safest . . . I mean, nothing could possibly—"

My face was hot. "No," I said.

"It's a condom," she said, tears starting up in her eyes, "my doctor got them for me they're . . . they're Swedish." Her face wrinkled up and she began to cry. "It's a condom," she sobbed, crying so hard the kimono fell open and I could see the outline of the thing against the swell of her nipples, "a full-body condom."

I was offended. I admit it. It wasn't so much her obsession with germs and contagion, but that she didn't trust me after all that time. I was clean. Quintessentially clean. I was a man of moderate habits and good health, I changed my underwear and socks daily—sometimes twice a day—and I worked in an office, with clean, crisp, unequivocal numbers, managing my late father's chain of shoe stores (and he died cleanly himself, of a myocardial infarction, at seventy-five). "But Breda," I said, reaching out to console her and brushing her soft, plastic-clad breast in the process, "don't you trust me? Don't you believe in me? Don't you, don't you love me?" I took her by the shoulders, lifted her head, forced her to look me in the eye. "I'm clean," I said. "Trust me."

She looked away. "Do it for me," she said in her smallest voice, "if you really love me."

In the end, I did it. I looked at her, crying, crying for me, and I looked at the thin sheet of plastic clinging to her, and I did it. She helped me into the thing, poked two holes for my nostrils, zipped the plastic zipper up the back, and pulled it tight over my head. It fit like a wetsuit. And the whole thing—the stroking and the tenderness and the gentle yielding—was everything I'd hoped it would be.

Almost.

She called me from work the next day. I was playing with sales figures and thinking of her. "Hello," I said, practically cooing into the receiver.

"You've got to hear this." Her voice was giddy with excitement.

"Hey," I said, cutting her off in a passionate whisper, "last night was really special."

"Oh, yes," she said, "yes, last night. It was. And I love you, I do . . ." She paused to draw in her breath. "But listen to this: I just got a piece from a man and his wife living among the Tuareg of Nigeria—these are the people who follow cattle around, picking up the dung for their cooking fires?"

I made a small noise of awareness.

"Well, they make their huts of dung too—isn't that wild? And guess what—when times are hard, when the crops fail and the cattle can barely stand up, you know what they eat?"

"Let me guess," I said. "Dung?"

She let out a whoop. "Yes! Yes! Isn't it too much? They *eat* dung!"

I'd been saving one for her, a disease a doctor friend had told me about. "Onchocerciasis," I said. "You know it?"

There was a thrill in her voice. "Tell me."

"South America and Africa both. A fly bites you and lays its eggs in your bloodstream and when the eggs hatch, the larvae—

these little white worms—migrate to your eyeballs, right underneath the membrane there, so you can see them wriggling around."

There was a silence on the other end of the line.

"Breda?"

"That's sick," she said. "That's really sick."

But I thought—? I trailed off. "Sorry," I said.

"Listen," and the edge came back into her voice, "the reason I called is because I love you, I think I love you, and I want you to meet somebody."

"Sure," I said.

"I want you to meet Michael. Michael Maloney."

"Sure. Who's he?"

She hesitated, paused just a beat, as if she knew she was going too far. "My doctor," she said.

You have to work at love. You have to bend, make subtle adjustments, sacrifices—love is nothing without sacrifice. I went to Dr. Maloney. Why not? I'd eaten tofu, bantered about leprosy and bilharziasis as if I were immune, and made love in a bag. If it made Breda happy—if it eased the nagging fears that ate at her day and night—then it was worth it.

The doctor's office was in Scarsdale, in his home, a two-tone mock Tudor with a winding drive and oaks as old as my grandfather's Chrysler. He was a young man—late thirties, I guessed—with a red beard, shaved head, and a pair of oversized spectacles in clear plastic frames. He took me right away—the very day I called—and met me at the door himself. "Breda's told me about you," he said, leading me into the floodlit vault of his office. He looked at me appraisingly a moment, murmuring "Yes, yes" into his beard, and then, with the aid of his nurses, Miss Archibald and Miss Slivovitz, put me through a battery of tests that would have embarrassed an astronaut.

First, there were the measurements, including digital joints, maxilla, cranium, penis, and earlobe. Next the rectal exam, the EEG and urine sample. And then the tests. Stress tests, patch tests, reflex tests, lung-capacity tests (I blew up yellow balloons till they popped, then breathed into a machine the size of a Hammond organ), the X-rays, sperm count, and a closely printed, twenty-four-page questionnaire that included sections on dream analysis, genealogy, and logic and reasoning. He drew blood too, of course—to test vital-organ function and exposure to disease. "We're testing for antibodies to over fifty diseases," he said, eyes dodging behind the walls of his lenses. "You'd be surprised how many people have been infected without even knowing it." I couldn't tell if he was joking or not. On the way out he took my arm and told me he'd have the results in a week.

That week was the happiest of my life. I was with Breda every night, and over the weekend we drove up to Vermont to stay at a hygiene center her cousin had told her about. We dined by candlelight—on real food—and afterward we donned the Saran Wrap suits and made joyous, sanitary love. I wanted more, of course—the touch of skin on skin—but I was fulfilled and I was happy. Go slow, I told myself. All things in time. One night, as we lay entwined in the big white fortress of her bed, I stripped back the hood of the plastic suit and asked her if she'd ever trust me enough to make love in the way of the centuries, raw and unprotected. She twisted free of her own wrapping and looked away, giving me that matchless patrician profile. "Yes," she said, her voice pitched low, "yes, of course. Once the results are in."

"Results?"

She turned to me, her eyes searching mine. "Don't tell me you've forgotten?"

I had. Carried away, intense, passionate, brimming with love, I'd forgotten.

"Silly you," she murmured, tracing the line of my lips with

a slim, plastic-clad finger. "Does the name Michael Maloney ring a bell?"

And then the roof fell in.

I called and there was no answer. I tried her at work and her secretary said she was out. I left messages. She never called back. It was as if we'd never known one another, as if I were a stranger, a door-to-door salesman, a beggar on the street.

I took up a vigil in front of her house. For a solid week I sat in my parked car and watched the door with all the fanatic devotion of a pilgrim at a shrine. Nothing. She neither came nor went. I rang the phone off the hook, interrogated her friends, haunted the elevator, the hallway, and the reception room at her office. She'd disappeared.

Finally, in desperation, I called her cousin in Larchmont. I'd met her once—she was a homely, droopy-sweatered, baleful-looking girl who represented everything gone wrong in the genes that had come to such glorious fruition in Breda—and barely knew what to say to her. I'd made up a speech, something about how my mother was dying in Phoenix, the business was on the rocks, I was drinking too much and dwelling on thoughts of suicide, destruction, and final judgment, and I had to talk to Breda just one more time before the end, and did she by any chance know where she was? As it turned out, I didn't need the speech. Breda answered the phone.

"Breda, it's me," I choked. "I've been going crazy looking for you."

Silence.

"Breda, what's wrong? Didn't you get my messages?"

Her voice was halting, distant. "I can't see you anymore," she said.

"Can't see me?" I was stunned, hurt, angry. "What do you mean?"

"All those feet," she said.

"Feet?" It took me a minute to realize she was talking about the shoe business. "But I don't deal with anybody's feet—I work in an office. Like you. With air-conditioning and sealed windows. I haven't touched a foot since I was sixteen."

"Athlete's foot," she said. "Psoriasis. Eczema. Jungle rot."

"What is it? The physical?" My voice cracked with outrage. "Did I flunk the damn physical? Is that it?"

She wouldn't answer me.

A chill went through me. "What did he say? What did the son of a bitch say?"

There was a distant ticking over the line, the pulse of time and space, the gentle sway of Bell Telephone's hundred million miles of wire.

"Listen," I pleaded, "see me one more time, just once—that's all I ask. We'll talk it over. We could go on a picnic. In the park. We could spread a blanket and, and we could sit on opposite corners—"

"Lyme disease," she said.

"Lyme disease?"

"Spread by tick bite. They're seething in the grass. You get Bell's palsy, meningitis, the lining of your brain swells up like dough."

"Rockefeller Center then," I said. "By the fountain."

Her voice was dead. "Pigeons," she said. "They're like flying rats."

"Helmut's. We can meet at Helmut's. Please. I love you."

"I'm sorry."

"Breda, please listen to me. We were so close—"

"Yes," she said, "we were close," and I thought of that first night in her apartment, the boy in the bubble and the Saran Wrap suit, thought of the whole dizzy spectacle of our romance till her voice came down like a hammer on the refrain, "but not that close."

H ARD S ELL

*S*o MAYBE I come on a little strong.

"Hey, babes," I say to him (through his interpreter, of course, this guy with a face like a thousand fists), "the beard's got to go. And that thing on your head too—I mean I can dig it and all; it's kinda wild, actually—but if you want to play with the big boys, we'll get you a toup." I wait right there a minute to let the interpreter finish his jabbering, but there's no change in the old bird's face—I might just as well have been talking to my shoes. But what the hey, I figure, he's paying me a hundred big ones up front, the least I can do is give it a try. "And this *jihad* shit, can it, will you? I mean that kinda thing might go down over here but on Santa Monica Boulevard, believe me, it's strictly from hunger."

Then the Ayatollah looks at me, one blink of these lizard eyes he's got, and he says something in this throat-cancer rasp—he's tired or he needs an enema or something—and the interpreter stands, the fourteen guys against the wall with the Uzis stand, some character out the window starts yodeling the midday prayers, and I stand too. I can feel it, instinctively—I mean, I'm perceptive, you know that, Bob—that's it for the first day. I mean, nothing. Zero. Zilch. And I go out of there shaking my head, all these clowns with the Uzis closing in on me like piranha, and I'm thinking how in christ does this guy expect to upgrade his image when half the country's in their bathrobe morning, noon, and night?

Okay. So I'm burned from jet lag anyway, and I figure I'll write the day off, go back to the hotel, have a couple Tanqueray rocks, and catch some z's. What a joke, huh? They don't have Tanqueray, Bob. Or rocks either. They don't have Beefeater's or Gordon's—they don't have a bar, for christsake. Can you believe it—the whole damn country, the cradle of civilization, and it's dry. All of a sudden I'm beginning to see the light— this guy really *is* a fanatic. So anyway I'm sitting at this table in the lobby drinking grape soda—yeah, grape soda, out of the can—and thinking I better get on the horn with Chuck back in Century City, I mean like I been here what—three hours?— and already the situation is going down the tubes, when I feel this like pressure on my shoulder.

I turn around and who is it but the interpreter, you know, the guy with the face. He's leaning on me with his elbow. Like I'm a lamppost or something, and he's wearing this big shit-eating grin. He's like a little Ayatollah, this guy—beard, bath-robe, slippers, hat, the works—and he's so close I can smell the roots of his hair.

"I don't like the tone you took with the Imam," he says in this accent right out of a Pepperidge Farm commercial, I mean like Martha's Vineyard all the way, and then he slides into the chair across from me. "This is not John Travolta you're ad-dressing, my very sorry friend. This is the earthly representative of the Qā'im, who will one day come to us to reveal the secrets of the divinity, Allah be praised." Then he lowers his voice, drops the smile, and gives me this killer look. "Show a little respect," he says.

You know me, Bob—I don't take shit from anybody, I don't care who it is, Lee Iacocca, Steve Garvey, Joan Rivers (all clients of ours, by the way), and especially not from some nimrod that looks like he just walked off the set of *Lawrence of Arabia*, right?

So I take a long swallow of grape soda, Mr. Cool all the way, and then set the can down like it's a loaded .44. "Don't tell me," I go, "—Harvard, right?"

And the jerk actually smiles. "Class of '68."

"Listen, pal," I start to say, but he interrupts me.

"The name is Hojatolislam."

Hey, you know me, I'm good with names—have to be in this business. But Hojatolislam? You got to be kidding. I mean I don't even attempt it. "Okay," I say, "I can appreciate where you're coming from, the guy's a big deal over here, yeah, all right . . . but believe me, you take it anyplace else and your Ayatollah's got about as positive a public image as the Son of Sam. That's what you hired us for, right? Hey, I don't care what people think of the man, to me, I'm an agnostic personally, and this is just another guy with a negative public perception that wants to go upscale. And I'm going to talk to him. Straight up. All the cards on the table."

And then you know what he does, the chump? He says I'm crass. (Crass—and I'm wearing an Italian silk suit that's worth more than this joker'll make in six lifetimes and a pair of hand-stitched loafers that cost me . . . but I don't even want to get into it.) Anway, I'm crass. I'm going to undermine the old fart's credibility, as if he's got any. It was so-and-so's party that wanted me in—to make the Ayatollah look foolish—and he, Hojatolislam, is going to do everything in his power to see that it doesn't happen.

"Whoa," I go, "don't let's mix politics up in this. I was hired to do a job here and I'm going to do it, whether you and the rest of the little ayatollahs like it or not."

Hoji kinda draws himself up and gives me this tight little kiss-my-ass smile. "Fine," he says, "you can do what you want, but you know how much of what you said this morning came across? In *my* translation, that is?"

Then it dawns on me: no wonder the Ayatollah looks like

he's in la-la land the whole time I'm talking to him—nothing's
getting through. "Let me guess," I say.

But he beats me to it, the son of a bitch. He leans forward
on his elbows and makes this little circle with his thumb and
index finger and then holds it up to his eye and peeks through
it—real cute, huh?

I don't say a word. But I'm thinking okay, pal, you want to
play hardball, we'll play hardball.

So it sounds like I'm in pretty deep, right? You're probably
thinking it's tough enough to market this turkey to begin with,
let alone having to deal with all these little ayatollahs and their
pet gripes. But the way I see it, it's no big problem. You got
to ask yourself, what's this guy got going for him? All right,
he's a fanatic. We admit it. Up front. But hell, you can capitalize
on anything. Now the big thing about a fanatic is he's sexy—
look at Hitler, Stalin, with that head of hair of his, look at Fidel—
and let's face it, he's got these kids, these so-called martyrs of
the revolution, dying for him by the thousands. The guy's got
charisma to burn, no doubt about it. Clean him up and put him
in front of the TV cameras, that's the way I see it—and no, I'm
not talking Merv Griffin and that sort of thing; I mean I can't
feature him up there in a luau shirt with a couple of gold chains
or anything like that—but he could show some chest hair, for
christsake. I mean he's old, but hell, he's a pretty sexy guy in
his way. A power trip like that, all those kids dying in the
swamps, giving the Iraqis hell, that's a very sexy thing. In a
weird way, I mean. Like it's a real turn-on. Classic. But my
idea is maybe get him a gig with GTE or somebody. You know,
coach up his English like with that French guy they had on
selling perfume a couple years back, real charming, sweet-guy
kinda thing, right? No, selling the man is the least of my worries.
But if I can't talk to him, I'm cooked.

So I go straight to my room and get Chuck on the horn.

"Chuck," I tell him, "they're killing me over here. Send me an interpreter on the next plane, will you? Somebody that's on our side."

Next morning, there's a knock on my door. It's this guy about five feet tall and five feet wide, with this little goatee and kinky hair all plastered down on his head. His name's Parviz. Yesterday he's selling rugs on La Brea, today he's in Tehran. Fine. No problem. Only thing is he's got this accent like Akim Tamiroff, I mean I can barely understand him myself, he's nodding off to sleep on me, and I've got an appointment with the big guy at one. There's no time for formalities, and plus the guy doesn't know from shit about PR anyway, so I sit him down and wire him up with about sixty cups of crank and then we're out the door.

"Okay, Parviz," I say, "let's run with it."

Of course, we don't even get in the door at the Ayatollah's place and these creeps with the Uzis have Parviz up against the wall, feeling him up and jabbering away at him in this totally weird language of theirs—sounds like a tape loop of somebody clearing their throat. I mean, they feel me up too, but poor Parviz, they strip him down to his underwear—this skinny-strap T-shirt with his big pregnant gut hanging out and these boxer shorts with little blue parrots on them—and the guy's awake now, believe me. Awake, and sweating like a pig. So anyway, they usher us into this room—different room, different house than yesterday, by the way—and there he is, the Ayatollah, propped up on about a hundred pillows and giving us his lizard-on-a-rock look. Hoji's there too, of course, along with all the other Ayatollah clones with their raggedy beards and pillbox hats.

Soon as Hoji gets a load of Parviz though, he can see what's coming and he throws some kind of fit, teeth flashing in his beard, his face bruised up like a bag of bad plums, pissing and moaning and pointing at me and Parviz like we just got done raping his mother or something. But hey, I've taken some meetings in my time and if I can't handle it, Bob, I mean who can? So I just kinda brush right by Hoji, a big closer's smile on my face, and shake the old bird's hand, and I mean nobody shakes his hand—nobody's laid skin on him in maybe ten years, at least since the revolution, anyway. But I figure the guy used to live in Paris, right? He's gotta have a nose for a good bottle of wine, a plate of crayfish, Havana cigars, the track, he's probably dying for somebody to press some skin and shoot the bull about life in the civilized world. So I shake his hand and the room tenses up, but at least it shuts up Hoji for a minute and I see my opening. "Parviz," I yell over my shoulder, "tell him that I said we both got the same goal, which is positive name/face recognition worldwide. I mean billboards on Sunset, the works, and if he listens to me and cleans up his act a little, I'm ninety-nine percent sure we're going home."

Well, Parviz starts in and right away Hoji cuts him off with this high-octane rap, but the Ayatollah flicks his eyes and it's like the guy just had the tongue ripped out of his head, I mean incredible, bang, that's it. Hoji ducks his head and he's gone. And me, I'm smiling like Mr. Cool. Parviz goes ahead and finishes and the old bird clears his throat and croaks something back.

I'm not even looking at Parviz, just holding the Ayatollah's eyes—by the way, I swear he dyes his eyebrows—and I go, "What'd he say?"

And Parviz tells me. Twice. Thing is, I can't understand a word he says, but the hell with it, I figure, be positive, right? "Okay," I say, seeing as how we're finally getting down to brass tacks, "about the beard. Tell him beards went out with Jim Morrison—and the bathrobe business is kinda kinky, and we can play to that if he wants, but wouldn't he feel more comfortable in a nice Italian knit?"

The big guy says nothing, but I can see this kinda glimmer in his eyes and I know he's digging it, I mean I can feel it, and I figure we'll worry about the grooming later and I cut right to the heart of it and lay my big idea on him, the idea that's going to launch the whole campaign.

This is genius, Bob, you're going to love it.

I ask myself, how do we soften this guy a little, you know, break down the barriers between him and the public, turn all that negative shit around? And what audience are we targeting here? Think about it. He can have all the camel drivers and Kalashnikov toters in the world, but let's face it, the bottom line is how does he go down over here and that's like no-wheresville. So my idea is this: baseball. Yeah, baseball. Where would Castro be without it? What can the American public relate to—and I'm talking the widest sector now, from the guys in the boardroom to the shlump with the jackhammer out the window there—better than baseball? Can you dig it: the Ayatollah's a closet baseball fan, but his people need him so much—love him, a country embattled, he's like a Winston Churchill to them—they won't let him come to New York for a Yankee game. Can you picture it?

No? Well, dig the photo. Yeah. From yesterday's *New York Times*. See the button there, on his bathrobe? Well, maybe it is a little fuzzy, AP is the pits, but that's a "Go Yankees!" button I gave him myself.

No, listen, he liked it, Bob, he liked it. I could tell. I mean I lay the concept on him and he goes off into this fucking solil-oquy, croaking up a storm, and then Parviz tells me it's okay but it's all over for today, he's gotta have his hat surgically removed or something, and the guys with the Uzis are closing in again . . . but I'm seeing green, Bob, I'm seeing him maybe throwing out the first ball this spring, Yankees versus the Reds or Pirates—okay, okay, wrong league—the Birds, then—I'm telling you, the sun on his face, Brooks Brothers draping his shoulders, the cameras whirring, and the arc of that ball just going on and on, out over the grass, across the airwaves and into the lap of every regular Joe in America.

Believe me, Bob, it's in the bag.

PEACE OF MIND

*F*IRST SHE TOLD THEM the story of the family surprised over their corn muffins by the masked intruder. "He was a black man," she said, dropping her voice and at the same time allowing a hint of tremolo to creep into it, "and he was wearing a lifelike mask of President Reagan. He just jimmied the lock and waltzed in the front door with the morning paper as if he was delivering flowers or something. . . . They thought it was a joke at first." Giselle's voice became hushed now, confidential, as she described how he'd brutalized the children, humiliated the wife—"Sexually, if you know what I mean"—and bound them all to the kitchen chair with twists of sheer pantyhose. Worse, she said, he dug a scratchy old copy of Sam and Dave's "Soul Man" out of the record collection and made them listen to it over and over as he looted the house. They knew he was finished when Sam and Dave choked off, the stereo rudely torn from the socket and thrown in with the rest of their things—she paused here to draw a calculated breath—"And at seven-thirty A.M., no less."

She had them, she could see it in the way the pretty little wife's eyes went dark with hate and the balding husband clutched fitfully at his pockets—she had them, but she poured it on anyway, flexing her verbal muscles, not yet noon and a sale, a big sale, already in the bag. So she gave them an abbreviated version of the story of the elderly lady and the overworked Mexican from the knife-sharpening service and wrung some hideous new

39

truths from the tale of the housewife who came home to find a strange car in her garage. "A strange car?" the husband prompted, after she'd paused to level a doleful, frightened look on the wife. Giselle sighed. "Two white men met her at the door. They were in their early forties, nicely dressed, polite— she thought they were real-estate people or something. They escorted her into the house, bundled up the rugs, the paintings, the Camcorder and VCR and then took turns desecrating"— that was the term she used, it got them every time—"desecrating her naked body with the cigarette lighter from her very own car."

The husband and wife exchanged a glance, then signed on for the whole shmeer—five thousand and some-odd dollars for the alarm system—every window, door, keyhole, and crevice wired— and sixty bucks a month for a pair of "Armed Response" signs to stick in the lawn. Giselle slid into the front seat of the Mercedes and cranked up the salsa music that made her feel as if every day was a fiesta, and then let out a long slow breath. She checked her watch and drew a circle around the next name on her list. It was a few minutes past twelve, crime was rampant, and she was feeling lucky. She tapped her foot and whistled along with the sour, jostling trumpets—no doubt about it, she'd have another sale before lunch.

The balding husband stood at the window and watched the Mercedes back out of the driveway, drift into gear, and glide soundlessly up the street. It took him a moment to realize he was still clutching his checkbook. "God, Hil," he said (or, rather, croaked—something seemed to be wrong with his throat), "it's a lot of money."

The pretty little wife, Hilary, crouched frozen on the couch, legs drawn up to her chest, feet bare, toenails glistening. "They stuff your underwear in your mouth," she whispered, "that's the worst thing. Can you imagine that, I mean the taste of it— your own underwear?"

Ellis didn't answer. He was thinking of the masked intruder—

that maniac disguised as the President—and of his own children, whose heedless squeals of joy came to him like hosannas from the swingset out back. He'd been a fool, he saw that now. How could he have thought, even for a minute, that they'd be safe out here in the suburbs? The world was violent, rotten, corrupt, seething with hatred and perversion, and there was no escaping it. Everything you worked for, everything you loved, had to be locked up as if you were in a castle under siege.

"I wonder what they did to her," Hilary said.

"Who?"

"That woman—the one with the cigarette lighter. I heard they burn their initials into you."

Yes, of course they did, he thought—why wouldn't they? They sold crack in the elementary schools, pissed in the alleys, battered old women for their Social Security checks. They'd cleaned out Denny Davidson while he was in the Bahamas and ripped the stereo out of Phyllis Steubig's Peugeot. And just last week they'd stolen two brand-new Ironcast aluminum garbage cans from the curb in front of the neighbor's house—just dumped the trash in the street and drove off with them. "What do you think, Hil?" he said. "We can still get out of it."

"I don't care what it costs," she murmured, her voice drained of emotion. "I won't be able to sleep till it's in."

Ellis crossed the room to gaze out on the sun-dappled back-yard. Mifty and Corinne were on the swings, pumping hard, lifting up into the sky and falling back again with a pure rhythmic grace that was suddenly so poignant he could feel a sob rising in his throat. "I won't either," he said, turning to his wife and spreading his hands as if in supplication. "We've got to have it."

"Yes," she said.

"If only for our peace of mind."

Giselle was pretty good with directions—she had to be, in her business—but still she had to pull over three times to consult her Thomas' Guide before she found the next address on her list. The house was in a seedy, run-down neighborhood of blasted trees, gutted cars, and tacky little houses, the kind of neighborhood that just made her blood boil—how could people live like that? she wondered, flicking off the tape in disgust. Didn't they have any self-respect? She hit the accelerator, scattering a pack of snarling, hyenalike dogs, dodged a stained mattress and a pair of overturned trash cans and swung into the driveway of a house that looked as if it had been bombed, partially reconstructed, and then bombed again. There has to be some mistake, she thought. She glanced up and caught the eye of the man sitting on the porch next door. He was fat and shirtless, his chest and arms emblazoned with lurid tattoos, and he was in the act of lifting a beer can to his lips when he saw that she was peering at him from behind the frosted window of her car. Slowly, as if it cost him an enormous effort, he lowered the beer can and raised the middle finger of his free hand.

She rechecked her list. 7718 Picador Drive. There was no number on the house in front of her, but the house to the left was 7716 and the one to the right 7720. This was it, all right. She stepped out of the car with her briefcase, squared her shoulders, and slammed the door, all the while wondering what in god's name the owner of a place like this would want with an alarm system. These were the sort of the people who broke into houses—and here she turned to give the fat man an icy glare—not the ones who had anything to protect. But then what did she care?—a sale was a sale. She set the car alarm with a fierce snap of her wrist, waited for the reassuring bleat of response from the bowels of the car, and marched up the walk.

The man who answered the door was tall and stooped—midfifties, she guessed—and he looked like a scholar in his wirerims and the dingy cardigan with the leather elbow patches. His hair was the color of freshly turned dirt and his eyes, slightly distorted and swimming behind the thick lenses, were as blue as the skies over Oklahoma. "Mr. Coles?" she said.

He looked her up and down, taking his time. "And what're

you supposed to be," he breathed in a wheezy humorless drawl, "the Avon Lady or something?" It was then that she noticed the nervous little woman frozen in the shadows of the hallway behind him. "Everett," the woman said in a soft, pleading tone, but the man took no notice of her. "Or don't tell me," he said, "you're selling Girl Scout cookies, right?"

When it came to sales, Giselle was unshakable. She saw her opening and thrust out her hand. "Giselle Nyerges," she said, "I'm from SecureCo? You contacted us about a home security system?"

The woman vanished. The fat man next door blew into his fist and produced a rude noise and Everett Coles, with a grin that showed too much gum, took her hand and led her into the house.

Inside, the place wasn't as bad as she'd expected. K-Mart taste, of course, furniture made of particle board, hopelessly tacky bric-a-brac, needlepoint homilies on the walls, but at least it was spare. And clean. The man led her through the living room to the open-beam kitchen and threw himself down in a chair at the Formica table. A sliding glass door gave onto the dusty expanse of the backyard. "So," he said. "Let's hear it."

"First I want to tell you how happy I am that you're considering a SecureCo home security system, Mr. Coles," she said, sitting opposite him and throwing the latches on her briefcase with a professional snap. "I don't know if you heard about it," she said, the conspiratorial whisper creeping into her voice, "but just last week they found a couple—both retirees, on a fixed income—bludgeoned to death in their home not three blocks from here. And they'd been security-conscious too—deadbolts on the doors and safety locks on the windows. The killer was this black man—a Negro—and he was wearing a lifelike mask of President Reagan. . . . Well, he found this croquet mallet . . ."

She faltered. The man was looking at her in the oddest way. Really, he was. He was grinning still—grinning as if she were telling a joke—and there was something wrong with his eyes. They seemed to be jerking back and forth in the sockets, jittering like the shiny little balls in a pinball machine. "I know it's not a pleasant story, Mr. Coles," she said, "but I like my customers to know that, that . . ." Those eyes were driving her crazy. She looked down, shuffling through the papers in her briefcase.

"They crowd you," he said.

"Pardon?" Looking up again.

"Sons of bitches," he growled, "they crowd you."

She found herself gazing over his shoulder at the neat little needlepoint display on the kitchen wall: SEMPER FIDELIS; HOME SWEET HOME; BURN, BABY, BURN.

"You like?" he said.

Burn, Baby, Burn?

"Did them myself." He dropped the grin and gazed out on nothing. "Got a lot of time on my hands."

She felt herself slipping. This wasn't the way it was supposed to go at all. She was wondering if she should hit him with another horror story or get down to inspecting the house and writing up an estimate, when he asked if she wanted a drink. "Thank you, no," she said. And then, with a smile, "It's a bit early in the day for me."

He said nothing, just looked at her with those jumpy blue eyes till she had to turn away. "Shit," he spat suddenly, "come down off your high horse, lady, let your hair down, loosen up."

She cleared her throat. "Yes, well, shouldn't we have a look around so I can assess your needs?"

"Gin," he said, and his voice was flat and calm again, "it's the elixir of life." He made no move to get up from the table. "You're a good-looking woman, you know that?"

"Thank you," she said in her smallest voice. "Shouldn't we—?"

"Got them high heels and pretty little ankles, nice earrings, hair all done up, and that smart little tweed suit—of course you know you're a good-looking woman. Bet it don't hurt the sales a bit, huh?"

She couldn't help herself now. All she wanted was to get up from the table and away from those jittery eyes, sale or no sale. "Listen," she said, "listen to me. There was this woman and she came home and there was this strange car in her garage—"

"No," he said, "you listen to me."

" 'Panty Rapist Escapes,' " Hilary read aloud in a clear declamatory tone, setting down her coffee mug and spreading out the "Metro" section as if it were a sacred text. " 'Norbert Baptiste, twenty-seven, of Silverlake, dubbed the Panty Rapist because he gagged his victims with their own underthings . . .' " She broke off to give her husband a look of muted triumph. "You see," she said, lifting the coffee mug to her lips, "I told you. *With their own underthings.*"

Ellis Hunsicker was puzzling over the boxscores of the previous night's ballgames, secure as a snail in its shell. It was early Saturday morning, Mifty and Corinne were in the den watching cartoons, and the house alarm was still set from the previous night. In a while, after he'd finished his muesli and his second cup of coffee, he'd punch in the code and disarm the thing and then maybe do a little gardening and afterward take the girls to the park. He wasn't really listening, and he murmured a half-hearted reply.

"And can you imagine Tina Carfarct trying to tell me we were just wasting our money on the alarm system?" She pinched her voice in mockery: " 'I hate to tell you, Hil, but this is the safest neighborhood in L.A.' Jesus, she's like a Pollyanna or something, but you know what it is, don't you?"

Ellis looked up from the paper.

"They're too cheap, that's what—her and Sid both. They're going to take their chances, hope it happens to the next guy, and all to save a few thousand dollars. It's sick. It really is."

Night before last they'd had the Carfarcts and their twelve-year-old boy, Brewster, over for dinner—a nice sole amandine and scalloped potatoes Ellis had whipped up himself—and the chief object of conversation was, of course, the alarm system. "I don't know," Sid had said (Sid was forty, handsome as a prince, an investment counselor who'd once taught high-school social studies), "it's kind of like being a prisoner in your own home."

"All that money," Tina chimed in, sucking at the cherry of her second Manhattan, "I mean I don't think I could stand it. Like Sid says, I'd feel like I was a prisoner or something, afraid to step out into my own yard because some phantom mugger might be lurking in the marigolds."

"The guy in the Reagan mask was no phantom," Hilary said, leaning across the table to slash the air with the flat of her hand, bracelets ajangle. "Or those two men—*white* men—who accosted that woman in her own garage—" She was so wrought up she couldn't go on. She turned to her husband, tears welling in her eyes. "Go on," she'd said, "tell them."

It was then that Tina had made her "safest neighborhood in L.A." remark and Sid, draining his glass and setting it down carefully on the table, had said in a phlegmy, ruminative voice, "I don't know, it's like you've got no faith in your fellow man," to which Ellis had snapped, "Don't be naive, Sid."

Even Tina scored him for that one. "Oh, come off it, Sid," she said, giving him a sour look.

"Let's face it," Ellis said, "it's a society of haves and have-nots, and like it or not, we're the haves."

"I don't deny there's a lot of crazies out there and all," Tina went on, swiveling to face Ellis, "it's just that the whole idea of having an alarm on everything—I mean you can't park your car at the mall without it—is just, well, it's a sad thing. I mean next thing you know people'll be wearing these body alarms to work, rub up against them in a crowd and—bingo!—lights flash and sirens go off." She sat back, pleased with herself, a tiny, elegant blonde in a low-cut cocktail dress and a smug grin, untouched, unafraid, a woman without a care in the world.

But then Sid wanted to see the thing and all four of them were at the front door, gathered round the glowing black plastic panel as if it were some rare jewel, some treasure built into the wall. Ellis was opening the closet to show them the big metal box that contained the system's "brain," as the SecureCo woman had called it, when Sid, taken by the allure of the thing, lightly touched the tip of his index finger to the neat glowing red strip at the bottom that read EMERGENCY.

Instantly, the scene was transformed. Whereas a moment earlier they'd been calm, civilized people having a drink before a calm, civilized meal, they were suddenly transformed into hand-wringing zombies, helpless in the face of the technology that assaulted them. For Sid had activated the alarm and no one, least of all Ellis, knew what to do about it. The EMERGENCY strip was flashing wildly, the alarm beep-beep-beeping, the girls and the Carfarcts' boy fleeing the TV room in confusion, four pairs of hands fluttering helplessly over the box, and Ellis trying to dredge up the disarm code from the uncertain pocket of memory in which it was stored. "One-two-two-one!" Hilary shouted. Tina was holding her ears and making a face. Sid looked abashed.

When at last—after two false starts—Ellis had succeeded in disarming the thing and they'd settled back with their drinks and exclamations of "Jesus!" and "I thought I was going to die," there was a knock at the door. It was a man in a SecureCo uniform, with nightstick and gun. He was tall and he had a mustache. He invited himself in. "There a problem?" he asked.

"No, no," Ellis said, standing in the entranceway, heart pounding, acutely aware of his guests' eyes on him, "it's a new system and we, uh—it was a mistake."

"Name?" the man said.

"Hunsicker. Ellis."

"Code word?"

Here Ellis faltered. The code word, to be used for purposes

of positive identification in just such a situation as this, was Hilary's inspiration. Pick something easy to remember, the SecureCo woman had said, and Hilary had chosen the name of the kids' pet rabbit, Honey Bunny. Ellis couldn't say the words. Not in front of this humorless man in the mustache, not with Sid and Tina watching him with those tight mocking smiles on their lips . . .

"Code word?" the man repeated.

Hilary was sunk into the couch at the far end of the coffee table. She leaned forward and raised her hand like a child in class, waving it to catch the guard's attention. "Honey Bunny," she said in a gasp that made the hair prickle at the back of Ellis' neck, "it's Honey Bunny."

That had been two nights ago.

But now, in the clear light of Saturday morning, after sleeping the sleep of the just—and prudent (Panty Rapist—all the Panty Rapists in the world could escape and it was nothing to him)—feeling self-satisfied and content right on down to the felt lining of his slippers, Ellis sat back, stretched, and gave his wife a rich little smile. "I guess it's a matter of priorities, honey," he said. "Sid and Tina can think what they want, but you know what I say—better safe than sorry."

When she talked about it afterward—with her husband at Gennaro's that night (she was too upset to cook), with her sister, with Betty Berger on the telephone—Giselle said she'd never been so scared in all her life. She meant it too. This was no horror story clipped from the newspaper, this was real. And it happened to her.

The guy was crazy. Creepy. Sick. He'd kept her there over four hours, and he had no intention of buying anything—she could see that in the first fifteen minutes. He just wanted an audience. Somebody to rant at, to threaten, to pin down with those jittery blue eyes. Richard had wanted her to go to the police, but she balked. What had he done, really? Scared her, yes. Bruised her arm. But what could the police do—she'd gone there of her own free will.

Her own free will. He'd said that. Those were his exact words.

Indignant, maybe a little shaken, she'd got up from the kitchen table to stuff her papers back into the briefcase. He was cursing under his breath, muttering darkly about the idiots on the free-way in their big-ass Mercedeses, crowding him, about spics and niggers and junior-high kids cutting through his yard—"Free country, my ass!" he'd shouted suddenly. "Free for every punk and weirdo and greaser to crap all over what little bit I got left, but let me get up from this table and put a couple holes in one of the little peckerheads and we'll see how it is. And I suppose you're going to protect me, huh, Miss Mercedes Benz with your heels and stockings and your big high-tech alarm system, huh?"

When she snapped the briefcase closed—no sale, nothing, just get me out of here, she was thinking—that was when he grabbed her arm. "Sit down," he snarled, and she tried to shake free but couldn't, he was strong with the rage of the psychopath, the lion in its den, the loony up against the wall.

"You're hurting me," she said as he forced her back down. "Mr. . . . Coles!" and she heard her own voice jump with anger, fright, pain.

"Yeah, that's right," he said, tightening his grip, "but you came here of your own free will, didn't you? Thought you were going to sucker me, huh? Run me a song and dance and lay your high-tech crap and your big bad SecureCo guards on me—oh, I've seen them, bunch of titsuckers and college wimps, who they going to stop? Huh?" He dropped her arm and challenged her with his jumpy mad tight-jawed glare.

She tried to get up but he roared, "Sit down! We got business here, goddamnit!" And then he was calling for his wife: "Glenys! Woman! Get your ass in here."

If she'd expected anything from the wife, any help or melioration, Giselle could see at a glance just how hopeless it was. The woman wouldn't look at her. She appeared in the doorway, pale as death, her hands trembling, staring at the carpet like a whipped dog. "Two G&T's," Coles said, sucking in his breath as if he were on the very edge of something, at the very beginning, "tall, with a wedge of lime."

"But—" Giselle began to protest, looking from Coles to the woman.

"You'll drink with me, all right." Coles' voice came at her like a blade of ice. "Get friendly, huh? Show me what you got." And then he turned away, his face violent with disgust. "SecureCo," he spat. He looked up, staring past her. "You going to keep the sons of bitches away from me, you going to keep them off my back, you going to give me any guarantees?" His voice rose. "I got a gun collection worth twelve thousand dollars in there—you going to answer for that? For my color TV? The goddamned trash can even?"

Giselle sat rigid, wondering if she could make a break for the back door and wondering if he was the type to keep it locked.

"Sell me," he demanded, looking at her now.

The woman set down the gin-and-tonics and then faded back into the shadows of the hallway. Giselle said nothing.

"Tell me about the man in the mask," he said, grinning again, grinning wide, too wide, "tell me about those poor old retired people. Come on," he said, his eyes taunting her, "sell me. I want it. I do. I mean I really need you people and your high-tech bullshit . . ."

He held her eyes, gulped half his drink, and set the glass down again. "I mean really," he said. "For my peace of mind."

It wasn't the fender-bender on the freeway the night before or the two hundred illegals lined up and looking for work on Canoga Avenue at dawn, and it wasn't the heart-clenching hate he still felt after being forced into early retirement two years

ago or the fact that he'd sat up all night drinking gin while
Glenys slept and the police and insurance companies filed their
reports—it wasn't any of that that finally drove Everett Coles
over the line. Not that he'd admit, anyway. It wasn't that little
whore from SecureCo either (that's what she was, a whore,
selling her tits and her lips and her ankles and all the rest of it
too) or the veiny old hag from Westec or even the self-satisfied,
smirking son of a bitch from Metropolitan Life, though he'd
felt himself slipping on that one ("Death and dismemberment!"
he'd hooted in the man's face, so thoroughly irritated, rubbed
wrong, and just plain pissed he could think of nothing but the
big glistening Mannlicher on the wall in the den). . . . No, it
was Rance Ruby's stupid, fat-faced, shit-licking excuse of a kid.

Picture him sitting there in the first faint glow of early morning, the bottle mostly gone now and the fire in his guts over
that moron with the barking face who'd run into him on the
freeway just about put out, and then he looks up from the
kitchen table and what does he see but this sorry lardassed spawn
of a sorry tattooed beer-swilling lardass of a father cutting through
the yard with his black death's-head T-shirt and his looseleaf
and book jackets, and that's it. There's no more thinking, no
more reason, no insurance or hope. He's up out of the chair like
a shot and into the den, and then he's punching the barrel of
the Mannlicher right through the glass of the den window. The
fat little fuck, he's out there under the grapefruit tree, shirttail
hanging out, turning at the sound, and then *ka-boom*, there's
about half of him left.

Next minute Everett Coles is in his car, fender rubbing against
the tire in back where that sorry sack of shit ran into him, and
slamming out of the driveway. He's got the Mannlicher on the
seat beside him and a couple fistfuls of ammunition and he's
peppering the side of Ruby's turd-colored house with a blast
from his Weatherby pump-action shotgun. He grazes a parked
camper on his way up the block, slams over a couple of garbage

cans, and leans out the window to take the head off somebody's yapping poodle as he careens out onto the boulevard, every wire gone loose in his head.

Ellis Hunsicker woke early. He'd dreamt he was a little cloud— the little cloud of the bedtime story he'd read Mifty and Corinne the night before—scudding along in the vast blue sky, free and untethered, the sun smiling on him as it does in picturebooks, when all at once he'd felt himself swept irresistibly forward, moving faster and faster, caught up in a huge, darkening, ma- levolent thunderhead that rose up faceless from the far side of the day . . . and then he woke. It was just first light. Hilary was breathing gently beside him. The alarm panel glowed soothingly in the shadow of the half-open door.

It was funny how quickly he'd got used to the thing, he reflected, yawning and scratching himself there in the muted light. A week ago he'd made a fool of himself over it in front of Sid and Tina, and now it was just another appliance, no more threatening or unusual—and no less vital—than the microwave, the Cuisinart, or the clock radio. The last two mornings, in fact, he'd been awakened not by the clock radio but by the insistent beeping of the house alarm—Mifty had set it off going out the back door to cuddle her rabbit. He thought now of getting up to shut the thing off—it was an hour yet before he'd have to be up for work—but he didn't. The bed was warm, the birds had begun to whisper outside, and he shut his eyes, drifting off like a little cloud.

When he woke again it was to the beep-beep-beep of the house alarm and to the hazy apprehension of some godawful crash— a jet breaking the sound barrier, the first rumbling clap of the quake he lived in constant fear of—an apprehension that some- thing was amiss, that this beep-beep-beeping, familiar though it seemed, was somehow different, more high-pitched and ad- monitory than the beep-beep-beeping occasioned by a child going out to cuddle a bunny. He sat up. Hilary rose to her elbows beside him, looking bewildered, and in that instant the alarm was silenced forever by the unmistakable roar of a gunblast. Ellis' heart froze. Hilary cried out, there was the heavy thump of footsteps below, a faint choked whimper as of little girls startled in their sleep and then a strange voice—high, hoarse, and raging—that chewed up the morning like a set of jaws. "Armed response!" the voice howled. "Armed response, god-damnit! Armed response!"

The couple strained forward like mourners at a funeral. Giselle had them, she knew that. They'd looked scared when she came to the door, a pair of timid rabbity faces peering out at her from behind the matching frames of their prescription glasses, and they seated themselves on the edge of the couch as if they were afraid of their own furniture. She had them wringing their hands and darting uneasy glances out the window as she described the perpetrator—"A white man, dressed like a schoolteacher, but with these wicked, jittery eyes that just sent a shiver through you." She focused on the woman as she described the victims. There was a boy, just fourteen years old, on his way to school, and a woman in a Mercedes driving down to the corner store for coffee filters. And then the family—they must have read about it—all of them, and not three blocks from where they were now sitting. "He was thirty-five years old," she said in a husky voice, "an engineer at Rocketdyne, his whole life ahead of him . . . and she, she was one of these supernice people who . . . and the children . . ." She couldn't go on. The man—Mr. Dunsinane, wasn't that the name?—leaned forward and handed her a Kleenex. Oh, she had them, all right. She could have sold them the super-deluxe laser alert system, stock in the company, mikes for every flower in the garden, but the old charge just wasn't there.

"I'm sorry," she whispered, fighting back a sob.

It was weird, she thought, pressing the Kleenex to her face, but the masked intruder had never affected her like this, or the knife-sharpening Mexican either. It was Coles, of course, and those sick jumpy eyes of his, but it was the signs too. She couldn't stop thinking about those signs—if they hadn't been there, that is, stuck in the lawn like a red flag in front of a bull . . . But there was no future in that. No, she told the story anyway, told it despite the chill that came over her and the thickening in her throat.

She had to. If only for her peace of mind.

WHEN MONTY'S LAST BREATH caught somewhere in the back of his throat with a sound like the tired wheeze of an old screen door, the first thing she did was turn on the water. She leaned over him a minute to make sure, then she wiped her hands on her dress and shuffled into the kitchen. Her fingers trembled as she jerked at the lever and felt the water surge against the porcelain. Steam rose in her face; a glitter of liquid leapt for the drain. Croak, that's what they called it. Now she knew why. She left the faucet running in the kitchen and crossed the gloomy expanse of the living room, swung down the hallway to the guest bedroom, and turned on both taps in the bathroom there. It was almost as an afterthought that she decided to fill the tub too.

For a long while she sat in the leather armchair in the living room. The sound of running water—pure, baptismal, as uncomplicated as the murmur of a brook in Vermont or a toilet at the Waldorf—soothed her. It trickled and trilled, burbling from either side of the house and driving down the terrible silence that crouched in the bedroom over the lifeless form of her husband.

The afternoon was gone and the sun plunging into the canopy of the big eucalyptus behind the Finkelsteins' when she finally pushed herself up from the chair. Head down, arms moving stiffly at her sides, she scuffed out the back door, crossed the patio, and bent to turn on the sprinklers. They sputtered and spat—not enough pressure, that much she understood—but finally came to life in halfhearted umbrellas of mist. She left the hose trickling in the rose garden, then went back into the house, passed through the living room, the kitchen, the master bedroom—not even a glance for Monty, no: she wouldn't look at him, not yet—and on into the master bath. The taps were weak, barely a trickle, but she left them on anyway, then flushed the toilet and pinned down the float with the brick Monty had used as a doorstop. And then finally, so weary she could barely lift her arms, she leaned into the stall and flipped on the shower.

Two weeks after the ambulance came for the old man next door, Meg Terwilliger was doing her stretching exercises on the prayer rug in the sunroom, a menthol cigarette glowing in the ashtray on the floor beside her, the new CD by Sandee and the Sharks thumping out of the big speakers in the corners. Meg was twenty-three, with the fine bones and haunted eyes of a poster child. She wore her black hair cut close at the temples, long in front, and she used a sheeny black eyeshadow to bring out the hunger in her eyes. In half an hour she'd have to pick up Tiffany at nursery school, drop off the dog at the veterinarian's, take Sonny's shirts to the cleaner's, buy a pound and a half of thresher shark, cilantro, and flour tortillas at the market, and start the burritos for supper. But now, she was stretching.

She took a deep drag on the cigarette, tugged at her right foot, and brought it up snug against her buttocks. After a moment she released it and drew back her left foot in its place. One palm flat on the floor, her head bobbing vaguely to the beat of the music, she did half a dozen repetitions, then paused to relight her cigarette. It wasn't until she turned over to do her straight-leg lifts that she noticed the dampness in the rug.

Puzzled, she rose to her knees and reached behind her to rub at the twin wet spots on the seat of her sweats. She lifted the corner of the rug, suspecting the dog, but there was no odor of urine. Looking closer, she saw that the concrete floor was a shade darker beneath the rug, as if it were bleeding moisture as it sometimes did in the winter. But this wasn't winter, this was high summer in Los Angeles and it hadn't rained for months. Cursing Sonny—he'd promised her ceramic tile and though she'd run all over town to get the best price on a nice Italian floral pattern, he still hadn't found the time to go look at it— she shot back the sliding door and stepped into the yard to investigate.

Immediately, she felt the Bermuda grass squelch beneath the soles of her aerobic shoes. She hadn't taken three strides—the sun in her face, Queenie yapping frantically from the fenced-in pool area—and her feet were wet. Had Sonny left the hose running? Or Tiffany? She slogged across the lawn, the pastel Reeboks spattered with wet, and checked the hose. It was innocently coiled on its tender, the tap firmly shut. Queenie's yapping went up an octave. The heat—it must have been ninety-five, a hundred—made her feel faint. She gazed up into the cloudless sky, then bent to check each of the sprinklers in succession.

She was poking around in the welter of bushes along the fence, looking for an errant sprinkler, when she thought of the old lady next door—Muriel, wasn't that her name? What with her husband dying and all, maybe she'd left the hose running and forgotten all about it. Meg rose on her tiptoes to peer over the redwood fence that separated her yard from the neighbors' and found herself looking into a glistening, sunstruck garden, with banks of impatiens, bird of paradise, oleander, and loquat, roses in half a dozen shades. The sprinklers were on and the hose was running. For a long moment Meg stood there, mesmerized by the play of light through the drifting fans of water; she was wondering what it would be like to be old, thinking of how it would be if Sonny died and Tiffany were grown up and gone. She'd probably forget to turn off the sprinklers too.

The moment passed. The heat was deadening, the dog hysterical. Meg knew she would have to do something about the sodden yard and wet floor in the sunroom, but she dreaded facing the old woman. What would she say—I'm sorry your husband died but could you turn off the sprinklers? She was thinking maybe she'd phone—or wait till Sonny got home and let him handle it—when she stepped back from the fence and sank to her ankles in mud.

When the doorbell rang, Muriel was staring absently at the cover of an old *National Geographic* which lay beneath a patina of dust on the coffee table. The cover photo showed the beige and yellow sands of some distant desert, rippled to the horizon with corrugations that might have been waves on a barren sea. Monty was dead and buried. She wasn't eating much. Or sleeping much either. The sympathy cards sat unopened on the table in the kitchen, where the tap overflowed the sink and water plunged to the floor with a pertinacity that was like a redemption. When it was quiet—in the early morning or late at night—she could distinguish the separate taps, each with its own voice and rhythm, as they dripped and trickled from the far corners of the house. In those suspended hours she could make out the comforting gurgle of the toilet in the guest room, the musical wash of the tub as water cascaded over the lip of its porcelain dam, the quickening rush of the stream in the hallway as it shot like a miniature Niagara down the chasm of the floor vent . . . she could hear the drip in the master bedroom, the distant hiss of a shower, and the sweet eternal sizzle of the sprinklers on the back lawn.

But now she heard the doorbell.

Wearily, gritting her teeth against the pain in her lower legs and the damp lingering ache of her feet, she pushed herself up from the chair and sloshed her way to the door. The carpet was black with water, soaked through like a sponge—and in a tidy corner of her mind she regretted it—but most of the runoff was finding its way to the heating vents and the gaps in the corners where Monty had miscalculated the angle of the baseboard. She heard it dripping somewhere beneath the house and for a moment pictured the water lying dark and still in a shadowy lagoon that held the leaking ship of the house poised on its trembling surface. The doorbell sounded again. "All right, all right," she muttered, "I'm coming."

A girl with dark circles round her eyes stood on the doorstep. She looked vaguely familiar, and for a moment Muriel thought she recognized her from a TV program about a streetwalker who rises up to kill her pimp and liberate all the other leather-clad, black-eyed streetwalkers of the neighborhood, but then the girl spoke and Muriel realized her mistake. "Hi," the girl said, and Muriel saw that her shoes were black with mud, "I'm your neighbor? Meg Terwilliger?"

Muriel was listening to the bathroom sink. She said nothing. The girl looked down at her muddy shoes. "I, uh, just wanted to tell you that we're, uh—Sonny and I, I mean—he's my husband?—we're sorry about your trouble and all, but I wondered if you knew your sprinklers were on out back?"

Muriel attempted a smile—surely a smile was appropriate at this juncture, wasn't it?—but managed only to lift her upper lip back from her teeth in a sort of wince or grimace.

The girl was noticing the rug now, and Muriel's sodden slippers. She looked baffled, perhaps even a little frightened. And young. So young. Muriel had had a young friend once, a girl from the community college who used to come to the house before Monty got sick. She had a tape recorder, and she would ask them questions about their childhood, about the days when the San Fernando Valley was dirt roads and orange groves. Oral history, she called it. "It's all right," Muriel said, trying to reassure her.

"I just—is it a plumbing problem?" the girl said, backing away from the door. "Sonny . . . " she said, but didn't finish the thought. She ducked her head and retreated down the steps, but when she reached the walk she wheeled around. "I mean you really ought to see about the sprinklers," she blurted, "the whole place is soaked, my sunroom and everything—"

"It's all right," Muriel repeated, and then the girl was gone and she shut the door.

"She's nuts, she is. Really. I mean she's out of her gourd."

Meg was searing chunks of thresher shark in a pan with green chilies, sweet red pepper, onion, and cilantro. Sonny, who was twenty-eight and so intoxicated by real estate he had to forgo the morning paper till he got home at night, was slumped in the breakfast nook with a vodka tonic and the sports pages. His white-blond hair was cut fashionably, in what might once have been called a flattop, though it was thinning, and his open, appealing face, with its boyish look, had begun to show signs of wear, particularly around the eyes, where years of escrow had taken their toll. Tiffany was in her room, playing quietly with a pair of six-inch dolls that had cost sixty-five dollars each.

"Who?" Sonny murmured, tugging unconsciously at the gold chain he wore around his neck.

"Muriel. The old lady next door. Haven't you heard a thing I've been saying?" With an angry snap of her wrist, Meg cut the heat beneath the saucepan and clapped a lid over it. "The floor in the sunroom is flooded, for god's sake," she said, stalking across the kitchen in her bare feet till she stood poised over him. "The rug is ruined. Or almost is. And the yard—"

Sonny slapped the paper down on the table. "All right! Just let me relax a minute, will you?"

She put on her pleading look. It was a look compounded of pouty lips, tousled hair, and those inevitable eyes, and it always had its effect on him. "One minute," she murmured. "That's all it'll take. I just want you to see the backyard."

She took him by the hand and led him through the living room to the sunroom, where he stood a moment contemplating the damp spot on the concrete floor. She was surprised herself at how the spot had grown—it was three times what it had been that afternoon, and it seemed to have sprouted wings and legs like an enormous Rorschach. She pictured a butterfly. Or no, a hovering crow or bat. She wondered what Muriel would have made of it.

Outside, she let out a little yelp of disgust—all the earthworms in the yard had crawled up on the step to die. And the lawn wasn't merely spongy now, it was soaked through, puddled like a swamp. "Jesus Christ," Sonny muttered, sinking in his wing-tips. He cakewalked across the yard to where the fence had begun to sag, the post leaning drunkenly, the slats bowed. "Will you look at this?" he shouted over his shoulder. Squeamish about the worms, Meg stood at the door to the sunroom. "The god-dam fence is falling down!"

He stood there a moment, water seeping into his shoes, a look of stupefaction on his face. Meg recognized the look. It stole over his features in moments of extremity, as when he tore open the phone bill to discover mysterious twenty-dollar calls to Bill-ings, Montana, and Greenleaf, Mississippi, or when his buyer called on the day escrow was to close to tell him he'd assaulted the seller and wondered if Sonny had five hundred dollars for bail. These occasions always took him by surprise. He was shocked anew each time the crisply surveyed, neatly kept world he so cherished rose up to confront him with all its essential sloppiness, irrationality, and bad business sense. Meg watched the look of disbelief turn to one of injured rage. She followed him through the house, up the walk, and into Muriel's yard, where he stalked up to the front door and pounded like the Gestapo.

There was no response.

"Son of a bitch," he spat, turning to glare over his shoulder at her as if it were her fault or something. From inside they could hear the drama of running water, a drip and gurgle, a sough and hiss. Sonny turned back to the door, hammering his fist against it till Meg swore she could see the panels jump.

It frightened her, this sudden rage. Sure, there was a problem here and she was glad he was taking care of it, but did he have to get violent, did he have to get crazy? "You don't have to beat her door down," she called, focusing on the swell of his shoulder and the hammer of his fist as it rose and fell in savage rhythm. "Sonny, come on. It's only water, for god's sake."

"Only?" he snarled, spinning round to face her. "You saw the fence—next thing you know the foundation'll shift on us. The whole damn house—" He never finished. The look on her face told him that Muriel had opened the door.

Muriel was wearing the same faded blue housecoat she'd had on earlier, and the same wet slippers. Short, heavyset, so big in front it seemed as if she were about to topple over, she clung to the doorframe and peered up at Sonny out of a stony face. Meg watched as Sonny jerked round to confront her and then stopped cold when he got a look at the interior of the house. The plaster walls were stained now, drinking up the wet in long jagged fingers that clawed toward the ceiling, and a dribble of coffee-colored liquid began to seep across the doorstep and puddle at Sonny's feet. The sound of rushing water was unmistakable, even from where Meg was standing. "Yes?" Muriel said, the voice withered in her throat. "Can I help you?"

It took Sonny a minute—Meg could see it in his eyes: this was more than he could handle, willful destruction of a domicile, every tap in the place on full, the floors warped, plaster ruined— but then he recovered himself. "The water," he said. "You— our fence—I mean you can't, you've got to stop this—"

The old woman drew herself up, clutching the belt of her housedress till her knuckles bulged with the tension. She looked first at Meg, still planted in the corner of the yard, and then turned to Sonny. "Water?" she said. "What water?"

The young man at the door reminded her, in a way, of Monty. Something about the eyes or the set of the ears—or maybe it was the crisp high cut of the sideburns . . . Of course, most young men reminded her of Monty. The Monty of fifty years ago, that is. The Monty who'd opened up the world to her over

the shift lever of his Model-A Ford, not the crabbed and abrasive
old man who called her bonehead and dildo and cuffed her like
a dog. Monty. When the stroke brought him down, she was
almost glad. She saw him pinned beneath his tubes in the hospital
and something stirred in her; she brought him home and changed
his bedpan, peered into the vaults of his eyes, fed him Gerber's
like the baby she'd never had, and she knew it was over. Fifty
years. No more drunken rages, no more pans flung against the
wall, never again his sour flesh pressed to hers. She was on
top now.

The second young man—he was a Mexican, short, stocky,
with a mustache so thin it could have been penciled on and
wicked little red-flecked eyes—also reminded her of Monty. Not
so much in the way he looked as in the way he held himself,
the way he swaggered and puffed out his chest. And the uniform
too, of course. Monty had worn a uniform during the war.

"Mrs. Burgess?" the Mexican asked.

Muriel stood at the open door. It was dusk, the heat cut as if
there were a thermostat in the sky. She'd been sitting in the
dark. The electricity had gone out on her—something to do
with the water and the wires. She nodded her head in response
to the policeman's question.

"We've had a complaint," he said.

Little piggy eyes. A complaint. *We've had a complaint.* He
wasn't fooling her, not for a minute. She knew what they wanted,
the police, the girl next door, and the boy she was married to—
they wanted to bring Monty back. Prop him up against the
bedframe, stick his legs back under him, put the bellow back
in his voice. Oh, no, they weren't fooling her.

She followed the policeman around the darkened house as he
went from faucet to faucet, sink to tub to shower. He firmly
twisted each of the taps closed and drained the basins, then
crossed the patio to kill the sprinklers and the hose too. "Are
you all right?" he kept asking. "Are you all right?"

She had to hold her chin in her palm to keep her lips from

trembling. "If you mean am I in possession of my faculties, yes, I am, thank you. I am all right."

They were back at the front door now. He leaned nonchalantly against the doorframe and dropped his voice to a confidential whisper. "So what's this with the water then?"

She wouldn't answer him. She knew her rights. What business was it of his, or anybody's, what she did with her own taps and her own sprinklers? She could pay the water bill. Had paid it, in fact. Eleven hundred dollars' worth. She watched his eyes and shrugged.

"Next of kin?" he asked. "Daughter? Son? Anybody we can call?"

Now her lips held. She shook her head.

He gave it a moment, then let out a sigh. "Okay," he said, speaking slowly and with exaggerated emphasis, as if he were talking to a child, "I'm going now. You leave the water alone—wash your face, brush your teeth, do the dishes. But no more of this." He swaggered back from her, fingering his belt, his holster, the dead weight of his nightstick. "One more complaint and we'll have to take you into custody for your own good. You're endangering yourself and the neighbors too. Understand?"

Smile, she told herself, smile. "Oh, yes," she said softly. "Yes, I understand."

He held her eyes a moment, threatening her—just like Monty used to do, just like Monty—and then he was gone.

She stood there on the doorstep a long while, the night deepening around her. She listened to the cowbirds, the wild parakeets that nested in the Murtaughs' palm, the whoosh of traffic from the distant freeway. After a while, she sat on the step. Behind her, the house was silent: no faucet dripped, no sprinkler hissed, no toilet gurgled. It was horrible. Insupportable. In the pit of that dry silence she could hear him, Monty, treading the buckled floors, pouring himself another vodka, cursing her in a voice like sandpaper.

She couldn't go back in there. Not tonight. The place was deadly, contaminated, sick as the grave—after all was said and done, it just wasn't clean enough. If the rest of it was a mystery—oral history, fifty years of Monty, the girl with the blackened eyes—that much she understood.

Meg was watering the cane plant in the living room when the police cruiser came for the old lady next door. The police had been there the night before and Sonny had stood out front with his arms folded while the officer shut down Muriel's taps and sprinklers. "I guess that's that," he said, coming up the walk in the oversized Hawaiian shirt she'd given him for Father's Day. But in the morning, the sprinklers were on again and Sonny called the local substation three times before he left for work. She's crazy, he'd hollered into the phone, irresponsible, a threat to herself and the community. He had a four-year-old daughter to worry about, for christ's sake. A dog. A wife. His fence was falling down. Did they have any idea what that amount of water was going to do to the substrata beneath the house?

Now the police were back. The patrol car stretched across the window and slid silently into the driveway next door. Meg set down the watering can. She was wearing her Fila sweats and a new pair of Nikes and her hair was tied back in a red scarf. She'd dropped Tiffany off at nursery school, but she had the watering and her stretching exercises to do and a pasta salad to make before she picked up Queenie at the vet's. Still, she went directly to the front door and then out onto the walk.

The police—it took her a minute to realize that the shorter of the two was a woman—were on Muriel's front porch, looking stiff and uncertain in their razor-creased uniforms. The man knocked first—once, twice, three times. Nothing happened. Then the woman knocked. Still nothing. Meg folded her arms and waited. After a minute, the man went around to the side gate and let himself into the yard. Meg heard the sprinklers die with a wheeze, and then the officer was back, his shoes heavy with mud.

Again he thumped at the door, much more violently now, and Meg thought of Sonny. "Open up," the woman called in a breathy contralto she tried unsuccessfully to deepen, "police."

It was then that Meg saw her, Muriel, at the bay window on the near side of the door. "Look," she shouted before she knew what she was saying, "she's there, there in the window!"

The male officer—he had a mustache and pale, fine hair like Sonny's—leaned out over the railing and gestured impatiently at the figure behind the window. "Police," he growled. "Open the door." Muriel never moved. "All right," he grunted, cursing under his breath, "all right," and he put his shoulder to the door. There was nothing to it. The frame splintered, water dribbled out, and both officers disappeared into the house.

Meg waited. She had things to do, yes, but she waited anyway, bending to pull the odd dandelion the gardener had missed, trying to look busy. The police were in there an awful long time—twenty minutes, half an hour—and then the woman appeared in the doorway with Muriel.

Muriel seemed heavier than ever, her face pouchy, arms swollen. She was wearing white sandals on her old splayed feet, a shapeless print dress, and a white straw hat that looked as if it had been dug out of a box in the attic. The woman had her by the arm; the man loomed behind her with a suitcase. Down the steps and up the walk, she never turned her head. But then, just as the policewoman was helping her into the backseat of the patrol car, Muriel swung round as if to take one last look at her house. But it wasn't the house she was looking at: it was Meg.

The morning gave way to the heat of afternoon. Meg finished the watering, made the pasta salad—bow-tie twists, fresh salmon, black olives, and pine nuts—ran her errands, picked up Tiffany, and put her down for a nap. Somehow, though, she just couldn't get Muriel out of her head. The old lady had stared at her for five seconds maybe, and then the policewoman was coaxing her into the car. Meg had felt like sinking into the ground. But then she realized that Muriel's look wasn't vengeful at all—it was just sad. It was a look that said this is what it comes to. Fifty years and this is what it comes to.

The backyard was an inferno, the sun poised directly over-head. Queenie, defleaed, shampooed, and with her toenails clipped, was stretched out asleep in the shade beside the pool. It was quiet. Even the birds were still. Meg took off her Nikes and walked barefoot through the sopping grass to the fence, or what was left of it. The post had buckled overnight, canting the whole business into Muriel's yard. Meg never hesitated. She sprang up onto the plane of the slats and dropped to the grass on the other side.

Her feet sank in the mud, the earth like pudding, like chocolate pudding, and as she lifted her feet to move toward the house the tracks she left behind her slowly filled with water. The patio was an island. She crossed it, dodging potted plants and wicker furniture, and tried the back door; finding it locked, she moved to the window, shaded her face with her hands, and peered in. The sight made her catch her breath. The plaster was crumbling, wallpaper peeling, the rug and floors ruined: she knew it was bad, but this was crazy, this was suicide.

Grief, that's what it was. Or was it? And then she was thinking of Sonny again—what if he was dead and she was old like Muriel? She wouldn't be so fat, of course, but maybe like one of those thin and elegant old ladies in Palm Springs, the ones who'd done their stretching all their lives. Or what if she wasn't an old lady at all—the thought swooped down on her like a bird out of the sky—what if Sonny was in a car wreck or something? It could happen.

She stood there gazing in on the mess through her own wavering reflection. One moment she saw the wreckage of the old lady's life, the next the fine mouth and expressive eyes everyone commented on. After a while, she turned away from the window and looked out on the yard as Muriel must have seen it. There were the roses, gorged with water and flowering madly, the impatiens, rigid as sticks, oleander drowning in their own yellowed leaves—and there, poking innocuously from the bushes at the far corner of the patio, was the steel wand that controlled the sprinklers. Handle, neck, prongs: it was just like theirs.

And then it came to her. She'd turn them on—the sprinklers—just for a minute, to see what it felt like. She wouldn't leave them on long—it could threaten the whole foundation of her house.

That much she understood.

THE HUMAN FLY

Just try to explain to anyone the art of fasting!
—Franz Kafka, "A Hunger Artist"

IN THE EARLY DAYS, before the press took him up, his outfit was pretty basic: tights and cape, plastic swim goggles and a bathing cap in the brightest shade of red he could find. The tights were red too, though they'd faded to pink in the thighs and calves and had begun to sag around the knees. He wore a pair of scuffed hightops—red, of course—and the cape, which looked as if it had last been used to line a trash can, was the color of poached salmon. He seemed to be in his thirties, though I never did find out how old he was, and he was thin, skinny, emaciated—so wasted you worried about his limbs dropping off. When he limped into the office that first afternoon, I didn't know what to think. If he brought an insect to mind, it was something spindly and frail—a daddy longlegs or one of those spidery things that scoot across the surface of the pool no matter how much chlorine the pool man dumps in.

"A gentleman here to see you," Crystal sang through the intercom.

My guard was down. I was vulnerable. I admit it. Basking in the glow of my first success (ten percent of a walk-on for Bettina Buttons, a nasally inflected twelve-year-old with pushy parents, in a picture called *Tyrannosaurus II*—no lines, but she did manage a memorable screech) and bloated with a celebratory lunch, I was feeling magnanimous, large-spirited, and saintly. Of course, the two splits of Sangre de Cristo, 1978, might have had something to do with it. I hit the button on the intercom. "Who is it?"

"Your name, sir?" I heard Crystal ask, and then, through the crackle of static, I heard him respond in the peculiar unmodulated rumble he associated with speech.

"Pardon?" Crystal said.

"La Mosca Humana," he rumbled.

Crystal leaned into the intercom. "Uh, I think he's Mexican or something."

At that stage in my career, I had exactly three clients, all inherited from my predecessor: the aforementioned Bettina; a comic with a harelip who did harelip jokes only; and a soft-rock band called Mu, who believed they were reincarnated court musicians from the lost continent of Atlantis. The phone hadn't rung all morning and my next (and only) appointment, with Bettina's mother, grandmother, acting coach, and dietician, was at seven. "Show him in," I said grandly.

The door pushed open, and there he was. He drew himself up with as much dignity as you could expect from a grown man in a red bathing cap and pink tights, and hobbled into the office. I took in the cap, the cape, the hightops and tights, the slumped shoulders and fleshless limbs. He wore a blond mustache, droopy and unkempt, the left side of his face was badly bruised, and his nose looked as if it had been broken repeatedly—and recently. The fluorescent light glared off his goggles.

My first impulse was to call security—he looked like one of those panhandling freaks out on Hollywood Boulevard—but I resisted it. As I said, I was full of wine and feeling generous. Besides, I was so bored I'd spent the last half-hour crumpling up sheets of high-fiber bond and shooting three-pointers into the wastebasket. I nodded. He nodded back. "So," I said, "what can I do for you, Mr., ah—?"

"Mosca," he rumbled, the syllables thick and muffled, as if he were trying to speak and clear his throat at the same time. "La Mosca Humana."

"The Human Fly, right?" I said, dredging up my high-school Spanish.

He looked down at the desk and then fixed his eyes on mine. "I want to be famous," he said.

How he found his way to my office, I'll never know. I've often wondered if it wasn't somebody's idea of a joke. In those days, I was nothing—I had less seniority than the guy who ran the Xerox machine—and my office was the smallest and farthest from the door of any in the agency. I was expected to get by with two phone lines, one secretary, and a workspace not much bigger than a couple of good-sized refrigerator boxes. There were no Utrillos or Demuths on my walls. I didn't even have a window.

I understood that the man hovering over my desk was a nut case, but there was more to it than that. I could see that he had something—a dignity, a sad elemental presence—that gave the lie to his silly outfit. I felt uneasy under his gaze. "Don't we all," I said.

"No, no," he insisted, "you don't understand," and he pulled a battered manila envelope from the folds of his cape. "Here," he said, "look."

The envelope contained his press clippings, a good handful of them, yellowed and crumbling, bleached of print. All but one were in Spanish. I adjusted the desk lamp, squinted hard. The datelines were from places like Chetumal, Tuxtla, Hidalgo, Tehuantepec. As best I could make out, he'd been part of a Mexican circus. The sole clipping in English was from the "Metro" section of the *Los Angeles Times*: MAN ARRESTED FOR SCALING ARCO TOWER.

I read the first line—"A man known only as 'The Human Fly' "—and I was hooked. What a concept: *a man known only as the Human Fly*! It was priceless. Reading on, I began to see him in a new light: the costume, the limp, the bruises. This was a man who'd climbed twenty stories with nothing more than a couple pieces of rope and his fingernails. A man who defied the authorities, defied death—my mind was doing backflips; we could run with this one, oh, yes, indeed. Forget your Rambos and Conans, this guy was the real thing.

"Five billion of us monkey on the planet," he said in his choked, moribund tones, "I want to make my mark."

I looked up in awe. I saw him on Carson, Letterman, grappling his way to the top of the Bonaventure Hotel, hurtling Niagara in a barrel, starring in his own series. I tried to calm myself. "Uh, your face," I said, and I made a broad gesture that took in the peach-colored bruise, the ravaged nose and stiffened leg, "what happened?"

For the first time, he smiled. His teeth were stained and ragged; his eyes flared behind the cracked plastic lenses of the goggles. "An accident," he said.

As it turned out, he wasn't Mexican at all—he was Hungarian. I saw my mistake when he peeled back the goggles and bathing cap. A fine band of skin as blanched and waxen as the cap of a mushroom outlined his ears, his hairline, the back of his neck, dead-white against the sun-burnished oval of his face. His eyes were a pale watery blue and the hair beneath the cap was as wispy and colorless as the strands of his mustache. His name was Zoltan Mindszenty, and he'd come to Los Angeles to live with his uncle when the Russian tanks rolled through Budapest in 1956. He'd learned English, Spanish, and baseball, practiced fire-eating and tightrope-walking in his spare time, graduated at the top of his high-school class, and operated a forklift in a cannery that produced refried beans and cactus salad. At the age of nineteen he joined the Quesadilla Brothers' Circus and saw the world. Or at least that part of it bounded by California, Arizona, New Mexico, and Texas to the north and Belize and Guatemala to the south. Now he wanted to be famous.

He moved fast. Two days after I'd agreed to represent him he made the eyewitness news on all three major networks when he suspended himself in a mesh bag from the twenty-second floor of the Sumitomo Building and refused to come down.

Terrific. The only problem was that he didn't bother to tell me about it. I was choking down a quick lunch—avocado and sprouts on a garlic-cheese croissant—already running late for an audition I'd set up for my harelipped comedian—when the phone rang. It was a Lieutenant Peachtree of the LAPD. "Listen," the lieutenant hissed, "if this is a publicity stunt . . ." and he trailed off, leaving the threat—heavy ire, the violation of penal codes, the arcane and merciless measures taken to deal with accessories—unspoken.

"Pardon?"

"The nutball up on the Sumitomo Building. Your client."

Comprehension washed over me. My first thought was to deny the connection, but instead I found myself stammering, "But, but how did you get my name?"

Terse and efficient, a living police report, Peachtree gave me the details. One of his men, hanging out of a window on the twenty-first floor, had pleaded with Zoltan to come down. "I am the Human Fly," Zoltan rumbled in response as the wind snapped and the traffic sizzled below, "you want to talk to me, call my agent."

"Twenty minutes," Peachtree added, and his tone was as flat and unforgiving as the drop of a guillotine, "I want you down here. Five minutes after that I want this clown in the back of the nearest patrol car—is that understood?"

It was. Perfectly. And twenty minutes later, with the help of an Officer Dientes, a screaming siren, and several hundred alert motorists who fell away from us on the freeway like swatted flies, I was taking the breeze on the twenty-first floor of the Sumitomo Building. Two of Peachtree's men gripped my legs and eased my torso out onto the slick glassy plane of the building's façade.

I was sick with fear. Before me lay the immensity of the city, its jaws and molars exposed. Above was the murky sky, half a dozen pigeons on a ledge, and Zoltan, bundled up like a sack of grapefruit and calmly perusing a paperback thriller. I choked back the remains of the croissant and cleared my throat. "Zoltan!" I shouted, the wind snatching the words from my lips and flinging them away. "Zoltan, what are you doing up there?"

There was a movement from the bag above me, Zoltan stirring himself like a great leathery fruit bat unfolding its wings, and then his skinny legs and outsized feet emerged from their confinement as the bag swayed gently in the breeze. He peered down at me, the goggles aflame with the sun, and gave me a sour look. "You're supposed to be my agent, and you have to ask me that?"

"It's a stunt, then—is that it?" I shouted.

He turned his face away, and the glare of the goggles died. He wouldn't answer. Behind me, I could hear Peachtree's crisp, efficient tones: "Tell him he's going to jail."

"They're going to lock you up. They're not kidding."

For a long moment, he didn't respond. Then the goggles caught the sun again and he turned to me. "I want the TV people, Tricia Toyota, 'Action News,' the works."

I began to feel dizzy. The pavement below, with its toy cars and its clots of tiny people, seemed to rush up at me and recede again in a pulsing wave. I felt Peachtree's men relax their grip. "They won't come!" I gasped, clutching the windowframe so desperately my fingers went numb. "They can't. It's network policy." It was true, as far as I knew. Every flake in the country would be out on that ledge if they thought they could get a ten-second clip on the evening news.

Zoltan was unimpressed. "TV," he rumbled into the wind, "or I stay here till you see the white of my bone."

I believed him.

As it turned out, he stayed there, aloft, for two weeks. And for some reason—because he was intractable, absurd, mad beyond hope or redemption—the press couldn't get enough of it.

TV included. How he passed the time, what he ate, how he relieved himself, no one knew. He was just a presence, a distant speck in a mesh sack, the faintest intrusion of reality on the clear smooth towering face of the Sumitomo Building. Peachtree tried to get him down, of course—harassing him with helicopters, sending a squad of window cleaners, firemen, and lederhosen up after him—but nothing worked. If anyone got close to him, Zoltan would emerge from his cocoon, cling to the seamless face of the building, and float—float like a big red fly—to a new position.

Finally, after the two weeks were up—two weeks during which my phone never stopped ringing, by the way—he decided to come down. Did he climb in the nearest window and take the elevator? No, not Zoltan. He backed down, inch by inch, uncannily turning up finger- and toe-holds where none existed. He sprang the last fifteen feet to the ground, tumbled like a sky diver, and came up in the grip of a dozen policemen. There was a barricade up, streets were blocked, hundreds of spectators had gathered. As they were hustling him to a patrol car, the media people converged on him. Was it a protest? they wanted to know. A hunger strike? What did it mean?

He turned to them, the goggles steamed over, pigeon feathers and flecks of airborne debris clinging to his cape. His legs were like sticks, his face nearly black with sun and soot. "I want to be famous," he said.

"A DC 10?"

Zoltan nodded. "The bigger, the better," he rumbled.

It was the day after he'd decamped from the face of the Sumitomo Building and we were in my office, discussing the next project. (I'd bailed him out myself, though the figure was right up there with what you'd expect for a serial killer. There were fourteen charges against him, ranging from trespassing to creating a public nuisance and refusing the reasonable request of a police officer to indecent exposure. I had to call in every favor that was ever owed me and go down on my knees to Sol Bank-off, the head of the agency, to raise the cash.) Zoltan was wearing the outfit I'd had specially made for him: new tights, a black silk cape without a wrinkle in it, a pair of Air Jordan basketball shoes in red and black, and most important of all, a red leather aviator's cap and goggles. Now he looked less like a geriatric at a health spa and more like the sort of fearless daredevil/superhero the public could relate to.

"But Zoltan," I pleaded, "those things go five hundred miles an hour. You'd be ripped to pieces. Climbing buildings is one thing, but this is insane. It's suicidal."

He was slouched in the chair, one skinny leg thrown over the other. "The Human Fly can survive anything," he droned in his lifeless voice. He was staring at the floor, and now he lifted his head. "Besides, you think the public have any respect for me if I don't lay it all on line?"

He had a point. But strapping yourself to the wing of a DC 10 made about as much sense as taking lunch at a sidewalk café in Beirut. "Okay," I said, "you're right. But you've got to draw the line somewhere. What good's it going to do you to be famous if you're dead?"

Zoltan shrugged.

"I mean already, just with the Sumitomo thing, I can book you on half the talk shows in the country. . . ."

He rose shakily to his feet, lifted his hand, and let it drop. Two weeks on the face of the Sumitomo Building with no apparent source of nourishment hadn't done him any good. If he was skinny before, he was nothing now—a shadow, a ghost, a pair of tights stuffed with straw. "Set it up," he rumbled, the words riding up out of the depths of his sunken abdomen, "I talk when I got something to talk about."

It took me a week. I called every airline in the directory, listened to a lifetime's worth of holding jingles, and talked to everyone from the forklift operator at KLM to the president and CEO of Texas Air. I was met by scorn, hostility, disbelief, and naked contempt. Finally I got hold of the schedules manager of Aero Masoquisto, the Ecuadorian national airline. It was going to cost me, he said, but he could hold up the regular weekly flight to Quito for a few hours while Zoltan strapped himself to the wing and took a couple passes round the airport. He suggested an airstrip outside Tijuana, where the officials would look the other way. For a price, of course.

Of course.

I went to Sol again. I was prepared to press my forehead to the floor, shine his shoes, anything—but he surprised me. "I'll front the money," he rasped, his voice ruined from forty years of whispering into the telephone, "no problem." Sol was seventy, looked fifty, and he'd had his own table in the Polo Lounge since before I was born. "If he bags it," he said, his voice as dry as a husk, "we got the rights to his life story and we'll do a paperback/miniseries/action-figure tie-in. Just get him to sign this, that's all." He slid a contract across the table. "And if he makes it, which I doubt—I mean I've seen some crazies in my time, but this guy is something else—if he makes it, we'll have a million and a half offers for him. Either way, we make out, right?"

"Right," I said, but I was thinking of Zoltan, his brittle limbs pressed to the unyielding metal, the terrible pull of the G-forces, and the cyclonic blast of the wind. What chance did he have?

Sol cleared his throat, shook a few lozenges into his fist, and rattled them like dice. "Your job," he said, "is to make sure the press shows up. No sense in this nimrod bagging it for nothing, right?"

I felt something clench in my gut.

Sol repeated himself. "Right?"

"Right," I said.

Zoltan was in full regalia as we boarded the plane at LAX, along with a handful of reporters and photographers and a hundred grim-looking Ecuadorians with plastic bags full of disposable diapers, cosmetics, and penlight batteries. The plan was for the pilot to announce a minor problem—a clogged air-conditioning vent or a broken handle in the flush toilet; we didn't want to panic anybody—and an unscheduled stop to repair it. Once on the ground, the passengers would be asked to disembark and we'd offer them free drinks in the spacious terminal while the plan taxied out of sight and Zoltan did his thing.

Problem was, there was no terminal. The landing strip looked as if it had been bombed during the Mexican Revolution, it was a hundred degrees inside the airplane and 120 out on the asphalt, and all I could see was heat haze and prickly-pear cactus. "What do you want to do?" I asked Zoltan.

Zoltan turned to me, already fumbling with his chin strap. "It's perfect," he whispered, and then he was out in the aisle, waving his arms and whistling for the passengers' attention. When they quieted down, he spoke to them in Spanish, the words coming so fast you might have thought he was a Mexican disc jockey, his voice riding on a current of emotion he never approached in English. I don't know what he said—he could have been exhorting them to hijack the plane, for all I knew—but the effect was dramatic. When he finished, they rose to their feet and cheered.

With a flourish, Zoltan threw open the emergency exit over the wing and began his preparations. Flashbulbs popped, reporters hung out the door and shouted questions at him—Had this ever been attempted before? Did he have his will made out? How high was he planning to go?—and the passengers pressed their faces to the windows. I'd brought along a TV crew to capture the death-defying feat for syndication, and they set up one camera on the ground while the other shot through the window.

Zoltan didn't waste any time. He buckled what looked like a huge leather truss around the girth of the wing, strapped himself into the pouch attached to it, tightened his chin strap a final time, and then gave me the thumbs-up sign. My heart was hammering. A dry wind breathed through the open window. The heat was like a fist in my face. "You're sure you want to go through with this?" I yelled.

"One hundred percent, A-OK," Zoltan shouted, grinning as the reporters crowded round me in the narrow passageway. Then the pilot said something in Spanish and the flight attendants pulled the window shut, fastened the bolts, and told us to take our seats. A moment later the big engines roared to life and we were hurtling down the runway. I could barely stand to look. At best, I consider flying an unavoidable necessity, a time to resurrect forgotten prayers and contemplate the end of all joy in a twisted howling heap of machinery; at worst, I rank it right up there with psychotic episodes and torture at the hands of malevolent strangers. I felt the wheels lift off, heard a shout from the passengers, and there he was—Zoltan—clinging to the trembling thunderous wing like a second coat of paint.

It was a heady moment, transcendent, the cameras whirring, the passengers cheering, Zoltan's greatness a part of us all. This was an event, a once-in-a-lifetime thing, like watching Hank Aaron stroke his seven hundred fifteenth homer or Neil Armstrong step out onto the surface of the moon. We forgot the heat, forgot the roar of the engines, forgot ourselves. He's doing it, I thought, he's actually doing it. And I truly think he would have pulled it off, if—well, it was one of those things no one could have foreseen. Bad luck, that's all.

What happened was this: just as the pilot was coming in for his final approach, a big black bird—a buzzard, somebody said— loomed up out of nowhere and slammed into Zoltan with a thump that reverberated throughout the plane. The whole thing took maybe half a second. This black bundle appears, there's a thump, and next thing Zoltan's goggles are gone and he's covered from head to toe in raw meat and feathers.

A gasp went through the cabin. Babies began to mewl, grown men burst into tears, a nun fainted. My eyes were riveted on Zoltan. He lay limp in his truss while the hot air sliced over the wing and the jagged yellow mountains, the prickly pear, and the pocked landing strip rushed past him like the backdrop of an old movie. The plane was still rolling when we threw open the emergency exit and staggered out onto the wing. The copilot was ahead of me, a reporter on my heels. "Zoltan!" I cried, scared and sick and trembling. "Zoltan, are you all right?"

There was no answer. Zoltan's head lolled against the flat hard surface of the wing and his eyes were closed, sunk deep behind the wrinkled flaps of his lids. There was blood everywhere. I bent to tear at the straps of the aviator's cap, my mind racing, thinking alternately of mouth-to-mouth and the medical team I should have thought to bring along, when an urgent voice spoke at my back. "Perdóneme, perdóneme, I yam a doaktor."

One of the passengers, a wizened little man in Mickey Mouse T-shirt and Bermudas, knelt over Zoltan, shoving back his eyelids and feeling for his pulse. There were shouts behind me. The wing was as hot as the surface of a frying pan. "Jes, I yam getting a pulse," the doctor announced and then Zoltan winked open an eye. "Hey," he rumbled, "am I famous yet?"

Zoltan was right: the airplane stunt fired the imagination of the country. The wire services picked it up, the news magazines ran stories—there was even a bit on the CBS evening news. A week later the *National Enquirer* was calling him the reincarnation of Houdini and the *Star* was speculating about his love life. I booked him on the talk-show circuit, and while he might not have had much to say, he just about oozed charisma. He appeared on the Carson show in his trademark outfit, goggles and all, limping and with his arm in a sling (he'd suffered a minor concussion, a shoulder separation, and a fractured kneecap when the bird hit him). Johnny asked him what it was like out there on the wing and Zoltan said: "Loud." And what was it like spending two weeks on the face of the Sumitomo Building? "Boring," Zoltan rumbled. But Carson segued into a couple of airline jokes ("Have you heard the new slogan for China Air-

lines?" Pause. "You've seen us drive, now watch us fly") and
the audience ate it up. Offers poured in from promoters, pro-
ducers, book editors, and toy manufacturers. I was able to book
David Mugillo, my harelipped comedian, on Zoltan's coattails,
and when we did the Carson show we got Bettina Buttons on
for three minutes of nasal simpering about *Tyrannosaurus II* and
how educational an experience it was for her to work with such
a sensitive and caring director as so-and-so.

Zoltan had arrived.

A week after his triumph on "The Tonight Show" he hobbled
into the office, the cape stained and torn, tights gone in the
knees. He brought a distinctive smell with him—the smell of
pissed-over gutters and fermenting dumpsters—and for the first
time I began to understand why he'd never given me an address
or a phone number. ("You want me," he said, "leave a message
with Ramón at Jiffy Cleaners.") All at once I had a vision of
him slinging his grapefruit sack from the nearest drainpipe and
curling up for the night. "Zoltan," I said, "are you okay? You
need some cash? A place to stay?"

He sat heavily in the chair across from me. Behind him, on
the wall, was an oil painting of an open window, a gift from
Mu's bass player. Zoltan waved me off. Then, with a weary
gesture, he reached up and removed the cap and goggles. I was
shocked. His hair was practically gone and his face was as seamed
and scarred as an old hockey puck. He looked about a hundred
and twelve. He said nothing.

"Well," I said, to break the silence, "you got your wish. You
made it." I lifted a stack of correspondence from the desk and
waved it at him. "You're famous."

Zoltan turned his head and spat on the floor. "Famous," he
mocked. "Fidel Castro is famous. Irving Berlin. Evel Knievel."
His rumble had turned bitter. "Peterbilt," he said suddenly.

This last took me by surprise. I'd been thinking of consolatory
platitudes, and all I could do was echo him weakly: "Peterbilt?"

"I want the biggest rig going. The loudest, the dirtiest."

I wasn't following him.

"Maine to L.A.," he rumbled.

"You're going to drive it?"

He stood shakily, fought his way back into the cap, and lowered the goggles. "Shit," he spat, "I ride the axle."

I tried to talk him out of it. "Think of the fumes," I said, "the road hazards. Potholes, dead dogs, mufflers. You'll be two feet off the pavement, going seventy-five, eighty miles an hour. Christ, a cardboard box'll tear you apart."

He wouldn't listen. Not only was he going through with it, but he wanted to coordinate it so that he ended up in Pasadena, for the swap meet at the Rose Bowl. There he would emerge from beneath the truck, wheel a motorcycle out of the back, roar up a ramp, and sail over twenty-six big rigs lined up fender to fender in the middle of the parking lot.

I asked Sol about it. Advance contracts had already made back the money he'd laid out for the airplane thing ten times over. And now we could line up backers. "Get him to wear a Pirelli patch on his cape," Sol rasped, "it's money in the bank."

Easy for Sol to say, but I was having problems with the whole business. This wasn't a plastic dinosaur on a movie lot or a stinko audience at the Improv, this was flesh and blood we were talking about here, a human life. Zoltan wasn't healthy—in mind or body. The risks he took weren't healthy. His ambition wasn't healthy. And if I went along with him, I was no better than Sol, a mercenary, a huckster who'd watch a man die for ten percent of the action. For a day or two I stayed away from the office, brooding around the kitchen in my slippers. In the end, though, I talked myself into it—Zoltan was going to do it with or without me. And who knew what kind of bloodsucker he'd wind up with next?

I hired a PR firm, got a major trucking company to carry him for the goodwill and free publicity, and told myself it was for the best. I'd ride in the cab with the driver, keep him awake, watch over Zoltan personally. And of course I didn't know how it was going to turn out—Zoltan *was* amazing, and if anyone could pull it off, he could—and I thought of the Sumitomo Building and Aero Masoquisto and hoped for the best.

We left Bangor in a cold drizzle on a morning that could have served as the backdrop for a low-budget horror picture: full-bellied clouds, gloom, mist, nose-running cold. By the time we reached Portland the drizzle had begun to crust on the windshield wipers; before we reached New Hampshire it was sleet. The driver was an American Indian by the name of Mink—no middle name, no surname, just Mink. He weighed close to five hundred pounds and he wore his hair in a single braided coil that hung to his belt loops in back. The other driver, whose name was Steve, was asleep in the compartment behind the cab. "Listen, Mink," I said, the windshield wipers beating methodically at the crust, tires hissing beneath us, "maybe you should pull over so we can check on Zoltan."

Mink shifted his enormous bulk in the seat. "What, the Fly?" he said. "No sweat. That guy is like amazing. I seen that thing with the airplane. He can survive that, he's got no problem with this rig—long's I don't hit nothin'."

The words were barely out of his mouth when an animal—a huge brown thing like a cow on stilts—materialized out of the mist. Startled, Mink jerked the wheel, the truck went into a skid, there was a jolt like an earthquake, and the cow on stilts was gone, sucked under the front bumper like a scrap of food sucked down a drain. When we finally came to a stop a hundred yards up the road, the trailer was perpendicular to the cab and Mink's hands were locked to the wheel.

"What happened?" I said.

"Moose," Mink breathed, adding a soft breathless curse. "We hit a fuckin' moose."

In the next instant I was down and out of the cab, racing the length of the trailer, and shouting Zoltan's name. Earlier, in the cold dawn of Bangor, I'd watched him stretch out his mesh bag and suspend it like a trampoline from the trailer's undercarriage, just ahead of the rear wheels. He'd waved to the reporters gathered in the drizzle, ducked beneath the trailer, and climbed into the bag. Now, my heart banging, I wondered what a moose might have done to so tenuous an arrangement. "Zoltan!" I shouted, going down on my knees to peer into the gloom beneath the trailer.

There was no moose. Zoltan's cocoon was still intact, and so was he. He was lying there on his side, a thin fetal lump rounding out of the steel and grime. "What?" he rumbled.

I asked him the question I always seemed to be asking him: was he all right?

It took him a moment—he was working his hand free—and then he gave me the thumbs-up sign. "A-OK," he said.

The rest of the trip—through the icy Midwest, the wind-torn Rockies, and the scorching strip between Tucson and Gila Bend—was uneventful. For me, anyway. I alternately slept, ate truck-stop fare designed to remove the lining of your stomach, and listened to Mink or Steve—their conversation was interchangeable—rhapsodize about Harleys, IROC Camaros, and women who went down on all fours and had "Truckers' Delite" tattooed across their buttocks. For Zoltan, it was business as usual. If he suffered from the cold, the heat, the tumbleweeds, beer cans, and fast-food containers that ricocheted off his poor lean scrag of a body day and night, he never mentioned it. True to form, he refused food and drink, though I suspected he must have had something concealed in his cape, and he never climbed down out of his cocoon, not even to move his bowels. Three days and three nights after we'd left Maine, we wheeled the big rig through the streets of Pasadena and into the parking lot outside the Rose Bowl, right on schedule.

There was a fair-sized crowd gathered, though there was no telling whether they'd come for the swap meet, the heavy-metal band we'd hired to give some punch to Zoltan's performance, or the stunt itself, but then who cared? They were there. As were the "Action News" teams, the souvenir hawkers and hot-dog vendors. Grunting, his face beaded with sweat, Mink guided the truck into place alongside the twenty-five others, straining to get it as close as possible: an inch could mean the difference between life and death for Zoltan, and we all knew it.

I led a knot of cameramen to the rear of the truck so they could get some tape of Zoltan crawling out of his grapefruit bag. When they were all gathered, he stirred himself, shaking off the froth of insects and road grime, the scraps of paper and cellophane, placing first one bony foot and then the other on the pavement. His eyes were feverish behind the lenses of the goggles and when he lurched out from under the truck I had to catch his arm to prevent him from falling. "So how does it feel to conquer the roadways?" asked a microphone-jabbing reporter with moussed hair and flawless teeth. "What was the worst moment?" asked another.

Zoltan's legs were rubber. He reeked of diesel fuel, his cape was in tatters, his face smeared with sweat and grease. "Twenty-six truck," he rumbled. "The Human Fly is invincible."

And then the band started in—smokebombs, megadecibels, subhuman screeches, the works—and I led Zoltan to his dressing room. He refused a shower, but allowed the makeup girl to sponge off his face and hands. We had to cut the old outfit off of him—he was too exhausted to undress himself—and then the girl helped him into the brand-new one I'd provided for the occasion. "Twenty-six truck," he kept mumbling to himself, "A-OK."

I wanted him to call it off. I did. He wasn't in his right mind, anybody could see that. And he was exhausted, beat, as starved and helpless as a refugee. He wouldn't hear of it. "Twenty-six truck," he rumbled, and when I put through a frantic last-minute call to Sol, Sol nearly swallowed the phone. "Damn straight he's going for it!" he shouted. "We got sponsors lined up here. ABC Sports wants to see the tape, for christsake." There was an outraged silence punctuated by the click of throat lozenges, and then Sol cut the connection.

Ultimately, Zoltan went for it. Mink threw open the trailer door, Zoltan fired up the motorcycle—a specially modified Harley Sportster with gas shocks and a bored engine—and one of our people signaled the band to cut it short. The effect was dynamic, the band cutting back suddenly to a punchy drum-and-bass thing and the growl of the big bike coming on in counterpoint . . . and then Zoltan sprang from the back of the trailer, his cape stiff with the breeze, goggles flashing, tires squealing. He made three circuits of the lot, coming in close on the line of trucks, dodging away from the ramp, hunched low and flapping over the handlebars. Every eye was on him. Suddenly he raised a bony fist in the air, swerved wide of the trucks in a great arcing loop that took him to the far end of the lot, and made a run for the ramp.

He was a blur, he was nothing, he was invisible, a rush of motion above the scream of the engine. I saw something—a shadow—launch itself into the thick brown air, cab after cab receding beneath it, the glint of chrome in the sun, fifteen trucks, twenty, twenty-five, and then the sight that haunts me to this day. Suddenly the shadow was gone and a blemish appeared on the broad side panel of the last truck, the one we'd taken across country, Mink's truck, and then, simultaneous with it, there was the noise. A single booming reverberation, as if the world's biggest drum had exploded, followed by the abrupt cessation of the motorcycle's roar and the sad tumbling clatter of dissociated metal.

We had medical help this time, of course, the best available: paramedics, trauma teams, ambulances. None of it did any good. When I pushed through the circle of people around him, Zoltan was lying there on the pavement like a bundle of broken twigs. The cape was twisted round his neck, and his limbs—the sorry fleshless sticks of his arms and legs—were skewed like a doll's. I bent over him as the paramedics brought up the stretcher.

"Twenty-five truck next time," he whispered, "promise me."

There was blood in his ears, his nostrils, his eye sockets. "Yes," I said, "yes. Twenty-five."

"No worries," he choked as they slid the stretcher under him, "the Human Fly . . . can survive . . . anything."

We buried him three days later.

It was a lonely affair, as funerals go. The uncle, a man in his seventies with the sad scrawl of time on his face, was the only mourner. The press stayed away, though the videotape of Zoltan's finale was shown repeatedly over the air and the freeze-frame photos appeared in half the newspapers in the country. I was shaken by the whole thing. Sol gave me a week off and I did some real soul-searching. For a while I thought of giving up the entertainment business altogether, but I was pulled back into it despite myself. Everybody, it seemed, wanted a piece of Zoltan. And as I sat down to sort through the letters, telegrams, and urgent callback messages, the phone ringing unceasingly, the sun flooding the windows of my new well-appointed and highflown office, I began to realize that I owed it to Zoltan to pursue them. This was what he'd wanted, after all.

We settled finally on an animated series, with the usual tie-ins. I knew the producer—Sol couldn't say enough about him—and I knew he'd do quality work. Sure enough, the show premiered number one in its timeslot and it's been there ever since. Sometimes I'll get up early on a Saturday morning just to tune in, to watch the jerky figures move against a backdrop of greed and corruption, the Human Fly ascendant, incorruptible, climbing hand over hand to the top.

THE HAT

THEY SENT a hit squad after the bear. Three guys in white parkas with National Forestry Service patches on the shoulders. It was late Friday afternoon, about a week before Christmas, the snow was coming down so fast it seemed as if the sky and earth were glued together, and Jill had just opened up the lodge for drinks and dinner when they stamped in through the door. The tall one—he ordered shots of Jim Beam and beers for all of them—could have been a bear himself, hunched under the weight of his shoulders in the big quilted parka, his face lost in a bristle of black beard, something feral and challenging in the clash of his blue eyes. "Hello, pretty lady," he said, looking Jill full in the face as he swung a leg over the barstool and pressed his forearms to the gleaming copper rail. "I hear you got a bear problem."

I was sitting in the shadows at the end of the bar, nursing a beer and watching the snow. Jill hadn't turned up the lights yet and I was glad—the place had a soothing underwater look to it, snow like a sheet stretched tight over the window, the fire in the corner gentle as a backrub. I was alive and moving—lighting a cigarette, lifting the glass to my lips—but I felt so peaceful I could have been dozing.

"That's right," Jill said, still flushing from the "pretty lady" remark. Two weeks earlier, in bed, she'd told me she hadn't felt pretty in years. What are you talking about? I'd said. She

88

dropped her lower lip and looked away. I gained twenty pounds, she said. I reached out to touch her, smiling, as if to say twenty pounds—what's twenty pounds? Little Ball of Suet, I said, referring to one of the Maupassant stories in the book she'd given me. It's not funny, she said, but then she'd rolled over and touched me back.

"Name's Boo," the big man said, pausing to throw back his bourbon and take a sip of beer. "This is Scott," nodding at the guy on his left, also in beard and watchcap, "and Josh." Josh, who couldn't have been more than nineteen, appeared on his right like a jack-in-the-box. Boo unzipped the parka to expose a thermal shirt the color of dried blood.

"Is this all together?" Jill asked.

Boo nodded, and I noticed the scar along the ridge of his cheekbone, thinking of churchkey openers, paring knives, the long hooked ivory claws of bears. Then he turned to me. "What you drinking, friend?"

I'd begun to hear sounds from the kitchen—the faint kiss of cup and saucer, the rattle of cutlery—and my stomach suddenly dropped like an elevator out of control. I hadn't eaten all day. It was the middle of the month, I'd read all the paperbacks in the house, listened to all the records, and I was waiting for my check to come. There was no mail service up here of course— the road was closed half the time in winter anyway—but Marshall, the lodgeowner and unofficial kingpin of the community, had gone down the mountain to lay in provisions against the holiday onslaught of tourists, ski-mobilers and the like, and he'd promised to pick it up for me. If it was there. If it was, and he made it back through the storm, I was going to have three or four shots of Wild Turkey, then check out the family dinner and sip coffee and Kahlua till Jill got off work. "Beer," I said.

"Would you get this man a beer, pretty lady?" said Boo in his backwoods basso, and when she'd opened me one and come back for his money, he started in on the bear. Had she seen him?

How much damage had he done? What about his tracks—anything unusual? His scat? He was reddish in color, right? Almost cinnamon? And with one folded ear?

She'd seen him. But not when he'd battered his way into the back storeroom, punctured a case of twelve-and-a-half-ounce cans of tuna, lapped up a couple of gallons of mountain red burgundy and shards of glass, and left a bloody trail that wound off through the ponderosa pines like a pink ribbon. Not then. No, she'd seen him under more intimate circumstances—in her own bedroom, in fact. She'd been asleep in the rear bedroom with her eight-year-old son, Adrian (they slept in the same room to conserve heat, shutting down the thermostat and tossing a handful of coal into the stove in the corner), when suddenly the back window went to pieces. The air came in at them like a spearthrust, there was the dull booming thump of the bear's big body against the outer wall, and an explosion of bottles, cans, and whatnot as he tore into the garbage on the back porch. She and Adrian had jolted awake in time to see the bear's puzzled shaggy face appear in the empty windowframe, and then they were up like Goldilocks and out the front door, where they locked themselves in the car. They came to me in their pajamas, trembling like refugees. By the time I got there with my Weatherby, the bear was gone.

"I've seen him," Jill said. "He broke the damn window out of my back bedroom and now I've got it all boarded up." Josh, the younger guy, seemed to find this funny, and he began a low snickering suck and blow of air like an old dog with something caught in his throat.

"Hell," Jill said, lighting up, centerstage, "I was in my nightie and barefoot too and I didn't hesitate a second—zoom, I grabbed my son by the hand and out the door we went."

"Your nightie, huh?" Boo said, a big appreciative grin transforming his face so that for a minute, in the dim light, he could have been a leering, hairy-hocked satyr come in from the cold.

"Maybe it wasn't just the leftovers he wanted," I offered, and everyone cracked up. Just then Marshall stepped through the door, arms laden, stamping the snow from his boots. I got up to help him, and when he began fumbling in his breast pocket, I felt a surge of relief: he'd remembered my check. I was on my way out the door to help with the supplies when I heard Boo's rumbling bass like distant thunder: "Don't you worry, pretty lady," he was saying, "we'll get him."

Regina showed up three days later. For the past few years she'd rented a room up here over the holidays, ostensibly for her health, the cross-country skiing, and the change of scene, but actually so she could display her backend in stretch pants to the sex-crazed hermits who lived year-round amidst the big pines and sequoias. She was from Los Angeles, where she worked as a dental hygienist. Her teeth were perfect, she smiled nonstop and with the serenity of the Mona Lisa, and she wore the kind of bra that was popular in the fifties—the kind that thrust the breasts out of her ski sweater like nuclear warheads. She's been known to give the tumble to the occasional tourist or one of the lucky locals when the mood took her, but she really had it for Marshall. For two weeks every Christmas and another week at Easter, she became a fixture at the bar, as much a part of the decor as the moosehead or the stuffed bear, perched on a barstool in Norwegian sweater, red ski pants, and mukluks, sipping a champagne cocktail and waiting for him to get off work. Sometimes she couldn't hold out and someone else would walk off with her while Marshall scowled from behind the grill, but usually she just waited there for him like a flower about to drop its petals.

She came into the white world that afternoon like a foretaste of the good times to come—city women, weekend cowboys, grandmas, children, dogs, and lawyers were on their way, trees and decorations going up, the big festival of the goose-eating

Christians about to commence—rolling into the snowbound parking lot in her Honda with the neat little chain-wrapped tires that always remind me of Tonka toys. It was about 4:00 P.M., the sky was a sorrowful gray, and a loose flurry was dusting the huge logs piled up on the veranda. In she came, stamping and shaking, the knit cap pulled down to her eyebrows, already on the lookout for Marshall.

I was sitting in my usual place, working on my fifth beer, a third of the way through the check Marshall had brought me three days previous and calculating gloomily that I'd be out of money by Christmas at this rate. Scooter was bartending, and his daughter-in-law Mae-Mae, who happened to be a widow, was hunched morosely over a Tom Collins three stools up from me. Mae-Mae had lost her husband to the mountain two years earlier (or, rather, to the tortuous road that connected us to civilization and snaked up 7300 feet from the floor of the San Joaquin Valley in a mere twenty-six miles, treacherous as a goat trail in the Himalayas), and hadn't spoken or smiled since. She was a Thai. Scooter's son, a Vietnam hero, had brought her back from Southeast Asia with him. When Jill was off, or the holiday crowd bearing down on the place, Scooter would drive up the mountain from his cabin at Little Creek, elevation 5500 feet, hang his ski parka on a hook in back, and shake, stir, and blend cocktails. He brought Mae-Mae with him to get her out of the house.

Scooter and I had been discussing some of the finer points of the prevent defense with respect to the coming pro-football playoffs when Regina's Honda rolled into the lot, and now we gave it up to gape at her as she shook herself like a go-go dancer, opened her jacket to expose the jutting armaments of her breasts, and slid onto a barstool. Scooter slicked back his white hair and gave her a big grin. "Well," he said, fumbling for her name, "um, uh, good to see you again."

She flashed him her fluoridated smile, glanced past the absorbed Mae-Mae to where I sat grinning like an overworked dog, then turned back to him. "Marshall around?"

Scooter informed her that Marshall had gone down the mountain on a supply run and should be back by dinnertime. And what would she like?

She sighed, crossed her legs, lit a cigarette. The hat she was wearing was part of a set—hand-knit, imported from Scandinavia, woven from ram's whiskers by the trolls themselves, two hundred bucks at I. Magnin. Or something like that. It was gray, like her eyes. She swept it from her head with a flourish, fluffed out her short black hair and ordered a champagne cocktail. I looked at my watch.

I'd read somewhere that nine out of ten adults in Alaska had a drinking problem. I could believe it. Snow, ice, sleet, wind, the dark night of the soul: what else were you supposed to do? It was the same way up on the mountain. Big Timber was a collection of maybe a hundred widely scattered cabins atop a broad-beamed peak in the southern Sierras. The cabins belonged to summer people from L.A. and San Diego, to cross-country skiers, gynecologists, talent agents, ad men, drunks, and nature lovers, for the most part, and to twenty-seven hard-core antisocial types who called the place home year-round. I was one of this latter group. So was Jill. Of the remaining twenty-five xenophobes and rustics, three were women, and two of them were married and post-menopausal to boot. The sole remaining female was an alcoholic poet with a walleye who lived in her parents' cabin on the outer verge of the development and hated men. TV reception was spotty, radio nonexistent, and the nearest library a one-room affair at the base of the mountain that boasted three copies of the *The Thorn Birds* and the complete works of Irving Wallace.

And so we drank.

Social Life, such as it was, revolved around Marshall's lodge, which dispensed all the amenities in a single huge room, from burgers and chili omelets to antacid pills, cold remedies, cans of pickled beets, and toilet paper, as well as spirits, human fraternity, and a chance to fight off alien invaders at the controls of the video game in the corner. Marshall organized his Friday-night family dinners, did a turkey thing on Thanksgiving and Christmas, threw a New Year's party, and kept the bar open on weekends through the long solitary winter, thinking not so much of profit, but of our sanity. The lodge also boasted eight woodsy hotel rooms, usually empty, but now—with the arrival of Boo and his fellow hit men, Regina, and a couple other tourists—beginning to fill up.

On the day Regina rolled in, Jill had taken advantage of the break in the weather to schuss down the mountain in her station wagon and do some Christmas shopping. I was supposed to have gone with her, but we'd had a fight. Over Boo. I'd come in the night before from my late-afternoon stroll to see Jill half spread across the bar with a blank bovine look on her face while Boo mumbled his baritone blandishments into her eyes from about six inches away. I saw that, and then I saw that she'd locked fingers with him, as if they'd been arm wrestling or something. Marshall was out in the kitchen, Josh was sticking it to the video game, and Scott must have been up in his room. "Hey," Boo said, casually turning his head, "what's happening?" Jill gave me a defiant look before extricating herself and turning her back to fool around with the cash register. I stood there in the doorway, saying nothing. *Bishzz, bishzz*, went the video game, *zoot-zoot-zoot*. Marshall dropped something out in the kitchen. "Buy this man a drink, honey," Boo said. I turned and walked out the door.

"Christ, I can't believe you," Jill had said when I came round to pick her up after work. "It's my job, you know? What am I supposed to do, hang a sign around my neck that says 'Property of M. Koerner'?"

I told her I thought that was a pretty good idea.

"Forget the ride," she said. "I'm walking."

"And what about the bear?" I said, knowing how the specter of it terrified her, knowing that she dreaded walking those dark snowlit roads for fear of chancing across him—knowing it and wanting for her to admit it, to tell me she needed me.

But all she said was "Screw the bear," and then she was gone.

Now I ordered another beer, sauntered along the bar, and sat down one stool up from Regina. "Hi," I said, "remember me? Michael Koerner? I live up back of Malloy's place?"

She narrowed her eyes and gave me a smile I could feel all the way down in the remotest nodes of my reproductive tract. She no more knew me than she would have known a Chinese peasant plucked at random from the faceless hordes. "Sure," she said.

We made small talk. How slippery the roads were—worse than last year. A renegade bear? Really? Marshall grew a beard?

I'd bought her two champagne cocktails and was working on yet another beer, when Jill catapulted through the door, arms festooned with foil-wrapped packages and eyes ablaze with goodwill and holiday cheer; Adrian tagged along at her side, looking as if he'd just sprung down from the back of a flying reindeer. If Jill felt put out by the spectacle of Regina—or more particularly by my proximity to and involvement in that spectacle—she didn't miss a beat. The packages hit the bar with a thump, Scooter and Mae-Mae were treated to joyous salutatory squeals, Regina was embraced and I was ignored. Adrian went straight for the video game, pausing only to scoop up the six quarters I held out to him like an offering. Jill ordered herself a cocktail and started in on Regina, bantering away about hairstyles, nails, shoes, blouses, and the like as if she were glad to see her. "I just love that hat!" she shouted at one point, reaching out to finger the material. I swung round on my stool and stared out the window.

It was then that Boo came into sight. Distant, snow-softened, trudging across the barren white expanse of the lot as if in a dream. He was wearing his white parka, hood up, a rifle was slung over his shoulder, and he was dragging something behind him. Something heavy and dark, a long low-slung form that raveled out from his heels like a shadow. When he paused to straighten up and catch his streaming breath, I saw with a shock that the carcass of an animal lay at his feet, red and raw like a gash in the snow. "Hey!" I shouted. "Boo got the bear!" And the next minute we were all out in the windblown parking lot, hemmed in by the forbidding ranks of the trees and the belly of the gray deflated sky, as Boo looked up puzzled from the carcass of a gutted deer. "What happened, the bar catch fire?" he said, his sharp blue eyes parrying briefly with mine, swooping past Scooter, Adrian, and Mae-Mae to pause a moment over Jill and finally lock on Regina's wide-eyed stare. He was grinning.

The deer's black lip was pulled back from ratty yellowed teeth; its eyes were opaque in death. Boo had slit it from chest to crotch, and a half-frozen bulb of grayish intestine poked from the lower end of the ragged incision. I felt foolish.

"Bait," Boo said in explanation, his eyes roving over us again. "I'm leaving a blood smear you could follow with your eyes closed and your nose stopped up. Then I'm going to hang the meat up a tree and wait for Mr. Bear."

Jill turned away, a bit theatrically I thought, and made small noises of protest and disgust on the order of "the poor animal," then took Adrian by the hand and pulled him back in the direction of the lodge. Mae-Mae stared through us all, this carnage like that other that had claimed her husband's life, end over end in the bubble of their car, blood on the slope. Regina looked at Boo. He stood over the fallen buck, grinning like a troglodyte with his prey, then bent to catch the thing by its antlers and drag it off across the lot as if it were an old rug for the church rummage sale.

*   *   *

That night the lodge was hopping. Tourists had begun to trickle in and there were ten or twelve fresh faces at the bar. I ate a chicken pot pie and a can of cold beets in the solitude of my cabin, wrapped a tacky black-and-gold scarf round my neck, and ambled through the dark featureless forest to the lodge. As I stepped through the door I smelled perfume, sweet drinks, body heat, and caught the sensuous click of the poolballs as they punctuated the swell of riotous voices churning up around me. Holiday cheer, oh, yes, indeed.

Jill was tending bar. Everyone in the development was there, including the old wives and the walleyed poetess. An array of roaring strangers and those recognized vaguely from previous seasons stood, slouched, and stamped round the bar or huddled over steaks in the booths to the rear. Marshall was behind the grill. I eased up to the bar between a bearded stranger in a gray felt cowboy hat and a familiar-looking character who shot me a glance of mortal dislike and then turned away. I was absently wondering what I could possibly have done to offend this guy (winter people—I could hardly remember what I'd said and done last week, let alone last year), when I spotted Regina. And Boo. They were sitting at a booth, the table before them littered with empty glasses and beer bottles. Good, I thought to myself, an insidious little smile of satisfaction creeping across my lips, and I glanced toward Jill.

I could see that she was watching them out of the corner of her eye, though an impartial observer might have guessed she was giving her full attention to Alf Cornwall, the old gas bag who sat across the bar from her and toyed with a glass of peppermint schnapps while he went on ad nauseam about the only subject dear to him—i.e., the lamentable state of his health. "Jill," I barked with malicious joy, "how about some service down here?"

She gave me a look that would have corroded metal, then heaved back from the bar and poured me a long slow shot of

Wild Turkey and an even slower glass of beer. I winked at her as she set the drinks down and scraped my money from the bar. "Not tonight, Michael," she said, "I don't feel up to it," and her tone was so dragged down and lugubrious she could have been a professional mourner. It was then that I began to realize just how much Boo had affected her (and by extension, how little I had), and I glanced over my shoulder to focus a quick look of jealous hatred on him. When Jill set down my change I grabbed her wrist. "What the hell do you mean 'not tonight,' " I hissed. "Now I can't even talk to you, or what?"

She looked at me like a martyr, like a twenty-eight-year-old woman deserted by her husband in the backend of nowhere and saddled with an unhappy kid and a deadbeat sometime beau to whom the prospect of marriage was about as appealing as a lobotomy, she looked at me like a woman who's give up on romance. Then she jerked her arm away and slouched off to hear all the fascinating circumstances attending Alf Cornwall's most recent bowel movement.

The crowd began to thin out about eleven, and Marshall came out from behind the grill to saunter up to the bar for a Remy Martin. He too seemed preternaturally interested in Alf Cornwall's digestive tract, and sniffed meditatively at his cognac for five minutes or so before he picked up the glass and strolled over to join Boo and Regina. He slid in next to Regina, nodding and smiling, but he didn't look too pleased.

Like Boo, Marshall was big. Big-headed, big-bellied, with grizzled hair and a beard flecked with white. He was in his mid-forties, twice divorced, and he had a casual folksy way about him that women found appealing, or unique—or whatever. Women who came up the mountain, that is. Jill had had a thing with him the year before I moved in, he was one of the chief reasons the walleyed poetess hated men, and any number of cross-country ski bunnies, doctors' wives, and day trippers had taken some extracurricular exercise in the oak-framed waterbed that dominated his room in the back of the lodge. Boo didn't stand a chance. Ten minutes after Marshall had sat down Boo was back up at the bar, a little unsteady from all he'd had to drink, and looking Jill up and down like he had one thing on his mind.

I was on my third shot and fifth beer, the lights were low, the fire going strong, and the twenty-foot Christmas tree lit up like a satellite. Alf Cornwall had taken his bullshit home with him; the poetess, the wives, and two-thirds of the new people had cleared out. I was discussing beach erosion with the guy in the cowboy hat, who as it turned out was from San Diego, and keeping an eye on Boo and Jill at the far end of the bar. "Well, Christ," San Diego roared as if I was half a mile away, "you put up them godforsaken useless damn seawalls and what have you got, I ask you? Huh?"

I wasn't listening. Boo was stroking Jill's hand like a glove salesman, Marshall and Regina were grappling in the booth, and I was feeling sore and hurt and left out. A log burned through and tumbled into the coals with a thud. Marshall got up to poke it, and all of a sudden I was seething. Turning my back on San Diego, I pushed off of my stool and strode to the end of the bar.

Jill saw the look on my face and drew back. I put my hand on Boo's shoulder and watched him turn to me in slow motion, his face huge, the scar glistening over his eyebrow. "You can't do that," I said.

He just looked at me.

"Michael," Jill said.

"Huh?" he said. "Do what?" Then he turned his head to look at Jill, and when he swung back round he knew.

I shoved him, hard, as he was coming up off the barstool, and he went down on one knee before he caught himself and lunged at me. He would have destroyed me if Marshall hadn't caught hold of him, but I didn't care. As it was, he gave me one terrific shot to the breastbone that flattened me against the bar and sent a couple of glasses flying. Bang, bang, they shat-

tered on the flagstone floor like lightbulbs dropped from a
ladder.

"Goddamnit," Marshall was roaring, "that's about enough."
His face was red to the roots of his whiskers. "Michael," he
said—or blared, I should say—and then he waved his hand in
disgust. Boo stood behind him, giving me a bad look. "I think
you've had enough, Michael," Marshall said. "Go on home."

I wanted to throw it right back in his face, wanted to shout
obscenities, take them both on, break up the furniture, and set
the tree afire, but I didn't. I wasn't sixteen: I was thirty-one
years old and I was reasonable. The lodge was the only bar in
twenty-six miles and I'd be mighty thirsty and mighty lonely
both if I was banished for good. "All right," I said. "All right."
And then, as I shrugged into my jacket: "Sorry."

Boo was grinning, Jill looked like she had the night the bear
broke in. Regina was studying me with either interest or amusement—I couldn't tell which—Scooter looked like he had to go
to the bathroom, and San Diego just stepped aside. I pulled the
door closed behind me. Softly.

Outside, it was snowing. Big, warm, healing flakes. It was
the kind of snow my father used to hold his hands out to,
murmuring, *God must be up there plucking chickens*. I wrapped the
scarf round my throat and was about to start off across the lot
when I saw something moving through the blur of falling flakes.
The first thing I thought of was some late arrival from down
below, some part-timer come to claim his cabin. The second
thing I thought of was the bear.

I was wrong on both counts. The snow drove down against
the dark branchless pillars of the treetrunks, chalk strokes on a
blackboard, I counted off three breaths, and then Mae-Mae
emerged from the gloom. "Michael?" she said, coming up to me.

I could see her face in the yellow light that seeped through
the windows of the lodge and lay like a fungus on the surface
of the snow. She gave me a rare smile, and then her face changed

as she touched a finger to the corner of my mouth. "What happen you?" she said, and her finger glistened with blood.

I licked my lip. "Nothing. Bit my lip, I guess." The snow caught like confetti in the feathery puff of her hair and her eyes tugged at me from the darkness. "Hey," I said, surprised by inspiration, "you want to maybe come up to my place for a drink?"

Next day, at dusk, I was out in the woods with my axe. The temperature was about ten degrees above zero, I had a pint of Presidente to keep me warm, and I was looking for a nice round-bottomed silver fir about five feet tall. I listened to the snow groan under my boots, watched my breath hang in the air; I looked around me and saw ten thousand little green trees beneath the canopy of the giants, none of them right. By the time I found what I was looking for, the snow had drunk up the light and the trees had become shadows.

As I bent to clear the snow from the base of the tree I'd selected, something made me glance over my shoulder. Failing light, logs under the snow, branches, hummocks. At first I couldn't make him out, but I knew he was there. Sixth sense. But then, before the shaggy silhouette separated itself from the gloom, a more prosaic sense took over: I could smell him. Shit, piss, sweat, and hair, dead meat, bad breath, the primal stink. There he was, a shadow among shadows, big around as a fallen tree, the bear, watching me.

Nothing happened. I didn't grin him down, fling the axe at him, or climb a tree, and he didn't lumber off in a panic, throw himself on me with a bloody roar, or climb a tree either. Frozen like an ice sculpture, not even daring to come out of my crouch for fear of shattering the moment, I watched the bear. Communed with him. He was a renegade, a solitary, airlifted in a groggy stupor from Yellowstone, where he'd become too familiar with people. Now he was familiar with me. I wondered if he'd studied my tracks as I'd studied his, wondered what he was doing out in the harsh snowbound woods instead of curled cozily in his den. Ten minutes passed. Fifteen. The woods went dark. I stood up. He was gone.

Christmas was a pretty sad affair. Talk of post-holiday depression, I had it before, during, and after. I was broke, Jill and I were on the outs, I'd begun to loathe the sight of three-hundred-foot trees and snow-capped mountains, and I liked the rest of humanity about as much as Gulliver liked the Yahoos. I did stop by Jill's place around six to share a miserable, tight-lipped meal with her and Adrian and exchange presents. I gave Adrian a two-foot-high neon-orange plastic dragon from Taiwan that spewed up puddles of reddish stuff that looked like vomit, and I gave Jill a cheap knit hat with a pink pompon on top. She gave me a pair of gloves. I didn't stay for coffee.

New Year's was different.

I gave a party, for one thing. For another, I'd passed from simple misanthropy to nihilism, death of the spirit, and beyond. It was 2:00 A.M., everybody in the lodge was wearing party hats, I'd kissed half the women in the place—including a reluctant Jill, pliant Regina, and sour-breathed poetess—and I felt empty and full, giddy, expansive, hopeful, despondent, drunk. "Party at my place," I shouted as Marshall announced last call and turned up the lights. "Everybody's invited."

Thirty bon vivants tramped through the snowy streets, blowing party horns and flicking paper ticklers at one another, fired up snowmobiles, Jeeps, and pickups, carried open bottles out of the bar, and hooted at the stars. They filled my little place like fish in a net, squirming against one another, grinning and shouting, making out in the loft, vomiting in the toilet, sniggering around the fireplace. Boo was there, water under the bridge. Jill too. Marshall, Regina, Scooter, Mae-Mae, Josh and Scott, the poetess, San Diego, and anybody else who happened

to be standing under the moosehead in a glossy dunc
I made my announcement. Somebody put on a reg
that sent seismic shudders through the floor, and ped
to dance. I was out in the kitchen fumbling with the ice-cube
tray when Regina banged through the door with a bar glass in
her hand. She gave me a crooked smile and held it out to me.
"What're you drinking?" she asked.

"Pink Boys," I said. "Vodka, crushed ice, and pink lemonade,
slushed in the blender."

"Pink Boys," Regina said, or tried to say. She was wearing
her knit hat and matching sweater, the hat pulled down to her
eyebrows, the sweater unbuttoned halfway to her navel. I took
the glass from her and she moved into me, caught hold of my
biceps, and stuck her tongue in my mouth. A minute later I had
her pinned up against the stove, exploring her exemplary den-
tition with the tip of my own tongue and dipping my hand into
that fabulous sweater as if into the mother lode itself.

I had no problems with any of this. I gave no thought to
motives, mores, fidelity, or tomorrow: I was a creature of nature, responding to natural needs. Besides which, Jill was locked
in an embrace with Marshall in the front room, the old satyr
and king of the mountain reestablishing a prior claim, Boo was
hunched over the fire with Mae-Mae, giving her the full flash
of his eyes and murmuring about bear scat in a voice so deep it
would have made Johnny Cash turn pale, and Josh and the
poetess were joyfully deflating Edna St. Vincent Millay while
swaying their bodies awkwardly to Bob Marley's voodoo
backbeat. New Year's Eve. It was like something out of *La
Ronde*.

By three-thirty, I'd been rejected by Regina, who'd obviously
been using me as a decoy, Marshall and Jill had disappeared and
rematerialized twice, Regina had tried unsuccessfully to lure Boo
away from Mae-Mae (who was now secreted with him in the
bedroom), San Diego had fallen and smashed my coffee table

to splinters, one half-gallon of vodka was gone and we were well into the second, and Josh and the poetess had exchanged addresses. Auld lang syne, I thought, surveying the wreckage and moodily crunching taco chips while a drunken San Diego raved in my ear about dune buggies, outboard engines, and tuna rigs. Marshall and Jill were holding hands. Regina sat across the room, looking dangerous. She'd had four or five Pink Boys, on top of what she'd consumed at the lodge, but who was counting? Suddenly she stood—or, rather, jumped to her feet like a marine assaulting a beachhead—and began to gather her things.

What happened next still isn't clear. Somehow her hat had disappeared—that was the start of it. At first she just bustled round the place, overturning piles of scarves and down jackets, poking under the furniture, scooting people from the couch and easy chair, but then she turned frantic. The hat was a keepsake, an heirloom. Brought over from Flekkefjord by her great-grandmother, who'd knitted it as a memento of Olaf the Third's coronation, or something like that. Anyway, it was irreplaceable. More precious than the Magna Carta, the Shroud of Turin, and the Hope Diamond combined. She grew shrill.

Someone cut the stereo. People began to shuffle their feet. One clown—a total stranger—made a show of looking behind the framed photograph of Dry Gulch, Wyoming, that hangs beside the fireplace. "It'll turn up," I said.

Regina had scattered a heap of newspapers over the floor and was frantically riffling through the box of kindling in the corner. She turned on me with a savage look. "The hell it will," she snarled. "Somebody stole it."

"Stole it?" I echoed.

"That's right," she said, the words coming fast now. She was looking at Jill. "Some bitch. Some fat-assed jealous bitch that just can't stand the idea of somebody showing her up. Some, some—"

She didn't get a chance to finish. Jill was up off the couch like something coming out of the gate at Pamplona and suddenly the two of them were locked in combat, pulling hair and raking at one another like Harpies. Regina was cursing and screeching at the same time; Jill went for the vitals. I didn't know what to do. San Diego made the mistake of trying to separate them, and got his cheek raked for the effort. Finally, when they careened into the pole lamp and sent it crashing to the floor with a climactic shriek of broken glass, Marshall took hold of Regina from behind and wrestled her out the door, while I did my best to restrain Jill.

The door slammed. Jill shrugged loose, heaving for breath, and turned her back on me. There were twenty pale astonished faces strung round the room like Japanese lanterns. A few of the men looked sheepish, as if they'd stolen a glimpse of something they shouldn't have. No one said a word. Just then Boo emerged from the bedroom, Mae-Mae in tow. "What's all the commotion?" he said.

I glanced around the room. All of a sudden I felt indescribably weary. "Party's over," I said.

I woke at noon with a hangover. I drank from the tap, threw some water in my face, and shambled down to the lodge for breakfast. Marshall was there, behind the grill, looking as if he was made of mashed potatoes. He barely noticed as I shuffled in and took a window seat among a throng of chipper, alert, and well-fed tourists.

I was leafing through the *Chronicle* and puffing away at my third cup of coffee when I saw Regina's car sail past the window, negotiate the turn at the end of the lot, and swing onto the road that led down the mountain. I couldn't be sure—it was a gloomy day, the sky like smoke—but as near as I could tell she was hatless. No more queen of the mountain for her, I thought. No more champagne cocktails and the tight thrilling clasp of spandex across the bottom—from here on out it was stinking mouths and receding gums. I turned back to the newspaper.

When I looked up again, Boo, Josh, and Scott were stepping

out of a Jeep Cherokee, a knot of gawkers and Sunday skiers gathered round them. Draped over the hood of the thing, still red at the edges with raw meat and blood, was a bearskin, head intact. The fur was reddish, almost cinnamon-colored, and one ear was folded down. I watched as Boo ambled up to the door, stepped aside for a pair of sixteen-year-old ski bunnies with layered hair, and then pushed his way into the lodge.

He took off his shades and stood there a moment in the doorway, carefully wiping them on his parka before slipping them into his breast pocket. Then he started toward the cash register, already easing back to reach for his wallet. "Hey," he said when he saw me, and he stopped to lean over the table for a moment. "We got him," he said, scraping bottom with his baritone and indicating the truck beyond the window with a jerk of his head. There was a discoloration across the breast of his white parka, a brownish spatter. I swiveled my head to glance out the window, then turned back to him, feeling as if I'd had the wind punched out of me. "Yeah," I said.

There was a silence. He looked at me, I looked at him. "Well," he said after a moment, "you take care," and then he strode up to the cash register to pay his bill and check out.

Jill came in about one. She was wearing shades too, and when she slipped behind the bar and removed them, I saw the black-and-blue crescent under her right eye. As for Marshall, she didn't even give him a glance. Later, after I'd been through the paper twice and figured it was time for a Bloody Mary or two and some Bowl games, I took a seat at the bar. "Hi, Michael," she said, "what'll you have?," and her tone was so soft, so contrite, so sweet and friendly and conciliatory, that I could actually feel the great big heaving plates of the world shifting back into alignment beneath my feet.

Oh, yes, the hat. A week later, when the soot and dust and woodchips around the cabin got too much for me, I dragged out the vacuum cleaner for my semiannual sweep around the place. I scooted over the rug, raked the drapes, and got the cobwebs in the corners. When I turned over the cushions on the couch, the wand still probing, I found the hat. There was a label inside. *J.C. Penney*, it read, *$7.95*. For a long moment I just stood there, turning the thing over in my hand. Then I tossed it in the fire.

ME CAGO EN LA LECHE
(ROBERT JORDAN IN NICARAGUA)

"So TELL ME, comrade, why do you wear your hair this way?"

Robert Jordan fingered the glistening, rock-hard corona of his spiked hair (dyed mud-brown now, with khaki highlights, for the sake of camouflage) and then loosened the cap of his flask and took a long burning hit of mescal. He waited till the flame was gone from his throat and the familiar glow lit his insides so that they felt radioactive, then leaned over the campfire to address the flat-faced old man in worn fatigues. "Because I shit in the milk of my mother, that's why," he said, the mescal abrading his voice. He caressed the copper stud that lay tight against the flange of his left nostril and wiped his hands with exaggerated care on his Hussong's T-shirt. "And come to think of it," he added, "because I shit in the milk of your mother too."

The old man, flat-faced though he was, said nothing. He wasn't that old, actually—twenty-eight or -nine, Robert Jordan guessed—but poor nutrition, lack of dental care, and too much squinting into the sun gave him the look of a retired caterer in Miami Beach. The fire snapped, monkeys howled. "La reputa que lo parió," the old man said finally, turning his head to spit.

Robert Jordan didn't catch it all—he'd dropped out of college in the middle of Intermediate Spanish—but he got the gist of it all right and gave the old man the finger. "Yeah," he said, "and screw you too."

Two nights earlier the old man had come to him in the Managua bus station as he gingerly lifted his two aluminum-frame superlightweight High Sierra mountain packs down from the overhead rack and exited the bus that had brought him from Mexico City. The packs were stuffed with soiled underwear, granola bars, hair gel, and plastic explosives, and Robert Jordan was suffering from a hangover. He was also suffering from stomach cramps, diarrhea, and dehydration, not to mention the general debilitating effects of having spent two days and a night on a third-class bus with a potpourri of drunks, chicken thieves, disgruntled pigs, and several dozen puking, mewling, loose-boweled niñitos. "Over here, comrade," the old man had whispered, taking him by the arm and leading him to a bench across the square.

The old man had hovered over him as Robert Jordan threw himself down on the bench and stretched his legs. Trucks rumbled by, burros brayed, campesinos hurried about their business. "You are the gringo for this of the Cup of Soup, no?" the old man asked.

Robert Jordan regarded him steadily out of the slits of his bloodshot eyes. The old man's face was as dry and corrugated as a strip of jerky and he wore the armband of the Frente, black letters—FSLN—against a red background. Robert Jordan was thinking how good the armband would look with his Dead Kennedys tour jacket, but he'd caught the "Cup of Soup" business and nodded. That nod was all the old man needed. He broke into a grin, bent to kiss him on both cheeks, and breathed rummy fumes in his face. "I am called Bayardo," the old man said, "and I am come to take you to the border."

Robert Jordan felt bone-weary, but this is what he'd come for, so he stood and shouldered one of the packs while Bayardo took the other. In a few minutes they'd be boarding yet another bus, this one north to Jinotega and the Honduran border that lay beyond it. There Robert Jordan would rendezvous with one of the counter-counter-revolutionary bands (Contra Contra) and he would, if things went well, annihilate in a roar of flying earth clods and shattered trees a Contra airstrip and warehouse where foodstuffs—Twinkies, Lipton Cup of Soup, and Rice Krispies among them—were flown in from Texas by the CIA. Hence the codename, "Cup of Soup."

But now—now they were camped somewhere on the Nicaraguan side of the border, listening to monkeys howl and getting their asses chewed off by mosquitoes, ticks, chiggers, leeches, and everything else that crawled, swam, or flew. It began to rain. The rain, Robert Jordan understood, would be bad for his hair. He finished a granola bar, exchanged curses with the old man, and crawled into his one-man pup tent. "You take the first watch," he growled through the wall of undulating nylon in his very bad Spanish. "And the second and third too. Come to think of it, why don't you just wake me at noon."

The camp was about what you'd expect, Robert Jordan thought, setting his pack down in a clump of poisonous-looking plants. He and the old man had hiked three days through the bug factory to get here, and what was it but a few banana-leaf hovels with cigarette cartons piled outside. Robert Jordan was thinking he'd be happy to blow this dump and get back to the drugs, whores, semi-clean linen, and tequila añejo of Mexico City and points north, when a one-eyed man emerged from the near hut, his face split with a homicidal grin. His name was Ruperto, and he wore the combat boots, baggy camouflage pants, and black T-shirt that even professors in Des Moines favored these days, and he carried a Kalashnikov assault rifle in his right hand. "Qué tal, old man," he said, addressing Bayardo, and then, turning to Robert Jordan and speaking in English: "And this is the gringo with the big boom-boom. Nice hair, gringo."

Robert Jordan traded insults with him, ending with the usual malediction about shit, milk, and mothers, and then pinched his voice through his nose in the nagging whine he'd perfected when he was four. "And so where's all the blow that's supposed to be dropping from the trees out here, huh? And what about maybe a hit of rum or some tortillas or something? I mean I been tramping through this craphole for three days and no sooner do I throw my pack down than I get some wiseass comment about my hair I could've stayed in Montana and got from some redneck cowboy. Hey," he shouted, leaning into Ruperto's face and twisting his voice till it broke in a snarl, "screw you too, Jack."

Ruperto said nothing. Just smiled his homicidal smile, one eye gleaming, the other dead in a crater of pale, scarred flesh. By now the others had begun to gather—Robert Jordan counted six of them, flat-faced Indians all—and a light rain was sizzling through the trees. "You want hospitality," Ruperto said finally, "go to Howard Johnson's." He spat at his feet. "Your mother," he said, and then turned to shout over his shoulder. "Muchacha!"

Everyone stopped dead to watch as the girl in skintight fatigues stepped out of the hut, shadowed by an older woman with the build of a linebacker. "Sí?" the girl said in a voice that inflamed Robert Jordan's groin.

Ruperto spat again. "Bring the gringo some chow."

"The Cup of Soup?" the girl asked.

Ruperto winked his mad wet eye at Robert Jordan. "Sí," he grunted, "the Cup of Soup."

As he lay in his pup tent that night, his limbs entwined in the girl's—her name was either Vidaluz or Concepción, he couldn't remember which—Robert Jordan thought of his grandmother. She was probably the only person in the world he didn't hate. His mother was a real zero, white wine and pasta salad all the way, and his friends back in Missoula were a bunch of dinks who thought Bryan Adams was god. His father was dead. When the old man had sucked on the barrel of his 30.06 Winchester, Robert was fourteen and angry. His role model was Sid Vicious and he was into glue and Bali Hai. It was his grandmother— she was Andalusian, really cool, a guerrilla who'd bailed out of

Spain in the '30s, pregnant with Robert Jordan II—who listened patiently to his gripes about the school jocks and his wimpy teachers and bought him tire chains to wrap around his boots. They sat for hours together listening to the Clash's Sandinista album, and when he blew off the tips of his pinky and ring fingers with a homemade bomb, it was she who gave him his first pair of studded black leather gloves. And what was best about her—what he liked more than anything else—was that she didn't take any shit from anybody. Once, when her third husband, Joe Thunderbucket, called her "Little Rabbit," she broke his arm in three places. It was she more than anyone who'd got him into all this revolution business—she and the Clash, anyway. And of course he'd always loved dynamite.

He lay there, slapping mosquitoes, his flesh sticky against the girl's, wondering what his grandmother was doing now, in the dark of this night before his first offensive. It was a Tuesday, wasn't it? That was bingo night on the reservation, and she usually went with Joe's sister Leona to punch numbers and drink boilermakers at the bingo hall. He pictured her in her black mantilla, her eyes cold and hard and lit maybe a little with the bourbon and Coors, and then he woke up Concepción or Vidaluz and gave it to her again, all his anger focused in the sharp tingling stab and rhythm of it.

It was still dark when the old man woke him. "Son of a bitch," Robert Jordan muttered. His hair was crushed like a Christmas-tree ornament and there was a sour metallic taste in his mouth. He didn't mind fighting for the revolution, but this was ridiculous—it wasn't even light yet. "Ándale," the old man said, "the Cup of Soup awaits."

"Are you out of your gourd, or what?" Robert Jordan twisted free of the girl and checked his watch. "It's four-fifteen, for christ's sake."

The old man shrugged. "Qué puta es la guerra," he said. "War's a bitch."

And then the smell of woodsmoke and frijoles came to him over Ruperto's high crazed whinny of a laugh, the girl was up and out of his sleeping bag, strolling heavy-haunched and naked across the clearing, and Robert Jordan was reaching for his hair gel.

After breakfast—two granola bars and a tin plate of frijoles that looked and tasted like humus—Robert Jordan vomited in the weeds. He was going into battle for the first time and he didn't have the stomach for it. This wasn't like blowing the neighbors' garbage cans at 2:00 A.M. or ganging up on some jerk in a frat jacket, this was the real thing. And what made it worse was that they couldn't just slip up in the dark, attach the plastique with a timer, and let it rip when they were miles away—oh, no, that would be too simple. His instructions, carried by the old man from none other than Ruy Ruiz, the twenty-three-year-old Sandinista poet in charge of counter-counter-revolutionary activities and occasional sestinas, were to blow it by hand the moment the cargo plane landed. Over breakfast, Robert Jordan, angry though he was, had begun to understand that there was more at risk here than his coiffure. There could be shooting. Rocket fire. Grenades. A parade of images from all the schlock horror films he'd ever seen—exploding guts, melting faces, ragged ghouls risen from the grave—marched witheringly through his head and he vomited.

"Hey, gringo," Ruperto called in English, "suck up your cojones and let's hit it."

Robert Jordan cursed him weakly with a barrage of shits and milks, but when he turned round to wipe the drool from his face he saw that Ruperto and his big woman had led a cluster of horses from the jungle. The big woman, her bare arms muscled like a weightlifter's, approached him leading a gelding the size of a buffalo. "Here, gringo," she breathed in her incongruously feminine voice, "mount up."

"Mount?" Robert Jordan squeaked in growing panic. "I thought we were walking."

The truth was, Robert Jordan had always hated horses. Growing up in Montana it was nothing but horses, horses, horses, morning, noon, and night. Robert Jordan was a rebel, a punk, a free spirit—he was no cowboy dildo—and for him it was dirt bikes and dune buggies. He'd been on horseback exactly twice in his life and both times he'd been thrown. Horses: they scared him. Anything with an eye that big—

"Vámonos," Ruperto snapped. "Or are you as gutless as the rest of the gringo wimps they send us?"

"Leche," Robert Jordan whinnied, too shaken even to curse properly. And then he was in the saddle, the big, broad-beamed monster of a horse peering back at him out of the flat wicked discs of its eyes, and they were off.

Hunkered down in the bug factory, weeds in his face, his coccyx on fire, and every muscle, ligament, and tendon in his legs and ass beaten to pulp by the hammer of the horse's backbone, Robert Jordan waited for the cargo plane. He was cursing his grandmother, the Sandinistas, the Clash, and even Sid Vicious. This was, without doubt, the stupidest thing he'd ever done. Still, as he crouched there with the hard black plastic box of the detonator in his hand, watching the pot-bellied crewcut rednecks and their runty flat-faced Indian allies out on the landing strip, he felt a surge of savage joy: he was going to blow the mother-fuckers to Mars and back.

Ruperto was somewhere to his left, dug in with the big woman and their Kalashnikovs. Their own flat-faced Indians, led by the flat-faced old man, were down to the right somewhere, bristling with rifles. The charges were in place—three in the high grass along the runway median and half a dozen under the prefab aluminum warehouse itself. The charges had been set by a scampering Ruperto just before dawn while the lone sentry dreamed of cold cerveza and a plate of fried dorado and banana chips. Ruperto had set them because when the time came Robert Jordan's legs hadn't worked and that was bad. Ruperto had called him a cheesebag, a faggot, and worse, and he'd lost face with the flat-faced Indians and the old man. But that was then, this was now.

Suddenly he heard it, the distant drone of propellers like the hum of a giant insect. He caressed the black plastic box, murmuring "Come on, baby, come on," all the slights and sneers he'd ever suffered, all the head slaps and jibes about his hair, his gloves, and his boots, all the crap he'd taken from his yuppie bitch of a mother and those dickheads at school—all of it had come down to this. If the guys could only see him now, if they could only see the all-out, hellbent, super-destructive, radical mess he was about to make . . . Yes! And there it was, just over the treetops. Coming in low like a pregnant goose, stuffed full of Twinkies. He began counting down: ten, nine, eight . . .

The blast was the most beautiful thing he'd ever witnessed. One minute he was watching the plane touch down, its wings and fuselage unmarked but for the painted-over insignia of the Flying Tigers, the world still and serene, the sack-bellies standing back expectantly, already tasting that first long cool Bud, and then suddenly, as if he'd clapped another slide in the projector, everything disappeared in a glorious killing thunderclap of fire and smoke. Hot metal, bits of molten glass and god knew how many Twinkies, Buds, and Cups of Soup went rocketing into the air, scorching the trees, and streaming down around Robert Jordan like a furious hissing rain. When the smoke cleared there was nothing left but twisted aluminum, the burned-out hulk of the plane, and a crater the size of Rockefeller Center. From the corner of his eye Robert Jordan could see Ruperto and the big woman emerge cautiously from the bushes, weapons lowered. In a quick low crouch they scurried across the open ground and stood for a moment peering into the smoking crater, then Ruperto let out a single shout of triumph—"Yee-haw!"— and fired off a round in the air.

It was then that things got hairy. Someone opened up on them from the far side of the field—some Contra Contra Contra, no doubt—and Ruperto went down. The flat-faced Indians let loose with all they had and for a minute the air screamed like a thousand babies torn open. The big woman threw Ruperto over her shoulder and flew for the jungle like a wounded crab. "Ándale!" she shouted and then the firing stopped abruptly as everyone, Robert Jordan included, bolted for the horses.

When he saw the fist-sized chunk torn out of Ruperto's calf, Robert Jordan wanted to vomit. So he did. The horses were half crazy from the blast and the rat-tat-tat of the Kalashnikovs and they stamped and snorted like fiends from hell. God, he hated horses. But he was puking, Ruperto's wound like raw meat flecked with dirt and bone, and the others were leaping atop their mounts, faces pulled tight with panic. Now there was firing behind them again and he straightened up and looked for his horse. There he was, Diablo, jerking wildly at his tether and kicking out his hoofs like a doped-up bronc at the rodeo. Shit. Robert Jordan wiped his lips and made a grab for the reins. It was a mistake. He might just as well have stabbed the horse with a hot poker—in that instant Diablo reared, snapped his tether, and brought all of his wet steaming nine hundred and fifty-eight pounds squarely down on Robert Jordan's left foot.

The sound of his toes snapping was unmusical and harsh and the pain that accompanied it so completely demanding of his attention that he barely noticed the retreating flanks of Diablo as he lashed off through the undergrowth. Robert Jordan let out a howl and broke into a string of inspired curses in two languages and then sat heavily, cradling his foot. The time he'd passed out having his nose pierced flashed through his mind and then the tears started up in his eyes. Stupid, stupid, stupid, he thought. And then he remembered where he was and who was shooting at him from across the field and he looked up to see his comrades already mounted—Ruperto included—and giving him a quick sad look. "Too bad, gringo," Ruperto said, grinning crazily despite the wound, "but it looks like we're short a horse."

"My toes, my toes!" Robert Jordan cried, trying to stand and falling back again.

Rat-tat. Rat-tat-tat, sang the rifles behind them.

Ruperto and his big woman spoke to their horses and they were gone. So too the flat-faced Indians. Only the old man lingered a moment. Just before he lashed his horse and disappeared, he leaned down in the saddle and gave Robert Jordan a wistful look. "Leche," he said, abbreviating the curse, "but isn't war a bitch."

THE LITTLE CHILL

HAL HAD KNOWN Rob and Irene, Jill, Harvey, Tootle, and Pesky since elementary school, and they were all forty going on sixty.

Rob and Irene had been high-school sweethearts, and now, after quitting their tenured teaching jobs, they brokered babies for childless couples like themselves. They regularly flew to Calcutta, Bahrain, and Sarawak to bring back the crumpled brown-faced little sacks of bones they located for the infertile wives of dry cleaners and accountants. Though they wouldn't admit it, they'd voted for Ronald Reagan.

Jill had a certain fragile beauty about her. She'd gone into a Carmelite nunnery after the obloquy of high school and the unrequited love she bore for Harvey, who at the time was hot for Tootle. She lived just up the street from Rob and Irene, in her late mother's house, and she'd given up the nun's life twelve years earlier to have carnal relations with a Safeway butcher named Eugene, who left her with a blind spot in one eye, a permanent limp, and triplets.

Harvey had been a high-school lacrosse star who quit college to join the Marines, acquiring a reputation for ferocity and self-less bravery during the three weeks he fought at Da Nang before taking thirty-seven separate bayonet wounds in his legs, chest, buttocks, and feet. He was bald and bloated, a brooding semi-invalid addicted to Quaalude, Tuinol, aspirin, cocaine, and Jack

Daniel's, and he lived in the basement of his parents' house, eating little and saying less. He despised Hal, Rob and Irene, Jill, Tootle, and Pesky because they hadn't taken thirty-seven bayonet wounds each and because they were communists and sellouts.

Tootle had been a cover girl; a macrobiot; the campaign manager for a presidential candidate from Putnam Valley, New York, who promised to push through legislation to animate all TV news features; and, finally, an environmentalist who spent all her waking hours writing broadsides for the Marshwort Preservationists' League. She was having an off/on relationship with an Italian race-car driver named Enzo.

Pesky was assistant manager of Frampold's LiquorMart, twice divorced and the father of a fourteen-year-old serial murderer whose twelve adult male victims all resembled Pesky in coloring, build, and style of dress.

And Hal? Hal was home from California. For his birthday.

Jill hosted the party. She had to. The triplets—Steve, Stevie, and Steven, now seven, seven, and seven, respectively—were hyperactive, antisocial, and twice as destructive as Hitler's Panzer Corps. She hadn't been able to get a baby-sitter for them since they learned to crawl. "All right," Hal had said to her on the phone, "your house then. Seven o'clock. Radical. Really." And then he hung up, thinking of the dingy cavern of her mother's house, with its stained wallpaper, battered furniture, and howling drafts, and of the mortified silence that would fall over the gang when they swung by to pick up Jill on a Friday night and Mrs. Morlock—that big-bottomed, horse-toothed parody of Jill—would insist they come in for hot chocolate. But no matter. At least the place was big.

As it turned out, Hal was two hours late. He was from California, after all, and this was his party. He hadn't seen any of these people in what—six years now?—and there was no way he was going to be cheated out of his grand entrance. At seven he pulled a pair of baggy parachute pants over his pink hightops, stuck a gold marijuana-leaf stud through the hole in his left earlobe, wriggled into an Ozzie Osbourne Barf Tour T-shirt though it was twenty-six degrees out and driving down sleet, and settled into the Barcalounger in which his deceased dad had spent the last two-thirds of his life. He sipped Scotch, watched the TV blip rhythmically, and listened to his own sad old failing mom dodder on about the Jell-O mold she'd bought for Mrs. Herskowitz across the street. Then, when he was good and ready, he got up, slicked back his thinning, two-tone, forty-year-old hair that looked more and more like mattress stuffing every day, shrugged into his trenchcoat, and slammed out into the storm.

There were two inches of glare ice on the road. Hal thumped his mother's stuttering Oldsmobile from tree to tree, went into a 180-degree spin, and schussed down Jill's driveway, narrowly avoiding the denuded azalea bush, three Flexible Flyers, and a staved-in Renault on blocks. He licked his fingertips and smoothed down his sideburns on the doorstep, knocked perfunctorily, and entered, grinning, in all his exotic, fair-haired, California glory. Unfortunately, the effect was wasted—no one but Jill was there. Hunched in the corner of a gutted sofa, she smiled wanly from behind a mound of soggy Fritos and half a gallon of California dip. "Hi," she said in a voice of dole, "they're coming, they're coming." Then she winked her bad eye at him and limped across the room to stick her tongue in his mouth.

She was clinging to him, licking at his mustache and telling him about her bout with breast cancer, when the doorbell rang and Rob and Irene came hurtling into the room shrieking "My God, look at you!" They were late, they screamed, because the baby-sitter never showed for their daughter, Soukamathandra-vaki, whose frightened little face peered in out of the night behind them.

An instant later, Harvey swung furiously up the walk on his silver crutches, Tootle and Pesky staggered in together with reddened noses and dilated pupils, and Steve, Stevie, and Steven emerged from the back of the house on their minibikes to pop wheelies in the middle of the room. The party was on.

"So," Harvey snarled, fencing Hal into the corner with the gleaming shafts of his crutches, "they tell me you're doing pretty good out there, huh, bub?"

Pesky and Tootle were standing beside him, grinning till Hal thought their lips would dry out and stick to their teeth, and Pesky had his arm around Tootle's shoulder. "Me?" Hal said, with a modest shrug. "Well, since you ask, my agent did say that—"

Harvey cut him off, turning to Pesky with a wild leer and shouting, "So how's the kid, what's his name—Damian?"

Dead silence fell over the room.

Rob and Irene froze, clutching Dixie cups of purple passion to their chests, and Jill, who'd been opening their eyes to the in-fighting, petty abuses, and catastrophic outrages of the food-stamp office where she worked, caught her tongue. Even Steve, Stevie, and Steven snapped to attention. They'd been playfully binding little Soukamathandravaki to one of the dining-room chairs with electrical tape, but at the mention of Damian, they looked round them in unison and vanished.

"You son of a bitch," Pesky said, his fingers dug so deep in Tootle's shoulder his knuckles went white. "You crippled fascist Marine Corps burnout."

Harvey jerked his big head to one side and spat on the floor. "What'd they give him, life plus a hundred and fifty years? Or'd they send him to Matteawan?"

"Hey," Irene shouted, a desperate keening edge to her voice, "hey, do you guys remember all those wild pranks we used to pull back in high school?" She tore across the room, waving her Dixie cup. "Like, like when we smeared that black stuff on our faces and burned the Jewish star on Dr. Rosenbaum's front lawn?"

Everyone ignored her.

"Harv," Hal said, reaching out to take his arm, but Harvey jerked violently away—"Get your stinking hands off me!" he roared—before he lost his balance and fell with a sad clatter of aluminum into the California dip.

"Serves you right, you bitter son of a bitch," Pesky growled, standing over him as if they'd just gone fifteen rounds. "The crippled war hero. Why don't you show us your scars, huh?"

"Pesky," Hal hissed, "leave it, will you?"

Rob and Irene were trying to help Harvey to his feet, but he fought them off, sobbing with rage. There was California dip on the collar of his campaign jacket. Hairless and pale, with his quivering jowls and splayed legs, he looked like a monstrous baby dropped there on the rug.

"Or the time Pesky ran up in front of Mrs. Gold's class in the third grade and blew on his thumb till he passed out, remember that?" Irene was saying, when the room was rent by a violent, predatory shriek, as if someone had torn a hawk in half. It was Tootle. She twisted out from under Pesky's arm and slammed her little white fist into his kidney. "You," she sputtered, "who are you to talk, lording it over Harvey as if he was some kind of criminal or something. At least he fought for his country. What'd you do, huh?" Her eyes were swollen. There was a froth of saliva caught in the corner of her mouth.

Pesky swung around. He was wearing his trademark Levi's— jeans, jacket, sweatshirt, socks, and big-buckled belt. If only they made shoes, he used to say. "Yeah, yeah, tell us about it," he sneered, "you little whore. Peddling your ass just like—"

"Canada, that's what you did about it. Like a typical wimp."

"Hey, hold on," Hal said, lurching out of the corner in his parachute pants, "I don't believe this. We all tried to get out of it—it was a rotten war, an illegal war, Nixon's and Johnson's war—what's the matter with you? Don't you remember?"

"The marches," Irene said.

"The posters," Rob joined in.

"A cheap whore, that's all. Cover girl, my ass."

"Shut up!" Tootle shrieked, turning on Hal. "You're just as bad as Pesky. Worse. You're a hypocrite. At least he knows he's a piece of shit." She threw back a cup of purple passion and leveled her green-eyed glare on him. "And you think you're so high and mighty, out there in Hollywood—well, la-de-da, that's what I say."

"He's an artist," Harvey said from the floor. "He co-wrote the immortal script for the 'Life with Beanie' show."

"Fuck you."

"Fuck you too."

And then suddenly, as if it signaled a visitation from another realm, there was the deep-throated cough of a precision engine in the driveway, a sputter and its dying fall. As one, the seven friends turned to the door. There was a thump. A knock—*dat dat-dat-dat da.* And then: "Allo, allo, anybody is home?"

It was Enzo. Tall, noble, with the nose of an emperor and a weave of silver in his hair so rich it might have been hammered from the mother lode itself. He was dressed in a coruscating jumpsuit with Pennzoil and Pirelli patches across the shoulder and chest, and he held his crash helmet in his hand. "Baby," he said, crossing the room in two strides and taking Tootle in his arms, "ciao."

No one moved. No one said a thing.

"Beech of a road," Enzo said. "Ice, you know." Outside, through the open door, the sleek low profile of his Lazaretto 2200 Pinin Farina coupe was visible, the windshield plated with ice, sleet driving down like straight pins. "Tooka me seventeen and a half minutes from La Guardia—a beech, huh? But baby, at least I'm here."

He looked round him, as if seeing the others for the first time, and then, without a word, crossed the room to the stereo, ran a quick finger along the spines of the albums, and flipped a black platter from its jacket as casually as if he were flipping pizzas in Napoli. He dropped the stylus, and as the room filled with music, he began to move his hips and mime the words: "Oooh-oooh, I heard it through the grapevine. . . ."

Marvin Gaye. Delectable, smooth, icy cool, ancient.

Pesky reached down to help Harvey from the floor. Jill took Hal's arm. Rob and Irene began to snap their fingers and Enzo swung Tootle out into the middle of the floor.

They danced till they dropped.

IN THE MAIL that morning there were two solicitations for life insurance, a coupon from the local car wash promising a "100% Brushless Wash," four bills, three advertising flyers, and a death threat from his ex-son, Anthony. Anthony had used green ink, the cyclonic scrawl of his longhand lifting off into the loops, lassos, and curlicues of heavy weather aloft, and his message was the same as usual: *I eat the royal jelly. I sting and you die. Bzzzzzzzz. Pat too, the bitch.* He hadn't bothered to sign it.

"Ken? What is it?"

Pat was right beside him now, peering over his elbow at the sheaf of ads and bills clutched in his hand. She'd been pruning the roses and she was still wearing her work gloves. They stood there out front of the house in the sunshine, hunched forward protectively, the mailbox rising up like a tombstone between them. "It's Anthony," she said, "isn't it?"

He handed her the letter.

"My god," she said, sucking in a whistle of breath like a wounded animal. "How'd he get the address?"

It was a good question. They'd known he was to be released from Juvenile Hall on his eighteenth birthday, and they'd taken precautions. Like changing their phone number, their address, their places of employment, and the city and state in which they lived. For a while, they'd even toyed with the idea of changing their name, but then Ken's father came for a visit from Wisconsin and sobbed over the family coat of arms till they gave it up. Over the years, they'd received dozens of Anthony's death threats—all of them bee-oriented; bees were his obsession—but nothing since they'd moved. This was bad. Worse than bad.

"You'd better call the police," he said. "And take Skippy to the kennel."

Nine years earlier, the Mallows had been childless. There was something wrong with Pat's fallopian tubes—some congenital defect that reduced her odds of conception to 222,000 to one— and to compound the problem, Ken's sperm count was inordinately low, though he ate plenty of red meat and worked out every other day on the racquetball court. Adoption had seemed the way to go, though Pat was distressed by the fact that so many of the babies available were—well, she didn't like to say it, but they weren't white. There were Thai babies, Guianese babies, Herero babies, babies from Haiti, Kuala Lumpur, and Kashmir, but Caucasian babies were at a premium. You could have a nonwhite baby in six days—for a price, of course—but there was an eleven-year waiting list for white babies—twelve for blonds, fourteen for blue-eyed blonds—and neither Ken nor Pat was used to being denied. "How about an older child?" the man from the adoption agency had suggested.

They were in one of the plush, paneled conference rooms of Adopt-A-Kid, and Mr. Denteen, a handsome, bold-faced man in a suit woven of some exotic material, leaned forward with a fatherly smile. He bore an uncanny resemblance to Robert Young of "Father Knows Best," and on the wall behind him was a photomontage of plump and cooing babies. Pat was mesmerized. "What?" she said, as if she hadn't heard him.

"An older child," Denteen repeated, his voice rich with insinuation. It was the voice of a seducer, a shrink, a blackmarketeer.

"No," Ken said, "I don't think so."

"How old?" Pat said.

Denteen leaned forward on his leather elbow patches. "I just happen to have a child—a boy—whose file just came to us this morning. Little Anthony Cademartori. Tony. He's nine years old. Just. Actually, his birthday was only last week."

The photo Denteen handed them showed a sunny, smiling, towheaded boy, a generic boy, archetypal, the sort of boy you envision when you close your eyes and think "boy." If they'd looked closer, they would have seen that his eyes were like two poked holes and that there was something unstable about his smile and the set of his jaw, but they were in the grip of a conceit and they didn't look that closely. Ken asked if there was anything wrong with him. "Physically, I mean," he said.

Denteen let a good-humored little laugh escape him. "This is your average nine-year-old boy, Mr. Mallow," he said. "Average height, weight, build, average—or above average—intelligence. He's all boy, and he's one heck of a lot fitter than I am." Denteen cast a look to the heavens—or, rather, to the ceiling tiles. "To be nine years old again," he sighed.

"Does he behave?" Pat asked.

"Does he behave?" Denteen echoed, and he looked offended, hurt almost. "Does the President live in the White House? Does the sun come up in the morning?" He straightened up, shot his cuffs, then leaned forward again—so far forward his hands dangled over the edge of the conference table. "Look at him," he said, holding up the picture again. "Mr. and Mrs. Mallow—Ken, Pat—let me tell you that this child has seen more heartbreak than you and I'll know in a lifetime. His birth parents were killed at a railway crossing when he was two, and then, the irony of it, his adoptive parents—they were your age, by the way—just dropped dead one day while he was at school. One minute they're alive and well and the next"—he snapped his fingers—"they're gone." His voice faltered. "And then poor little Tony . . . poor little Tony comes home. . . ."

Pat looked stunned. Ken reached out to squeeze her hand.

"He needs love, Pat," Denteen said. "He has love to give. A
lot of love."

Ken looked at Pat. Pat looked at Ken.

"So," Denteen said, "when would you like to meet him?"

They met him the following afternoon, and he seemed fine. A
little shy, maybe, but fine. Super-polite, that's what Pat thought.
May I this and may I that, please, thank you, and it's a pleasure
to meet you. He was adorable. Big for his age—that was a
surprise. They'd expected a lovable little urchin, the kind of kid
Norman Rockwell might have portrayed in the barber's chair
atop a stack of phone books, but Anthony was big, already the
size of a teenager—big-headed, big in the shoulders, and big in
the rear. Tall too. At nine, he was already as tall as Pat and
probably outweighed her. What won them over, though, was
his smile. He turned his smile on them that first day in Denteen's
office—a blooming angelic smile that showed off his dimples
and the perfection of his tiny white glistening teeth—and Pat
felt something give way inside her. At the end of the meeting
she hugged him to her breast.

The smile was a regular feature of those first few months—
the months of the trial period. Anthony smiled at breakfast, at
dinner, smiled when he helped Ken rake the leaves from the
gutters or tidy up the yard, smiled in his sleep. He stopped
smiling when the trial period was over, as if he'd suddenly lost
control of his facial muscles. It was uncanny. Almost to the day
the adoption became formal—the day that he was theirs and
they were his—Anthony's smile vanished. The change was abrupt
and it came without warning.

"Scooter," Ken called to him one afternoon, "you want to
help me take those old newspapers to the recycling center and
then maybe stop in at Baskin and Robbins?"

Anthony was upstairs in his room, the room they'd decorated
with posters of ballplayers and airplanes. He didn't answer.

"Scooter?"

Silence.

Puzzled, Ken ascended the stairs. As he reached the landing, he became aware of an odd sound emanating from Anthony's room—a low hum, as of an appliance kicking in. He paused to knock at the door and the sound began to take on resonance, to swell and shrink again, a thousand muted voices speaking in unison. "Anthony?" he called, pushing open the door.

Anthony was seated naked in the middle of his bed, wearing a set of headphones Ken had never seen before. The headphones were attached to a tape player the size of a suitcase. Ken had never seen the tape player before either. And the walls—gone were the dazzling sunstruck posters of Fernando Valenzuela, P-38s, and Mitsubishi Zeroes, replaced now by black-and-white photos of insects—torn, he saw, from library books. The books lay scattered across the floor, gutted, their spines broken.

For a long moment, Ken merely stood there in the doorway, the sizzling pulse of that many-voiced hum leaking out of Anthony's headphones to throb in his gut, his chest, his bones. It was as if he'd stumbled upon some ancient rite in the Australian Outback, as if he'd stepped out of his real life in the real world and into some cheap horror movie about demonic possession and people whose eyes lit up like Christmas-tree ornaments. Anthony was seated in the lotus position, his own eyes tightly closed. He didn't seem to be aware of Ken. The buzzing was excruciating. After a moment, Ken backed out of the room and gently shut the door.

At dinner that evening, Anthony gave them their first taste of his why-don't-you-get-off-my-back look, a look that was to become habitual. His hair stood up jaggedly, drawn up into needlelike points—he must have greased it, Ken realized—and he slouched as if there were an invisible piano strapped to his shoulders. Ken didn't know where to begin—with the scowl, the nudity, the desecration of library books, the tape player and its mysterious origins (had he borrowed it—perhaps from school? a friend?). Pat knew nothing. She served chicken croquettes, biscuits with honey, and baked beans, Anthony's favorite meal. She was at the stove, her back to them, when Ken cleared his throat.

"Anthony," he said, "is there anything wrong? Anything you want to tell us?"

Anthony shot him a contemptuous look. He said nothing. Pat glanced over her shoulder.

"About the library books . . ."

"You were spying on me," Anthony snarled.

Pat turned away from the stove, stirring spoon in hand. "What do you mean? Ken? What's this all about?"

"I wasn't spying, I—" Ken faltered. He felt the anger rising in him. "All right," he said, "where'd you get the tape player?"

Anthony wiped his mouth with the back of his hand, then looked past Ken to his adoptive mother. "I stole it," he said.

Suddenly Ken was on his feet. "Stole it?" he roared. "Don't you know what that means, library books and now, now stealing?"

Anthony was a statue, big-headed and serene. "Bzzzzzzzz," he said.

The scene at the library was humiliating. Clearly, the books had been willfully destroyed. Mrs. Tutwillow was outraged. And no matter how hard Ken squeezed his arm, Anthony remained pokerfaced and unrepentant. "I won't say I'm sorry," he sneered, "because I'm not." Ken gave her a check for $112.32, to cover the cost of replacing the books, plus shipping and handling. At Steve's Stereo Shoppe, the man behind the counter—Steve, presumably—agreed not to press charges, but he had a real problem with offering the returned unit to the public as new goods, if Ken knew what he meant. Since he'd have to sell it used now, he wondered if Ken had the $87.50 it was going to cost him to mark it down. Of course, if Ken didn't want to cooperate, he'd have no recourse but to report the incident to the police. Ken cooperated.

At home, after he'd ripped the offending photos from the walls and sent Anthony to his room, he phoned Denteen. "Ken, listen. I know you're upset," Denteen crooned, his voice as soothing as a shot of whiskey, "but the kid's life has been real hell, believe me, and you've got to realize that he's going to need some time to adjust." He paused. "Why don't you get him a dog or something?"

"A dog?"

"Yeah. Something for him to be responsible for for a change. He's been a ward—I mean, an adoptee—all this time, with people caring for him, and maybe it's that he feels like a burden or something. With a dog or a cat he could do the giving."

A dog. The idea of it sprang to sudden life and Ken was a boy himself again, roaming the hills and stubble fields of Wisconsin, Skippy at his side. A dog. Yes. Of course.

"And listen," Denteen was saying, "if you think you're going to need professional help with this, the man to go to is Maurice Barebaum. He's one of the top child psychologists in the state, if not the country." There was a hiss of shuffling papers, the flap of Rolodex cards. "I've got his number right here."

"I don't want a dog," Anthony insisted, and he gave them a strained, histrionic look.

We're onstage, Ken was thinking, that's what it is. He looked at Pat, seated on the couch, her legs tucked under her, and then at his son, this stranger with the staved-in eyes and tallowy arms who'd somehow won the role.

"But it would be so nice," Pat said, drawing a picture in the air, "you'd have a little friend."

Anthony was wearing a black T-shirt emblazoned with red and blue letters that spelled out MEGADETH. On the reverse was the full-color representation of a stupendous bumblebee. "Oh, come off it, Pat," he sang, a keening edge to his voice, "that's so stupid. Dogs are so slobbery and shitty."

"Don't use that language," Ken said automatically.

"A little one, maybe," Pat said, "a cocker or a sheltie."

"I don't want a dog. I want a hive. A beehive. That's what I want." He was balancing like a tightrope walker on the edge of the fireplace apron.

"Bees?" Ken demanded. "What kind of pet is that?" He was angry. It seemed he was always angry lately.

Pat forestalled him, her tone soft as a caress. "Bees, darling?" she said. "Can you tell us what you like about them? Is it because they're so useful, because of the honey, I mean?"

Anthony was up on one foot. He tipped over twice before he answered. "Because they have no mercy."

"Mercy?" Pat repeated.

"Three weeks, that's how long a worker lasts in the summer," Anthony said. "They kick the drones out to die. The spent workers too." He looked at Ken. "You fit in or you die."

"And what the hell is that supposed to mean?" Ken was shouting; he couldn't help himself.

Anthony's face crumpled up. His cheeks were corrugated, the spikes of his hair stood out like thorns. "You hate me," he whined. "You fuck, you dickhead—you hate me, don't you, don't you?"

"Ken!" Pat cried, but Ken already had him by the arm. "Don't you ever—" he said.

"Ever what? Ever what? Say 'fuck'? You do it, you do it, you do it!" Anthony was in a rage, jerking away, tears on his face, shouting. "Upstairs, at night. I hear you. Fucking. That's what you do. Grunting and fucking just like, like, like *dogs!*"

"I'll need to see him three days a week," Dr. Barebaum said. He was breathing heavily, as if he'd just climbed several flights of stairs.

Anthony was out in the car with Pat. He'd spent the past forty-five minutes sequestered with Barebaum. "Is he—is he all right?" Ken asked. "I mean, is he normal?"

Barebaum leaned back in his chair and made a little pyramid

of his fingers. "Adjustment problems," he breathed. "He's got a lot of hostility. He's had a difficult life."

Ken stared down at the carpet.

"He tells me," Barebaum dredged up the words as if from some inner fortress, "he tells me he wants a dog."

Ken sat rigid in the chair. This must be what it feels like before they switch on the current at Sing Sing, he thought. "No, you've got it wrong. *We* wanted to get *him* a dog, but he said no. In fact, he went schizoid on us."

Barebaum's nose wrinkled up at the term "schizoid." Ken regretted it instantly. "Yes," the doctor drawled, "hmmph. But the fact is the boy quite distinctly told me the whole blow-up was because he does indeed want a dog. You know, Mr., ah—"

"Mallow."

"—Mallow, we often say exactly the opposite of what we mean; you are aware of that, aren't you?"

Ken said nothing. He studied the weave of the carpet.

After a moment, the doctor cleared his throat. "You do have health insurance?" he said.

In all, Anthony was with them just over three years. The dog— a sheltie pup Ken called "Skippy" and Anthony referred to alternately as "Ken" and "Turd"—was a mistake, they could see that now. For the first few months or so, Anthony had ignored it, except to run squealing through the house, the puppy's warm excreta cupped in his palms, shouting, "It shit! It shit! The dog shit!" Ken, though, got to like the feel of the pup's wet nose on his wrist as he skimmed the morning paper or sat watching TV in the evening. The pup was alive, it was high-spirited and joyful, and it brought him back to his own childhood in a way that Anthony, with his gloom and his sneer, never could have. "I want a hive," Anthony said, over and over again. "My very own hive."

Ken ignored him—bees were dangerous, after all, and this

was a residential neighborhood—until the day Anthony finally did take an interest in Skippy. It was one of those rare days when Pat's car was at the garage, so Ken picked her up at work and they arrived home together. The house was quiet. Skippy, who usually greeted them at the door in a paroxysm of licking, rolling, leaping, and tail-thumping, was nowhere to be seen. And Anthony, judging from the low-threshold hum washing over the house, was up in his room listening to the bee tapes Pat had given him for Christmas. "Skippy," Ken called, "here, boy!" No Skippy. Pat checked the yard, the basement, the back room. Finally, together, they mounted the stairs to Anthony's room.

Anthony was in the center of the bed, clad only in his underwear, reprising the ritual Ken had long since grown to accept (Dr. Barebaum claimed it was nothing to worry about—"It's his way of meditating, that's all, and if it calms him down, why fight it?"). Huge color photographs of bees obliterated the walls, but these were legitimate photos, clipped from the pages of *The Apiarian's Monthly,* another gift from Pat. Anthony looked bloated, fatter than ever, pale and white as a grub. When he became aware of them, he slipped the headphones from his ears. "Honey," Pat said, reaching down to ruffle his hair, "have you seen Skippy?"

It took him a moment to answer. He looked bewildered, as if she'd asked him to solve an equation or name the twenty biggest cities in Russia. "I put him in his cell," he said finally.

"Cell?" Ken echoed.

"In the hive," Anthony said. "The big hive."

It was Ken who noticed the broomstick wedged against the oven door, and it was Ken who buried Skippy's poor singed carcass and arranged to have the oven replaced—Pat wouldn't, couldn't cook in it, ever again. It was Ken too who lost control of himself that night and slapped Anthony's sick pale swollen face till Pat pulled him off. In the end, Anthony got his hive,

thirty thousand honeybees in a big white wooden box with fifteen frames inside, and Barebaum got to see Anthony two more
days a week.

At first, the bees seemed to exert a soothing influence on the
boy. He stopped muttering to himself, used his utensils at the
table, and didn't seem quite as vulnerable to mood swings as he
had. After school and his daily sessions with Barebaum, he'd
spend hours tending the hive, watching the bees at their compul-
sive work, humming softly to himself as if in a trance. Ken was
worried he'd be stung and bought him a gauze bonnet and
gloves, but he rarely wore them. And when he was stung—
daily, it seemed—he displayed the contusions proudly, as if they
were battle scars. For Ken and Pat, it was a time of accommoda-
tion, and they were quietly optimistic. Gone was the smiling
boy they'd taken into their home, but at least now he wasn't
so—there was no other word for it—so odd, and he seemed less
agitated, less ready to fly off the handle.

The suicide attempt took them by surprise.

Ken found him, at dusk, crouched beneath the hive and quietly bleeding from both wrists. Pat's X-ACTO knife lay in the
grass beside him, black with blood. In the hospital the next day,
Anthony looked lost and vulnerable, looked like a little boy
again. Barebaum was there with them. "It's a phase," he said,
puffing for breath. "He's been very depressed lately."

"Why?" Pat asked, sweeping Anthony's hair back from his
forehead, stroking his swollen hands. "Your bees," she choked.
"What would your bees do without you?"

Anthony let his eyes fall shut. After a moment he lifted his lids
again. His voice was faint. "Bzzzzzzzz," he said.

They kept him at the Hart Mental Health Center for nine
months, and then they let him come home again. Ken was
against it. He'd contacted a lawyer about voiding the adoption
papers—Anthony was just too much to handle; he was emotionally unstable, disturbed, dangerous; the psychiatric bills alone

were killing them—but Pat overruled him. "He needs us," she said. "He has no one else to turn to." They were in the living room. She bent forward to light a cigarette. "Nobody said it would be easy," she said.

"Easy?" he retorted. "You talk like it's a war or something. I didn't adopt a kid to go to war—or to save the world either."

"Why did you adopt him then?"

The question took him by surprise. He looked past Pat to the kitchen, where one of Anthony's crayon drawings—of a lopsided bee—clung to the refrigerator door, and then past the refrigerator to the window and the lush still yard beyond. He shrugged. "For love, I guess."

As it turned out, the question was moot—Anthony didn't last six months this time. When they picked him up at the hospital—"Hospital," Ken growled, "nut hatch is more like it"—they barely recognized him. He was taller and he'd put on weight. Pat couldn't call it baby fat anymore—this was true fat, adult fat, fat that sank his eyes and strained at the seams of his pants. And his hair, his rich fine white-blond hair, was gone, shaved to a transparent stubble over a scalp the color of boiled ham. Pat chattered at him, but he got into the car without a word. Halfway home he spoke for the first time. "You know what they eat in there," he said, "in the hospital?"

Ken felt like the straightman in a comedy routine. "What do they eat?" he said, his eyes fixed on the road.

"Shit," Anthony said. "They eat shit. Their own shit. That's what they eat."

"Do you have to use that language?"

Anthony didn't bother to respond.

At home, they discovered that the bees had managed to survive on their own, a fact that somehow seemed to depress Anthony, and after shuffling halfheartedly through the trays and getting stung six or seven times, he went up to bed.

The trouble—the final trouble, the trouble that was to take Anthony out of their hands for good—started at school. Anthony was almost twelve now, but because of his various problems, he was still in fifth grade. He was in a special program, of course, but he took lunch and recess with the other fifth-graders. On the playground, he towered over them, plainly visible a hundred yards away, like some great unmoving statue of the Buddha. The other children shied away from him instinctively, as if they knew he was beyond taunting, beyond simple joys and simple sorrows. But he was aware of them, aware in a new way, aware of the girls especially. Something had happened inside him while he was away—"Puberty," Barebaum said, "he has urges like any other boy"—and he didn't know how to express it.

One afternoon, he and Oliver Monteiros, another boy from the special program, cornered a fifth-grade girl behind one of the temporary classrooms. There they "stretched" her, as Anthony later told it—Oliver had her hands, Anthony her feet—stretched her till something snapped in her shoulder and Anthony felt his pants go wet. He tried to tell the principal about it, about the wetness in his pants, but the principal wouldn't listen. Dr. Conarroe was a gray-bearded black man who believed in dispensing instant justice. He was angry, gesturing in their faces, his beard jabbing at them like a weapon. When Anthony unzipped his fly to show him what had happened, Dr. Conarroe suspended him on the spot.

Pat spoke with Anthony, and they both—she and Ken—went in to meet with Dr. Conarroe and the members of the school board. They brought Barebaum with them. Together, they were able to overcome the principal's resistance, and Anthony, after a week's suspension, was readmitted. "One more incident," Conarroe said, his eyes aflame behind the discs of his wire-framed glasses, "and I don't care how small it is, and he's out. Is that understood?"

At least Anthony didn't keep them in suspense. On his first day back he tracked down the girl he'd stretched, chased her into the girls' room, and as he told it, put his "stinger" in her.

The girl's parents sued the school district, Anthony was taken into custody and remanded to Juvenile Hall following another nine-month stay at Hart, and Ken and Pat finally threw in the towel. They were exhausted, physically and emotionally, and they were in debt to Barebaum for some thirty thousand dollars above what their insurance would cover. They felt cheated, bitter, worn down to nothing. Anthony was gone, adoption a sick joke. But they had each other, and after a while—and with the help of Skippy II—they began to pick up the pieces.

And now, six years later, Anthony had come back to haunt them. Ken was enraged. He, for one, wasn't about to be chased out of this house and this job—they'd moved once, and that was enough. If he'd found them, he'd found them—so much the worse. But this was America, and they had their rights too. While Pat took Skippy to the kennel for safekeeping, Ken phoned the police and explained the situation to an Officer Ocksler, a man whose voice was so lacking in inflection he might as well have been dead. Ken was describing the incident with Skippy the First when Officer Ocksler interrupted him. "I'm sorry," he said, and there was a faint animation to his voice now, as if he were fighting down a belch or passing gas, "but there's nothing we can do."

"Nothing you can do?" Ken couldn't help himself: he was practically yelping. "But he broiled a harmless puppy in the oven, raped a fifth-grade girl, sent us thirty-two death threats, and tracked us down even though we quit our jobs, packed up and moved, and left no forwarding address." He took a deep breath. "He thinks he's a bee, for christsake."

Officer Ocksler inserted his voice into the howling silence that succeeded this outburst. "He commits a crime," he said, the words stuck fast in his throat, "you call us."

The next day's mail brought the second threat. It came in the form of a picture postcard, addressed to Pat, and postmarked locally. The picture—a Japanese print—showed a pale fleshy couple engaged in the act of love. The message, which took some deciphering, read as follows:

> *Dear Mother Pat,*
>
> *I'm a King Bee,*
> *Gonna buzz round your hive,*
> *Together we can make honey*
> *Let me come inside.*
>
> *Your son, Anthony*

Ken tore it to pieces. He was red in the face, trembling. White babies, he thought bitterly. An older child. They would have been better off with a seven-foot Bantu, an Eskimo, anything. "I'll kill him," he said. "He comes here, I'll kill him."

It was early the next morning—Pat was in the kitchen, Ken upstairs shaving—when a face appeared in the kitchen window. It was a large and familiar face, transformed somewhat by the passage of the years and the accumulation of flesh, but unmistakable nonetheless. Pat, who was leaning over the sink to rinse her coffee cup, gave a little gasp of recognition.

Anthony was smiling, beaming at her like the towheaded boy in the photograph she'd kept in her wallet all these years. He was smiling, and suddenly that was all that mattered to her. The sweetness of those first few months came back in a rush—he was her boy, her own, and the rest of it was nothing—and before she knew what she was doing she had the back door open. It was a mistake. The moment the door swung open, she heard them. Bees. A swarm that blackened the side of the house, the angry hiss of their wings like grease in a fryer. They were right there, right beside the door. First one bee, then another, shot past her head. "Mom," Anthony said, stepping up onto the porch, "I'm home."

She was stunned. It wasn't just the bees, but Anthony. He was huge, six feet tall at least, and so heavy. His pants—they were pajamas, hospital-issue—were big as a tent, and it looked as if he'd rolled up a carpet beneath his shirt. She could barely make out his eyes, sunk in their pockets of flesh. She didn't know what to say.

He took hold of the door. "I want a hug," he said. "Give me a hug."

She backed away from him instinctively. "Ken!" she called, and the catch in her throat turned it into a mournful, drawn-out bleat. "Ken!"

Anthony was poised on the threshold. His smile faded. Then, like a magician, he reached out his hand and plunged it into the mass of bees. She saw him wince as he was stung, heard the harsh sizzle of the insects rise in crescendo, and then he drew back his hand, ever so slowly, and the bees came with him. They moved so fast—glutinous, like meringue clinging to a spoon—that she nearly missed it. There was something in his hand, a tiny box, some sort of mesh, and then his hand was gone, his arm, the right side of his body, his face and head and the left side too. Suddenly he was alive with bees, wearing them, a humming, pulsating ball of them.

She felt a sharp pain in her ankle, then another at her throat. She backed up a step.

"You sent me away," Anthony scolded, and the bees clung to his lips. "You never loved me. Nobody ever loved me."

She heard Ken behind her—"What is this?" he said, and then a weak curse escaped him—but she couldn't turn. The hum of the bees mesmerized her. They clung to Anthony, one mind, thirty thousand bodies.

And then the blazing ball of Anthony's hand separated itself from his body and his bee-thick fingers opened to reveal the briefest glimpse of the gauze-covered box. "The queen," Anthony said. "I throw her down and you're"—she could barely hear him, the bees raging, Ken shouting out her name—"you're history. Both of you."

For a long moment Anthony stood there motionless, afloat

in bees. Huge as he was, he seemed to hover over the linoleum, derealized in the mass of them. And then she knew what was going to happen, knew that she was barren then and now and forever and that it was meant to be, and that this, her only child, was beyond human help or understanding.

"Go away," Anthony said, the swarm thrilling louder, "go . . . into the . . . next room . . . before, before—" and then Ken had her by the arm and they were moving. She thought she heard Anthony sigh, and as she darted a glance back over her shoulder he crushed the box with a snap loud as the crack of a limb. There was an answering roar from the bees, and in her last glimpse of him he was falling, borne down by the terrible animate weight of them.

"I'll kill him," Ken spat, his shoulder pressed to the parlor door. Bees rattled against the panels like hailstones.

She couldn't catch her breath. She felt a sudden stab under her collar, and then another. Ken's words didn't make sense—Anthony was gone from them now, gone forever—didn't he understand that? She listened to the bees raging round her kitchen, stinging blindly, dying for their queen. And then she thought of Anthony, poor Anthony, in his foster homes, in the hospital, in prison, thought of his flesh scored a thousand, ten thousand times, wound in his cerement of bees.

He was wrong, she thought, leaning into the door as if bracing herself against a storm, they do have mercy. They do.

THAWING OUT

THEY WERE FEET that he loved, feet that belonged in high heels, calfskin, furry slippers with button eyes and rabbit ears, and here they were, naked to the snow. He was hunched in his denim jacket, collar up, scarf wound tight round his throat, and his fingers were so numb he could barely get a cigarette lit. She stood beside him in her robe, barely shivering, the wild ivy of her hair gone white with a dusting of snow. He watched her lift her arms, watched her breasts rise gently as she fought back her hair and pulled the bathing cap tight to her skull. He took a quick drag on the cigarette and looked away.

There were maybe twenty cars in the lot: station wagons, Volvos, VW Bugs, big steel-blue Buicks with their crushproof bumpers and nautical vents. An inch of new snow softened the frozen ruts and the strips of yellowed ice that lay like sores beneath it. Beyond the lot, a short slope, the white rails of the dock, and the black lapping waters of the Hudson. It was five of two—he checked his watch—but the belly of the sky hung so low it might have been dusk.

A moment earlier, when Naina had stepped from her car, a chain reaction had begun, and now the car doors were flung open one by one and the others began to emerge. They were old, all of them, as far as he could see. A few middle-aged, maybe. Some in robes, some not. The men were ghosts in baggy trunks, bowlegged, splay-footed, and bald, with fallen bellies

142

and dead gray hair fringing their nipples. He thought of Buster Keaton, in his antiquated swimsuit and straw boater. The women were heavier, their excrescences forced like sausage stuffing into the black spandex casings of their one-piece suits. Their feet were bloated and red, their thighs mottled with disuse, their upper arms heavy, bulbous, the color of suet. They called out to one another gaily, like schoolgirls at a picnic, in accents thick with another time and place.

"Jesus, Naina," he whispered, turning to her, "this is crazy. It's like something out of Fellini. Look at them."

Naina gave him a soft tight-lipped smile—a tolerant smile, understated, serene, a smile that stirred his groin and made him go weak with something like hunger—and then her mother's car schussed into the lot. The whole group turned as one to watch as the ancient, rust-eaten Pontiac heaved over the ruts toward them. He could see the grin on Mama Vyshensky's broad, faintly mustachioed face as she fought the wheel and rode the bumps. He froze for an instant, certain her final, veering skid would send her careening into the side of his Camaro, but the big splotched bumper jerked to a halt six feet short of him. "Naina!" she cried, lumbering from the car to embrace her daughter as if she hadn't seen her in twenty years. "And Marty," turning to envelop him in a quick bear hug. "Nice weather, no?"

The breath streamed from her nostrils. She was a big woman with dimples and irrepressible eyes, a dead ringer for Nina Khrushchev. Her feet—as swollen and red as any of the others'—were squeezed into a pair of cheap plastic thongs and she wore a tentlike swimsuit in a shade of yellow that made the Camaro look dull. "Sonia!" she shouted, turning away and flagging her hand. "Marfa!" A gabble of Ukrainian, and then the group began to gather.

Marty felt the wind on his exposed hand and he took a final drag on his cigarette, flicked the butt away, and plunged his hand deep in his pocket. This was really something. Crazy. He felt like a visitor to another planet. One old bird was rubbing snow into the hair of his bare chest, another skidding down the slope on his backside. "A toast!" someone shouted, and they all gathered round a bottle of Stolichnaya, thimble-sized glasses materializing in their hands. And when one old man with red-dened ears asked him where his swim trunks were, Marty said it wasn't cold enough for him, not by half.

They drank. One round, then another, and then they shouted something he didn't catch and flung the glasses over their shoul-ders. Two ponderous old women began fighting playfully over a towel while Naina's mother shouted encouragement and the others laughed like wizened children. And Naina? Naina stood out among them like a virgin queen, the youngest by thirty years. At least. That's what it was, he suddenly realized—an ancient rite, sacrifice of the virgin. But they were a little late in this case, he thought, and felt his groin stir again. He squeezed her hand, gazed off into the curtain of falling snow, and saw the mountains fade and reappear in the distance.

Then he heard the first splash and turned to see a flushed bald head bobbing in the water and the old man with reddened ears suspended in the air, knees clutched tightly to his chest. There was a second splash—a real wallop—and then another, and then they were all in, frolicking like seals. Naina was one of the last to go, tucking her chin, planting her feet, her thighs flexing as she floated out into the tumult of the storm and cut the flat black surface in perfect grace and harmony.

The whole thing left him cold.

They'd been going together a month when she first took him to meet her mother. It was mid-October, chilly, a persistent rain beating the leaves from the trees. He didn't want to meet her mother. He wanted to stay in bed and touch every part of her. He was twenty-three and he'd had enough of mothers.

"Don't expect anything fancy," Naina said, sitting close as he drove. "It's the house I grew up in. Mama's no housekeeper."

He glanced at her, her face as open as a doll's, high forehead, thick eyebrows, eyes pale as ice, and that hair. That's what caught him the first time he saw her. That and her voice, as hushed and placid as the voice talking inside his head. "How long do we have to stay?" he said.

The house was in Cold Spring, two stories, white with green trim, in need of paint. It was an old house, raked back from the steep hill that dropped through town to the foot of the river. Naina's mother was waiting for them at the door. "This is Marty," she pronounced, as if he could have been anyone else, and to his horror, she embraced him. "In," she said, "in," sweeping them before her and slamming the door with a boom. "Such nasty day."

Inside, it was close and hot, the air heavy with the odor of cooking. He was no gourmet, and he couldn't identify the aroma, but it brought him back to high school and the fat-armed women who stood guard over the big simmering pots in the cafeteria. It wasn't a good sign.

"Sit," said Naina's mother, gesturing toward a swaybacked sofa draped with an afghan and three overfed cats. "Shoo," she said, addressing the cats, and he sat. He looked round him. There were doilies everywhere, lamps with stained shades, mounds of newspapers and magazines. On the wall above the radiator, the framed portrait of a blue-eyed Christ.

Naina sat beside him while her mother trundled back and forth, rearranging the furniture, fussing with things, and all the while watching him out of the corner of her eye. He was sleeping with her daughter, and she knew it. "A peppermint," she said, whirling round on him with a box the size of a photo album, "maybe you want? Beer maybe? A nice glass of buttermilk?"

He didn't want anything. "No thanks," he managed, the voice stuck in his throat. Naina took a peppermint.

Finally the old woman settled into the sofa beside him—beside him, when there were six other chairs in the room—and he felt himself sinking into the cushions as into a morass. Something was-boiling over in the kitchen: he could smell it, hear it hissing. Sitting, she towered over him. "You like my Naina?" she asked.

The question stunned him. She'd tossed him a medicine ball and he was too weak to toss it back. Like? Did he like her Naina? He lingered over her for hours at a time, hours that became days, and he did things to her in the dark and with the lights on too. Did he like her? He wanted to jump through the roof.

"You call me Mama," she said, patting his hand. "None of this Mrs. business." She was peering into his eyes like an ophthalmologist. "So. You like her?" she repeated.

Miserable, squirming, glancing at Naina—that smile, tight-lipped and serene, her eyes dancing—and then back at her mother, he couldn't seem to find anything to focus on but his shoes. "Yeah," he whispered.

"Um," the old woman grunted, narrowing her eyes as if she were deciding something. Then she rose heavily to her feet, and as he looked up in surprise and mortification, she spread her arms above him in a grand gesture. "All this," she said, "one day is yours."

"So what do you mean, like love and marriage and all that crap?"

Marty was staring down into his Harvey Wallbanger. It was November. Naina was at art class and he was sitting in the bar of the Bum Steer, talking about her. With Terry. Terry was just back from San Francisco and he was wearing a cowboy hat and an earring. "No," Marty protested, "I mean she's hot, that's all. And she's a great person. You're going to like her. Really. She's—"

"What's her mother look like?"

Mama Vyshensky rose up before his eyes, her face dark with a five o'clock shadow, her legs like pylons, the square of her shoulders and the drift of her collapsed bosom. "What do you mean?"

Terry was drinking a mug of beer with a shot of tomato juice on the side. He took a swallow of beer, then upended the tomato juice in the mug. The stain spread like blood. "I mean, they all wind up looking like their mother. And they all want something from you." Terry stirred the tomato beer with his forefinger and then sucked it thoughtfully. "Before you know it you got six slobbering kids, a little pink house, and you're married to her mother."

The thought of it made him sick. "Not me," he said. "No way."

Terry tilted the hat back on his head and fiddled briefly with the earring. "You living together yet?"

Marty felt his face flush. He lifted his drink and put it down again. "We talked about it," he said finally, "like why pay rent in two places, you know? She's living in an apartment in Yorktown and I'm still in the bungalow. But I don't know."

Terry was grinning at him. He leaned over and gave him a cuff on the shoulder. "You're gone, man," he said. "It's all over. Birdies singing in the trees."

Marty shrugged. He was fighting back a grin. He wanted to talk about her—he was full of her—but he was toeing a fine line here. He and Terry were both men of the world, and men of the world didn't moon over their women. "There's one rule," he said, "they've got to love you first. And most. Right?"

"Amen," Terry said.

They were quiet a moment, mulling over this nugget of wisdom. Marty drained his glass and ordered another. "What the hell," Terry said, "give me another one too."

The drinks came. They sipped meditatively. "Shit," Terry said, "you know what? I saw your mother. At La Guardia. It was weird. I mean I'm coming in after six months out there and I get off the plane and there's your mother."

"Who was she with?"

"I don't know. Some skinny old white-haired dude with a string tie and a suit. She said hello to me and I shook the guy's hand. They were going to Bermuda, I think she said."

Marty said nothing. He sipped at his drink. "She's a bitch," he said finally.

"Yeah," Terry said, reprising the ceremony of the beer and the tomato juice, "whatever. But listen," turning to him now, his face lit beneath the brim of his ten-gallon hat, "let me tell you about San Francisco—I mean that's where it's really happening."

In January, a month after he'd watched her part the frigid waters of the Hudson, the subject of living arrangements came up again. She'd cooked for him, a tomato-and-noodle dish she called spaghetti but that was pure Kiev in flavor, texture, and appearance—which is not to say it was bad, just that it wasn't spaghetti as he knew it. He had three helpings, then he built a fire and they lay on the sofa together. "You know, this is crazy," she said in her softest voice, the one with the slight catch to it.

It had been a long day—he was in his first year of teaching, Special Ed, and the kids had been wild. They'd sawed the oak handles off the tools in shop class and chucked stones at the schoolbus during lunch break. He was drowsy. "Hm?" was all the response he could manage.

Her voice purred in his ear. "Spending all my time here; I mean, half my clothes here and half at my place. It's crazy."

He said nothing, but his eyes were open.

She was silent too. A log shifted in the fireplace. "It's just such a waste, is all," she said finally. "The rent alone, not to mention gas and wear and tear on my car . . ."

He got up to poke the fire, his back to her. "Terry's going back to the West Coast this summer. He wants me to go along. For a vacation. I mean, I've never seen it."

"So what does that mean?" she said.

He poked the fire.

"You know I can't go," she said after a moment. "I've got courses to take at New Paltz. You know that, right?"

He felt guilty. He looked guilty. He shrugged.

Later, he made Irish coffee, heavy on sugar, cream, and whiskey. She was curled up in the corner of the sofa, her legs bare, feet tucked under her. She was spending the night.

The wind had come up and sleet began to rattle the windows. He brought the coffee to her, sat beside her and took her hand. It was then that the picture of her perched at the edge of the snowy dock came back to him. "Tell me again," he said, "about the water, how it felt."

"Hm?"

"You know, with the Polar Bear Club?"

He watched her slow smile, watched the snowy afternoon seep back into her eyes. "Oh, that—I've been doing it since I was three. It's nothing. I don't even think about it." She looked past him, staring into the flames. "You won't believe this, but it's not that cold—almost the opposite."

"You're right," he said. "I won't."

"No, really," she insisted, looking him full in the face now. She paused, shrugged, took a sip of her coffee. "It depends on your frame of mind, I guess."

At the end of June, just before he left for San Francisco, they took a trip together. He'd heard about a fishing camp in northern Quebec, a place called Chibougamau, where pike and walleye attacked you in the boat. There were Eskimos there, or near there, anyway. And the last four hours of driving was on dirt roads.

She had no affection for pike or walleye either, but this was their vacation, their last chance to be together for a while. She smiled her quiet smile and packed her bag. They spent one night in Montreal and then drove the rest of the way the following day. When they got there—low hills, a scattering of crude cabins, and a river as raw and hard as metal—Marty was so excited his hands trembled on the wheel. "I want to fish," he said to the guide who greeted them.

The guide was in his forties, hard-looking, with a scar that ran in a white ridge from his ear to his Adam's apple. He was dressed in rubber knee boots, jeans, and a lumberjack shirt. "Hi" and "thank you" was about all the English he could manage. He gestured toward the near cabin.

"Ours?" Marty said, pointing first to Naina and then himself. The guide nodded.

Marty looked up at the sun; it squatted on the horizon, bloated and misshapen.

"Listen, Naina," he said, "honey, would you mind if . . . I mean, I'm dying to wet my line and since we're paying for today and all—"

"Sure," she said. "I'll unpack. Have fun." She grinned at the guide. The guide grinned back.

A moment later, Marty was out on the river, experimentally manning the oars while the guide stood in the bow, discoursing on technique. Marty tried to listen, but French had never been his strong suit; in the next instant the guide cast a lure ahead of them and immediately connected with a fish that bent the rod double. Marty pulled at the oars, and the guide, fighting his fish, said something over his shoulder. This time, though, the guide's face was alive with urgency and the something came in an angry rush, as if he were cursing. Pull harder? Marty thought. Is that what he wants?

He dug in a bit harder, his eyes on the line and the distant explosion where the fish—it was a walleye—cut the surface. But now the guide was raving at him, nonstop, harsh and guttural, and all the while looking desperately from Marty to the bent rod and back again. Marty looked round him. The river was loud as a freight train. "What?" he shouted. "What's the matter?" And then all at once, his eyes wild, the guide heaved the pole into the water, knocked Marty aside, and took up the oars in a frenzy. Then Marty saw it, the precipice yawning before them, the crash and flow of the water, spray in his face, the shore looming up, and the guide snatching frantically at the brush shooting past them. With ten feet to spare, the guide caught a low-hanging branch, the boat jerked back, and all of a sudden Marty was in the water.

But what water! The shock of it beat the breath from him and he went under. He grasped at the air and then he was swept over the falls like a bit of fluff, pounded on the rocks, and flung ashore with the flotsam below. He was lucky. Nothing broken. The guide, muttering under his breath and shooting him murderous looks, sewed up the gash in his thumb with fishing line while Marty gritted his teeth and drank off a glass of whiskey like the wounded sheriff in an old western. It took him two hours to stop shivering.

In bed that night they heard the howling of wolves, a sound that opened up the darkness like a surgeon's blade. "It was a communication problem," Marty insisted, "that's all." Naina pressed her lips to his bruises, kneaded his back, nursed him with a sad, tender, tireless grace.

He woke at dawn, aching. She lay stiff beside him, her eyes open wide. "Will you miss me?" she said.

At first, he'd written her every day—postcards, mainly—from Des Moines, Albuquerque, the Grand Canyon. But then he got to San Francisco, found a job bartending, and drifted into another life. For a while he and Terry stayed with a girl Terry knew from his last trip, then they found a room for sixty dollars a week in a tenement off Geary, but Terry got mugged one night and the two of them moved in with a cocktail waitress Marty knew from work. Things were loose. He stopped writing. And when September came around, he didn't write to the principal at school either.

December was half gone by the time he got back.

The Camaro had broken down on him just outside Chicago—a burnt valve—and the repairs ate up everything he had. He slept in the bus station for three nights while a Pakistani with mad black eyes worked over his car, and if it wasn't for the hitchhiker who split the cost of gas with him, he'd still be there.

When he finally coasted into Yorktown and pulled up at the curb outside Naina's apartment, he was running on empty. For a long while, he stood there in the street looking up at her window. It had been a joyless trip back and he'd thought of her the whole way—her mouth, her eyes, the long tapering miracle of her body, especially her body—and twice he'd stopped to send her a card. Both times he changed his mind. Better to see her, try to explain himself. But now that he was here, outside her apartment, his courage failed him.

He stood there in the cold for fifteen minutes, then started up the driveway. There was ice on the steps and he lost his footing and fell against the door with a thump that shook the frame. Then he rang the bell and listened to the crashing in his chest. A stranger came to the door, a big fat-faced woman of thirty with a baby in her arms. No, Naina didn't live there anymore. She'd left in September. No, she didn't know where she was.

He sat in the car and tried to collect himself. Her mother's, he thought, she's probably at her mother's. He patted down his pockets and counted the money. Two dollars and sixty-seven cents. A dollar for gas, a pack of cigarettes, and two phone calls.

He called his landlord first. Mr. Weiner answered the phone himself, his breathing ravaged with emphysema. He was sorry, Mr. Weiner was, but when he hadn't heard from him he'd gone ahead and rented the place to someone else. His things were in the basement—and if he didn't pick them up within the week he'd have to put them out for the trash, was that understood?

The other call was to his mother. She sounded surprised to hear from him—surprised and defensive. But had he heard? Yes, she was remarried. And no, she didn't think Roger would like it if he spent the night. It was a real shame about his teaching job, but then he always was irresponsible. She punctuated each phrase with a sigh, as if the very act of speaking were torture. All right, she sighed finally, she'd loan him a hundred dollars till he got back on his feet.

It was getting dark when he pulled up in front of the house in Cold Spring. He didn't hesitate this time—he was too miserable. Get it over with, he told himself, one way or the other.

Naina's mother answered the door, peering myopically into the cold fading light. He could smell cabbage, cat, and vinegar, felt the warmth wafting out to him. "Marty?" she said.

He'd grown his hair long and the clipped mustache had become a patchy beard. His denim jacket was faded and it was torn across the shoulder where he'd fallen flat one afternoon in Golden Gate Park, laughing at the sky and the mescaline percolating inside his brain. He wore an earring like Terry's. He wondered that she recognized him, and somehow it made him feel sorrowful—sorrowful and guilty. "Yes," he said.

There was no embrace. She didn't usher him in the door. She just stood there, the support hose sagging round her ankles.

"I, uh . . . I was looking for Naina," he said, and then, attempting a smile, "I'm back."

The old woman's face was heavy, stern, hung with folds and pouches. She didn't respond. But she was watching him in her shrewd way, totting up the changes, deciding something. "All right," she said finally, "come," and she swung back the door for him.

Inside, it was as he remembered it, nothing changed but for an incremental swelling of the heaps of magazines in the corners. She gestured for him to sit on the swaybacked sofa and took the chair across from him. A cat sprang into his lap. It was so quiet he could hear the ticking of the kitchen clock. "So, is she," he faltered, "is she living here now?—I mean, I went out to Yorktown first thing. . . ."

Mama Vyshensky slowly shook her head. "College," she said. She shrugged her big shoulders and looked away, busying herself with the arrangement of the doily on the chair arm. "When she doesn't hear from you, she goes back to college. For the Master."

He didn't know what to say. She was accusing him, he knew

it. And he had no defense. "I'm sorry," he said. He stood to go.

The old woman was studying him carefully, her chin propped on one hand, eyes reduced to slits. "Your house," she said, "the bungalow. Where do you sleep tonight?"

He didn't answer. He was going to sleep in the car, in a rubble of crumpled newspaper and fast-food containers, the greasy sleeping bag pulled up over his head.

"I have a cot," she said. "In the closet."

"I was going to go over to my mother's . . ." he said, trailing off. He couldn't seem to keep his right foot still, the heel tapping nervously at the worn floorboards.

"Sit," she said.

He did as he was told. She brought him a cup of hot tea, a bowl of boiled cabbage and ham, and a plate of cold pirogen. Eating, he tried to explain himself. "About Naina," he began, "I—"

She waved her hand in dismissal. "Don't tell me," she said. "I'm not the one you should tell."

He set the cup down and looked at her—really looked at her—for the first time.

"Day after tomorrow," she said, "the solstice, shortest day of year. You come to dock on river." She held his eyes and he thought of the day she'd offered him the whole shabby pile of the house as if it were Hyde Park itself. "Same time as last year," she said.

The day was raw, cold, the wind gusting off the river. A dead crust of snow clung to the ground, used up and discolored, dirt showing through in streaks that were like wounds. Marty got there early. He pulled into the lot and parked the Camaro behind a Cadillac the size of a Rose Parade float. He didn't want her to see him right away. He let the car run, heater going full, and lit a cigarette. For a while he listened to the radio, but that didn't feel right, so he flicked it off.

The lot gradually filled. He recognized some of the cars from the previous year, watched the white-haired old masochists maneuver over the ruts as if they were bringing 747s in for a landing. Mama Vyshensky was late, as usual, and no one made a move till her battered Pontiac turned the corner and jolted into the lot. Then the doors began to open and bare feet gripped the snow.

Still, he waited. The driver's door of the Pontiac swung open, and then the passenger's door, and he felt something rising in him, a metallic compound of hope and despair that stuck in the back of his throat. And then Naina stepped out of the car. Her back was to him, her legs long and naked, a flash of her blood-red nails against the tarnished snow. He watched her toss her head and then gather her hair in a tight knot and force it under the bathing cap. He'd slept in the car the past two nights, he'd hunkered over cups of coffee at McDonald's like a bum. He saw her and he felt weak.

The crowd began to gather around Mama Vyshensky, ancient, all of them, spindly-legged, their robes like shrouds. He recognized the old man with red ears, bent double now and hunched over a cane. And a woman he'd seen last year, heaving along in a one-piece with a ballerina fringe round the hips. They drank a toast and shouted. Then another, and they flung their glasses. Naina stood silent among them.

He waited till they began to move down the slope to the dock and then he stepped noiselessly from the car, heart pounding in his chest. By the time they'd reached the dock, Naina and her mother at the head of the group, he was already passing the stragglers. "You bring a towel?" one old woman called out to him, and another tittered. He just gave her a blank stare, hurrying now, his eyes on Naina.

As he stepped onto the dock, Naina stood poised at the far end. She dropped her robe. Then she turned and saw him. She saw him—he could read it in her eyes—though she turned away as if she hadn't. He tried to get to her, wedging himself between two heavy-breasted women and a hearty-looking old man with a white goatee, but the dock was too crowded. And then came the first splash. Naina glanced back at him and the soft smile seemed to flicker across her lips. She held his eyes now, held them across the field of drooping flesh, the body hair, the toothless mouths. Then she turned and dove.

All right, he thought, his pulse racing, all right. And then he had a boot in his hand and he was hopping on one leg. Then the other boot. A confusion of splashes caromed around him, water flew, the wind cut across the dock. He tore off his jacket, sweater, T-shirt, dropped his faded jeans, and stood there in his briefs, scanning the black rollicking water. There she was, her head bobbing gently, arms flowing across her breast in an easy tread.

He never hesitated. His feet pounded against the rough planks of the dock, the wind caught his hair, and he was up and out over the churning water, hanging suspended for the briefest, maddest, most lucid instant of his life, and then he was in.

Funny. It was warm as a bath.

THE DEVIL AND IRV CHERNISKE

JUST OUTSIDE the sleepy little commuter village of Irvington, New York, there stands a subdivision of half-million-dollar homes, each riding its own sculpted acre like a ship at sea and separated from its neighbors by patches of scrub and the forlorn-looking beeches that lend a certain pricy and vestigial air to the place. The stockbrokers, lawyers, doctors, and software salesmen who live here with their families know their community as Beechwood, in deference to the legend hammered into the slab of pink marble at the entrance of Beechwood Drive. This slab was erected by the developer, Sal Maggio, in the late nineteen-sixties, though there are few here now who can remember that far back. For better or worse, Beechwood is the sort of community in which the neighbors don't know one another and don't really care to, though they do survey each other's gardeners and automobiles with all the perspicacity of appraisers, and while the proper names of the people next door may escape them, they are quick to invent such colorful sobriquets as the Geeks, the Hackers, the Volvos, and the Chinks by way of compensation.

For the most part, the handsome sweeping macadam streets go untrodden but for the occasional backward jogger, and the patches of wood are ignored to the point at which they've begun to revert to the condition of the distant past, to the time before Maggio's bulldozer, when the trees stretched unbroken all the way to Ardsley. Fieldmice make their home in these woods, moths, spiders, sparrows, and squirrels. In the late afternoon, garter snakes silently thread the high rank thick-stemmed morass of bluegrass gone wild, and toads thump from one fetid puddle to another. An unpropitious place, these woods. A forgotten place. But it was here, in one of these primordial pockets, beneath a wind-ravaged maple and within earshot of the chit-chit-chit of the gray squirrel, that Irv Cherniske made the deal of his life.

Irv was one of the senior residents of Beechwood, having moved into his buff-and-chocolate Tudor with the imitation flagstone façade some three years earlier. He was a hard-nosed cynic in his early forties, a big-headed, heavy-paunched, irascible stock trader who'd seen it all—and then some. The characteristic tone of his voice was an unmodulated roar, but this was only the daintiest of counterpoint to the stentorian bellow of his wife, Tish. The two fought so often and at such a pitch that their young sons, Shane and Morgan, often took refuge in the basement game room while the battle raged over their heads and out across the placid rolling lawns of Beechwood Estates. To the neighbors, these battles were a source of rueful amusement: separately, yet unanimously, they had devised their own pet nickname for the Cherniskes. A torn, ragged cry would cut the air around dinnertime each evening, and someone would lift a watery gimlet to his lips and remark, with a sigh, that the Screechers were at it again.

One evening, after a particularly bracing confrontation with his wife over the question of who had last emptied the trash receptacle in the guest room, Irv was out in the twilit backyard, practicing his chip shot and swatting mosquitoes. It was the tail end of a long Fourth of July weekend, and an unearthly stillness had settled over Beechwood, punctuated now and again by the distant muffled pop of leftover fireworks. The air was muggy and hot, a fiery breath of the tropics more suitable to Rangoon than New York. Irv bent in the fading light to address a neon-orange Titleist. Behind him, in the house which seemed almost to sink under the weight of its mortgage, Tish and his sons were watching TV, the muted sounds of conflict and sorrow carrying fitfully to where he stood in the damp grass, awash in birdsong. He raised the nine-iron, dropped it in a fluid rush, and watched the ball rise mightily into the darkening belly of the sky. Unfortunately, he overshot the makeshift flag he'd set up at the foot of the lawn and carried on into the ragged clump of trees beyond it.

With a curse, Irv trundled down the hill and pushed his way through the mounds of cuttings the gardener had piled up like breastworks at the edge of the woods and a moment later found himself in the hushed and shadowy stand of beeches. An odor of slow rot assaulted his nostrils. Crickets chirruped. There was no sign of the ball. He was kicking aimlessly through the leaves, all but certain it was gone for good—two and a half bucks down the drain—when he was startled by a noise from the gloom up ahead.

Something—or someone—was coming toward him, a presence announced by the crush of brittle leaves and the hiss of uncut grass. "Who is it?" he demanded, and the crickets fell silent. "Is someone there?"

The shape of a man began to emerge gradually from the shadows—head and shoulders first, then a torso that kept getting bigger. And bigger. His skin was dark—so dark Irv at first took him to be a Negro—and a wild feral shock of hair stood up jaggedly from his crown like the mane of a hyena. The man said nothing.

Irv was not easily daunted. He believed in the Darwinian struggle, believed, against all signs to the contrary, that he'd risen to the top of the pack and that the choicest morsels of the feast of life were his for the taking. And though he wasn't nearly the bruiser he'd been when he started at nose tackle for Fox Lane High, he was used to wielding his paunch like a weapon and blustering his way through practically anything, from a

potential mugging right on down to putting a snooty maître d'
in his place. For all that, though, when he saw the size of the
man, when he factored in his complexion and considered the
oddness of the circumstances, he felt uncertain of himself. Felt
as if the parameters of the world as he knew it had suddenly
shifted. Felt, unaccountably, that he was in deep trouble. Char-
acteristically, he fell back on bluster. "Who in hell are you?" he
demanded.

The stranger, he now saw, wasn't black at all. Or, rather, he
wasn't a Negro, as he'd first supposed, but something else altogether. Swarthy, that's what he was. Like a Sicilian or a Greek.
Or maybe an Arab. He saw too that the man was dressed almost
identically to himself, in a Lacoste shirt, plaid slacks, and white
Adidas. But this was no golf club dangling from the stranger's
fingertips—it was a chainsaw. "Hell?" the big man echoed, his
voice starting down low and then rising in mockery. "I don't
believe it. Did you actually say 'Who in hell are you?'?" He
began to laugh in a shallow, breathy, and decidedly unset-
tling way.

It was getting darker by the minute, the trunks of the trees
receding into the shadows, stars dimly visible now in the dome
of the sky. There was a distant sound of fireworks and a sharp
sudden smell of gunpowder on the air. "Are you . . . are you
somebody's gardener or something?" Irv asked, glancing uncomfortably at the chainsaw.

This got the stranger laughing so hard he had to pound his
breastbone and wipe the tears from his eyes. "Gardener?" he
hooted, stamping around in the undergrowth and clutching his
sides with the sheer hilarity of it. "You've got to be kidding.
Come on, tell me you're kidding."

Irv felt himself growing annoyed. "I mean, because if you're
not," he said, struggling to control his voice, "then I want to
know what you're doing back here with that saw. This is private
property, you know."

Abruptly, the big man stopped laughing. When he spoke, all

trace of amusement had faded from his voice. "Oh?" he growled. "And just who does it belong to, then—it wouldn't be yours, by any chance, would it?"

It wasn't. As Irv well knew. In fact, he'd done a little title-searching six months back, when Tish had wanted to mow down the beeches and put in an ornamental koi pond with little pink bridges and mechanical waterfalls. The property, useless as it was, belonged to the old bird next door—"the Geek" was the only name Irv knew him by. Irv thought of bluffing, but the look in the stranger's eye made him think better of it. "It belongs to the old guy next door—Beltzer, I think his name is. Bitzer. Something like that."

The stranger was smiling now, but the smile wasn't a comforting one. "I see," he said. "So I guess you're trespassing too."

Irv had had enough. "We'll let the police decide that," he snapped, turning to stalk back up the lawn.

"Hey, Irv," the stranger said suddenly, "don't get huffy—old man Belcher won't be needing this plot anymore. You can hide all the golf balls you want down here."

The gloom thickened. Somewhere a dog began to howl. Irv felt the tight hairs at the base of his neck begin to stiffen. "How do you know my name?" he said, whirling around. "And how do you know what Belcher needs or doesn't need?" All of a sudden, Irv had the odd feeling that he'd seen this stranger somewhere before—real estate, wasn't it?

"Because he'll be dead five minutes from now, that's how." The big man let out a disgusted sigh. "Let's quit pissing around here—you know damn well who I am, Irv." He paused. "October twenty-two, 1955, Our Lady of the Immaculate Heart Church in Mount Kisco. Monsignor O'Kane. The topic is the transubstantiation of the flesh and you're screwing around with Alfred LaFarga in the back pew, talking 'Saturday Night Creature Features.' 'Did you see it when the mummy pulled that guy's eyes out?' you whispered. Alfred was this ratty little clown, looked like his shoulders were going to fall through his chest—

now making a killing in grain futures in Des Moines, by the way—and he says, 'That wasn't his eye, shit-for-brains, it was his tongue.' "

Irv was stunned. Shocked silent for maybe the first time in his life. He'd seen it all, yes—but not this. It was incredible, it really was. He'd given up on all that God and Devil business the minute he left parochial school—no percentage in it—and now here it was, staring him in the face. It took him about thirty seconds to reinvent the world, and then he was thinking there might just be something in it for him. "All right," he said, "all right, yeah, I know who you are. Question is, what do you want with me?"

The stranger's face was consumed in shadow now, but Irv could sense that he was grinning. "Smart, Irv," the big man said, all the persuasion of a born closer creeping into his voice. "What's in it for me, right? Let's make a deal, right? The wife isn't working, the kids need designer jeans, PCs, and dirt bikes, and the mortgage has you on the run, am I right?"

He was right—of course he was right. How many times, bullying some loser over the phone or wheedling a few extra bucks out of some grasping old hag's retirement account, had Irv wondered if it was all worth it? How many times had he shoved his way through a knot of pink-haired punks on the subway only to get home all the sooner to his wife's nagging and his sons' pale, frightened faces? How many times had he told himself he deserved more, much more—ease and elegance, regular visits to the track and the Caribbean, his own firm, the two or maybe three million he needed to bail himself out for good? He folded his arms. The stranger, suddenly, was no more disturbing than sweet-faced Ben Franklin gazing up benevolently from a mountain of C-notes. "Talk to me," Irv said.

The big man took him by the arm and leaned forward to whisper in his ear. He wanted the usual deal, nothing less, and he held out to Irv the twin temptations of preternatural business success and filthy lucre. The lucre was buried right there in that shabby patch of woods, a hoard of Krugerrands, bullion, and silver candlesticks socked away by old man Belcher as a hedge against runaway inflation. The business success would result from the collusion of his silent partner—who was leaning into him now and giving off an odor oddly like that of a Szechuan kitchen—and it would take that initial stake and double and redouble it till it grew beyond counting. "What do you say, Irv?" the stranger crooned.

Irv said nothing. He was no fool. Poker face, he told himself. Never look eager. "I got to think about it," he said. He was wondering vaguely if he could rent a metal detector or something and kiss the creep off. "Give me twenty-four hours."

The big man drew away from him. "Hmph," he grunted contemptuously. "You think I come around every day? This is the deal of a lifetime I'm talking here, Irv." He paused a moment to let this sink in. "You don't want it, I can always go to Joe Luck across the street over there."

Irv was horrified. "You mean the Chinks?"

At that moment the porch light winked on in the house behind them. The yellowish light caught the big man's face, bronzing it like a statue. He nodded. "Import/export. Joe's got connections with the big boys in Taiwan—and believe me, it isn't just backscratchers he's bringing in in those crates. But I happen to know he's hard up for capital right now, and I think he'd jump at the chance—"

Irv cut him off. "Okay, okay," he said. "But how do I know you're the real thing? I mean, what proof do I have? Anybody could've talked to Alfred LaFarga."

The big man snorted. Then, with a flick of his wrist, he fired up the chainsaw. *Rrrrrrrrrrow*, it sang as he turned to the nearest tree and sent it home. Chips and sawdust flew off into the darkness as he guided the saw up and down, back and across, carving something in the bark, some message. Irv edged forward. Though the light was bad, he could just make out the jagged uppercase *B*, and then the *E* that followed it. When the big man reached the *L*, Irv anticipated him, but waited, arms folded, for the sequel. The stranger spelled out BELCHER, then sliced into the base of the tree; in the next moment the tree was toppling into the gloom with a shriek of clawing branches.

Irv waited till the growl of the saw died to a sputter. "Yeah?" he said. "So what does that prove?"

The big man merely grinned, his face hideous in the yellow light. Then he reached out and pressed his thumb to Irv's forehead and Irv could hear the sizzle and feel the sting of his own flesh burning. "There's my mark," the stranger said. "Tomorrow night, seven o'clock. Don't be late." And then he strode off into the shadows, the great hulk of him halved in an instant, and then halved again, as if he were sinking down into the earth itself.

The first thing Tish said to him as he stepped in the door was "Where the hell have you been? I've been shouting myself hoarse. There's an ambulance out front of the neighbor's place."

Irv shoved past her and parted the living-room curtains. Sure enough, there it was, red lights revolving and casting an infernal glow over the scene. There were voices, shouts, a flurry of people clustered round a stretcher and a pair of quick-legged men in hospital whites. "It's nothing," he said, a savage joy rising in his chest—it was true, true after all, and he was going to be rich—"just the old fart next door kicking off."

Tish gave him a hard look. She was a year younger than he—his college sweetheart, in fact—but she'd let herself go. She wasn't so much obese as muscular, big, broad-beamed—every inch her husband's match. "What's that on your forehead?" she asked, her voice pinched with suspicion.

He lifted his hand absently to the spot. The flesh seemed rough and abraded, raised in an annealed disc the size of a quarter. "Oh, this?" he said, feigning nonchalance. "Hit my head on the barbecue."

She was having none of it. With a move so sudden it would have surprised a cat, she shot forward and seized his arm. "And what's that I smell—Chinese food?" Her eyes leapt at him; her jaw clenched. "I suppose the enchiladas weren't good enough for you, huh?"

He jerked his arm away. "Oh, yeah, I know—you really slaved over those enchiladas, didn't you? Christ, you might have chipped a nail or something tearing the package open and shoving them in the microwave."

"Don't give me that shit," she snarled, snatching his arm back and digging her nails in for emphasis. "The mark on your head, the Chinese food, that stupid grin on your face when you saw the ambulance—I know you. Something's up, isn't it?" She clung to his arm like some inescapable force of nature, like the tar in the La Brea pits or the undertow at Rockaway Beach. "Isn't it?"

Irv Cherniske was not a man to confide in his wife. He regarded marriage as an arbitrary and essentially adversarial relationship, akin to the yoking of prisoners on the chain gang. But this once, because the circumstances were so arresting and the stranger's proposal so unique (not to mention final), he relented and let her in on his secret.

At first, she wouldn't believe it. It was another of his lies, he was covering something up—*devils:* did he think she was born yesterday? But when she saw how solemn he was, how shaken, how feverish with lust over the prospect of laying his hands on the loot, she began to come around. By midnight she was urging him to go back and seal the bargain. "You fool. You idiot. What do you need twenty-four hours for? Go. Go now."

Though Irv had every intention of doing just that—in his own time, of course—he wasn't about to let her push him into anything. "You think I'm going to damn myself forever just to please you?" he sneered.

Tish took it for half a beat, then she sprang up from the sofa as if it were electrified. "All right," she snapped. "I'll find the son of a bitch myself and we'll both roast—but I tell you I want those Krugerrands and all the rest of it too. And I want it now."

A moment later, she was gone—out the back door and into the soft suburban night. Let her go, Irv thought in disgust, but despite himself he sat back to wait for her. For better than an hour he sat there in his mortgaged living room, dreaming of crushing his enemies and ascending the high-flown corridors of power, envisioning the cut-glass decanter in the bar of the Rolls and breakfast on the yacht, but at last he found himself nodding and decided to call it a day. He rose, stretched, and then padded through the dining room and kitchen to the back porch. He swung open the door and halfheartedly called his wife's name. There was no answer. He shrugged, retraced his steps, and wearily mounted the stairs to the bedroom: devil or no devil, he had a train to catch in the morning.

Tish was sullen at breakfast. She looked sorrowful and haggard and there were bits of twig and leaf caught in her hair. The boys bent silently over their caramel crunchies, waiflike in the khaki jerseys and oversized shorts they wore to camp. Irv studied his watch while gulping coffee. "Well," he said, addressing his stone-faced wife, "any luck?"

At first she wouldn't answer him. And when she did, it was in a voice so constricted with rage she sounded as if she were being throttled. Yes, she'd found the sorry son of a bitch, all right—after traipsing all over hell and back for half the night—and after all that he'd had the gall to turn his back on her. He wasn't in the mood, he said. But if she were to come back at noon with a peace offering—something worth talking about, something to show she was serious—he'd see what he could do for her. That's how he'd put it.

For a moment Irv was seized with jealousy and resentment—was she trying to cut him out, was that it?—but then he remembered how the stranger had singled him out, had come to him, and he relaxed. He had nothing to worry about. It was Tish. She just didn't know how to bargain, that was all. Her idea of a give and take was to reiterate her demands, over and over, each time in a shriller tone than the last. She'd probably pushed and pushed till even the devil wouldn't have her. "I'll be home early," he said, and then he was driving through a soft misting rain to the station.

It was past seven when finally he did get home. He pulled into the driveway and was surprised to see his sons sitting glumly on the front stoop, their legs drawn up under them, rain drooling steadily from the eaves. "Where's your mother?" he asked, hurrying up the steps in alarm. The elder, Shane, a pudgy, startled-looking boy of eight, whose misfortune it was to favor Tish about the nose and eyes, began to whimper. "She, she never came back," he blubbered, smearing snot across his lip.

Filled with apprehension—and a strange, airy exhilaration too: maybe she was gone, gone for good!—Irv dialed his mother. "Ma?" he shouted into the phone. "Can you come over and watch the kids? It's Tish. She's missing." He'd no sooner set the phone down than he noticed the blank space on the wall above the sideboard. The painting was gone. He'd always hated the thing—a gloomy dark swirl of howling faces with the legend "Cancer Dreams" scrawled in red across the bottom, a small monstrosity Tish had insisted on buying when he could barely make the car payments—but it was worth a bundle, that much he knew. And the moment he saw that empty space on the wall he knew she'd taken it to the big man in the woods—but what else had she taken? While the boys sat listlessly before the TV with a bag of taco chips, he tore through the house. Her jewelry would have been the first thing to go, and he wasn't surprised to see that it had disappeared, teak box and all. But in growing consternation he discovered that his coin collection was gone too, as were his fly rod and his hip waders and the bottle of V.S.O.P. he'd been saving for the World Series. The whole business had apparently been bundled up in the Irish-linen cloth that had shrouded the dining-room table for as long as he could remember.

Irv stood there a moment over the denuded table, overcome

with grief and rage. She *was* cutting him out, the bitch. She and the big man were probably down there right now, dancing round a gaping black hole in the earth. Or worse, she was on the train to New York with every last Krugerrand of Belcher's hoard, heading for the Caymans in a chartered yacht, hurtling out of Kennedy in a big 747, two huge, bursting, indescribably heavy trunks nestled safely in the baggage compartment beneath her. Irv rushed to the window. There were the woods: still, silent, slick with wet. He saw nothing but trees.

In the next instant, he was out the back door, down the grassy slope, and into the damp fastness of the woods. He'd forgotten all about the kids, his mother, the house at his back—all he knew was that he had to find Tish. He kicked through dead leaves and rotting branches, tore at the welter of grapevine and sumac that seemed to rise up like a barrier before him. "Tish!" he bawled.

The drizzle had turned to a steady, pelting rain. Irv's face and hands were scratched and insect-bitten and the hair clung to his scalp like some strange species of mold. His suit—all four hundred bucks' worth—was ruined. He was staggering through a stubborn tangle of briars, his mind veering sharply toward the homicidal end of the spectrum, when a movement up ahead made him catch his breath. Stumbling forward, he flushed a great black carrion bird from the bushes; as it rose silently into the darkening sky, he spotted the tablecloth. Still laden, it hung from the lower branches of a pocked and leprous oak. Irv looked round him cautiously. All was still, no sound but for the hiss of the rain in the leaves. He straightened up and lumbered toward the pale damp sack, thinking at least to recover his property.

No such luck. When he lifted the bundle down, he was disappointed by its weight; when he opened it, he was shocked to the roots of his hair. The tablecloth contained two things only: a bloody heart and a bloody liver. His own heart was beating so hard he thought his temples would burst; in horror he flung the thing to the ground. Only then did he notice that the undergrowth round the base of the tree was beaten down and trampled, as if a scuffle had taken place beneath it. There was a fandango of footprints in the mud and clumps of stiff black hair were scattered about like confetti—and wasn't that blood on the bark of the tree?

"Irv," murmured a voice at his back, and he whirled round in a panic. There he was, the big man, his swarthy features hooded in shadow. This time he was wearing a business suit in a muted gray check, a power yellow tie, and an immaculate trenchcoat. In place of the chainsaw, he carried a shovel, which he'd flung carelessly over one shoulder. "Whoa," he said, holding up a massive palm, "I didn't mean to startle you." He took a step forward and Irv could see that he was grinning. "All's I want to know is do we have a deal or not?"

"Where's Tish?" Irv demanded, his voice quavering. But even as he spoke he saw the angry red welt running the length of the big man's jaw and disappearing into the hair at his temple, and he knew.

The big man shrugged. "What do you care? She's gone, that's all that matters. Hey, no more of that nagging whiny voice, no more money down the drain on face cream and high heels— just think, you'll never have to wake up again to that bitchy pout and those nasty red little eyes. You're free, Irv. I did you a favor."

Irv regarded the stranger with awe. Tish was no mean adversary, and judging from the look of the poor devil's face, she'd gone down fighting.

The big man dropped his shovel to the ground and there was a clink of metal on metal. "Right here, Irv," he whispered. "Half a million easy. Cash. Tax-free. And with my help you'll watch it grow to fifty times that."

Irv glanced down at the bloody tablecloth and then back up at the big man in the trenchcoat. A slow grin spread across his lips.

Coming to terms wasn't so easy, however, and it was past

dark before they'd concluded their bargain. At first the stranger had insisted on Irv's going into one of the big Hollywood talent agencies, but when Irv balked, he said he figured the legal profession was just about as good—but you needed a degree for that, and begging Irv's pardon, he was a bit old to be going back to school, wasn't he? "Why can't I stay where I am," Irv countered, "—in stocks and bonds? With all this cash I could quit Tiller Ponzi and set up my own office."

The big man scratched his chin and laid a thoughtful finger alongside his nose. "Yeah," he murmured after a moment, "yeah, I hadn't thought of that. But I like it. You could promise them thirty percent and then play the futures market and gouge them till they bleed."

Irv came alive at the prospect. "Bleed 'em dry," he hooted. "I'll scalp and bucket and buy off the CFTC investigators, and then I'll set up an offshore company to hide the profits." He paused, overcome with the beauty of it. "I'll screw them right and left."

"Deal?" the devil said.

Irv took the big calloused hand in his own. "Deal."

Ten years later, Irv Cherniske was one of the wealthiest men in New York. He talked widows into giving him their retirement funds to invest in ironclad securities and sure bets, lost them four or five hundred thousand, and charged half that again in commissions. With preternatural luck his own investments paid off time and again and he eventually set up an inside-trading scheme that made guesswork superfluous. The police, of course, had been curious about Tish's disappearance, but Irv showed them the grisly tablecloth and the crude hole in which the killer had no doubt tried to bury her, and they launched an intensive manhunt that dragged on for months but produced neither corpse nor perpetrator. The boys he shunted off to his mother's, and when they were old enough, to a military school in Tangiers. Two months after his wife's disappearance, the newspapers uncovered a series of ritual beheadings in Connecticut and dropped all mention of the "suburban ghoul," as they'd dubbed Tish's killer; a week after that, Tish was forgotten and Beechwood went back to sleep.

It was in the flush of his success, when he had everything he'd ever wanted—the yacht, the sweet and compliant young mistress, the pair of Rolls Corniches, and the houses in the Bahamas and Aspen, not to mention the new wing he'd added to the old homestead in Beechwood—that Irv began to have second thoughts about the deal he'd made. Eternity was a long time, yes, but when he'd met the stranger in the woods that night it had seemed a long way off too. Now he was in his fifties, heavier than ever, with soaring blood pressure and flat feet, and the end of his career in this vale of profits was drawing uncomfortably near. It was only natural that he should begin to cast about for a loophole.

And so it was that he returned to the church—not the Roman church, to which he'd belonged as a boy, but the Church of the Open Palm, Reverend Jimmy, Pastor. He came to Reverend Jimmy one rainy winter night with a fire in his gut and an immortal longing in his heart. He sat through a three-hour service in which Reverend Jimmy spat fire, spoke in tongues, healed the lame, and lectured on the sanctity of the one and only God—profit—and then distributed copies of the *Reverend Jimmy Church-Sponsored Investment Guide* with the chili and barbecue recipes on the back page.

After the service, Irv found his way to Reverend Jimmy's office at the back of the church. He waited his turn among the other supplicants with growing impatience, but he reminded himself that the way to salvation lay through humility and forbearance. At long last he was ushered into the presence of the Reverend himself. "What can I do for you, brother?" Reverend Jimmy asked. Though he was from Staten Island, Reverend Jimmy spoke in the Alabama hog-farmer's dialect peculiar to his tribe.

"I need help, Reverend," Irv confessed, flinging himself down on a leather sofa worn smooth by the buttocks of the faithful.

Reverend Jimmy made a small pyramid of his fingers and leaned back in his adjustable chair. He was a youngish man— no older than thirty-five or so, Irv guessed—and he was dressed in a flannel shirt, penny loafers, and a plaid fishing hat that masked his glassy blue eyes. "Speak to me, brother," he said.

Irv looked down at the floor, then shot a quick glance round the office—an office uncannily like his own, right down to the computer terminal, mahogany desk, and potted palms—and then whispered, "You're probably not going to believe this."

Reverend Jimmy lit himself a cigarette and shook out the match with a snap of his wrist. "Try me," he drawled.

When Irv had finished pouring out his heart, Reverend Jimmy leaned forward with a beatific smile on his face. "Brother," he said, "believe me, your story's nothin' new—I handle just as bad and sometimes worser ever day. Cheer up, brother: salvation is on the way!"

Then Reverend Jimmy made a number of pointed inquiries into Irv's financial status and fixed the dollar amount of his tithe—to be paid weekly in small bills, no checks please. Next, with a practiced flourish, he produced a copy of Adam Smith's *Wealth of Nations*, the text of which was interspersed with biblical quotes in support of its guiding theses, and pronounced Irv saved. "You got your holy book," the Reverend Jimmy boomed as Irv ducked gratefully out the door, "—y'all keep it with you every day, through sleet and snow and dark of night, and old Satan he'll be paarless against you."

And so it was. Irv gained in years and gained in wealth. He tithed the Church of the Open Palm, and he kept the holy book with him at all times. One day, just after his sixtieth birthday, his son Shane came to the house to see him. It was a Sunday and the market was closed, but after an early-morning dalliance with Sushoo, his adept and oracular mistress, he'd placed a half dozen calls to Hong Kong, betting on an impending monsoon in Burma to drive the price of rice through the ceiling. He was in the Blue Room, as he liked to call the salon in the west wing, eating a bit of poached salmon and looking over a coded letter from Butram, his deep man in the SEC. The holy book lay on the desk beside him.

Shane was a bloated young lout in his late twenties, a sorrowful, shameless leech who'd flunked out of half a dozen schools and had never held a job in his life—unlike Morgan, who'd parlayed the small stake his father had given him into the biggest used-car dealership in the country. Unwashed, unshaven, the gut he'd inherited from his father peeping out from beneath a Hawaiian shirt so lurid it looked as if it had been used to stanch wounds at the emergency ward, Shane loomed over his father's desk. "I need twenty big ones," he grunted, giving his father a look of beery disdain. "Bad week at the track."

Irv looked up from his salmon and saw Tish's nose, Tish's eyes, saw the greedy, worthless, contemptible slob his son had become. In a sudden rage he shot from the chair and hammered the desk so hard the plate jumped six inches. "I'll be damned if I give you another cent," he roared.

Just then there was a knock at the door. His face contorted with rage, Irv shoved past his son and stormed across the room, a curse on his lips for Magdalena, the maid, who should have known better than to bother him at a time like this. He tore open the door only to find that it wasn't Magdalena at all, but his acquaintance of long ago, the big black man with the wild mane of hair and the vague odor of stir-fry on his clothes. "Time's up, Irv," the big man said gruffly. In vain did Irv look over his shoulder to where the Reverend Jimmy's holy book sat forlorn on the desk beside the plate of salmon that was already growing cold. The big man took his arm in a grip of steel and whisked him through the hallway, down the stairs, and out across the lawn to where a black BMW with smoked windows sat running at the curb. Irv turned his pale fleshy face to the house and saw his son staring down at him from above, and then the big man laid an implacable hand on his shoulder and shoved him into the car.

The following day, of course, as is usual in these cases, all of Irv's liquid assets—his stocks and bonds, his Swiss and Bahamian bankbooks, even the wads of new-minted hundred-dollar bills he kept stashed in safe-deposit boxes all over the country—turned to cinders. Almost simultaneously, the house was gutted by a fire of mysterious origin, and both Rolls-Royces were destroyed. Joe Luck, who shuffled out on his lawn in a silk dressing gown at the height of the blaze, claimed to have seen a great black bird emerge from the patch of woods behind the house and mount into the sky high above the roiling billows of steam and smoke, but for some reason, no one else seemed to have shared his vision.

The big refurbished house on Beechwood Drive has a new resident now, a corporate lawyer by the name of O'Faolain. If he's bothered by the unfortunate history of the place—or even, for that matter, aware of it—no one can say. He knows his immediate neighbors as the Chinks, the Fat Family, and the Turf Builders. They know him as the Shyster.

THE MIRACLE AT BALLINSPITTLE

THERE THEY ARE, the holybugs, widows in their weeds and fat-ankled mothers with palsied children, all lined up before the snotgreen likeness of the Virgin, and McGahee and McCarey among them. This statue, alone among all the myriad three-foot-high snotgreen likenesses of the Virgin cast in plaster by Finnbar Finnegan & Sons, Cork City, was seen one grim March afternoon some years back to move its limbs ever so slightly, as if seized suddenly by the need of a good sinew-cracking stretch. Nuala Nolan, a young girl in the throes of Lenten abnegation, was the only one to witness the movement—a gentle beckoning of the statue's outthrust hand—after a fifteen-day vigil during which she took nothing into her body but Marmite and soda water. Ever since, the place has been packed with tourists.

Even now, in the crowd of humble countrymen in shit-smeared boots and knit skullcaps, McGahee can detect a certain number of Teutonic or Manhattanite faces above cableknit sweaters and pendant cameras. Drunk and in debt, on the run from a bad marriage, two DWI convictions, and the wheezy expiring gasps of his moribund mother, McGahee pays them no heed. His powers of concentration run deep. He is forty years old, as lithe as a boxer though he's done no hard physical labor since he took a construction job between semesters at college twenty years back, and he has the watery eyes and doleful, doglike expression of the saint. Twelve hours ago he was in New York, at Paddy

Flynn's, pouring out his heart and enumerating his woes for McCarey, when McCarey said, "Fuck it, let's go to Ireland." And now here he is at Ballinspittle, wearing the rumpled Levi's and Taiwanese sportcoat he'd pulled on in his apartment yesterday morning, three hours off the plane from Kennedy and flush with warmth from the venerable Irish distillates washing through his veins.

McCarey—plump, stately McCarey—stands beside him, bleary-eyed and impatient, disdainfully scanning the crowd. Heads are bowed. Infants snuffle. From somewhere in the distance come the bleat of a lamb and the mechanical call of the cuckoo. McGahee checks his watch: they've been here seven minutes already and nothing's happened. His mind begins to wander. He's thinking about orthodontia—thinking an orthodontist could make a fortune in this country—when he looks up and spots her, Nuala Nolan, a scarecrow of a girl, an anorectic, bones-in-a-sack sort of girl, kneeling in front of the queue and reciting the Mysteries in a voice parched for food and drink. Since the statue moved she has stuck to her diet of Marmite and soda water until the very synapses of her brain have become encrusted with salt and she raves like a mariner lost at sea. McGahee regards her with awe. A light rain has begun to fall.

And then suddenly, before he knows what's come over him, McGahee goes limp. He feels lightheaded, transported, feels himself sinking into another realm, as helpless and cut adrift as when Dr. Beibelman put him under for his gallbladder operation. He breaks out in a sweat. His vision goes dim. The murmur of the crowd, the call of the cuckoo, and the bleat of the lamb all meld into a single sound—a voice—and that voice, ubiquitous, timeless, all-embracing, permeates his every cell and fiber. It seems to speak through him, through the broad-beamed old hag beside him, through McCarey, Nuala Nolan, the stones and birds and fishes of the sea. "Davey," the voice calls in the sweetest tones he ever heard, "Davey McGahee, come to me, come to my embrace."

As one, the crowd parts, a hundred stupefied faces turned toward him, and there she is, the Virgin, snotgreen no longer but radiant with the aquamarine of actuality, her eyes glowing, arms beckoning. McGahee casts a quick glance around him. McCarey looks as if he's been punched in the gut, Nuala Nolan's skeletal face is clenched with hate and jealousy, the humble countrymen and farmwives stare numbly from him to the statue and back again . . . and then, as if in response to a subconscious signal, they drop to their knees in a human wave so that only he, Davey McGahee, remains standing. "Come to me," the figure implores, and slowly, as if his feet were encased in cement, his head reeling and his stomach sour, he begins to move forward, his own arms outstretched in ecstasy.

The words of his catechism, forgotten these thirty years, echo in his head: "Mother Mary, Mother of God, pray for us sinners now and at the hour of our—"

"Yesssss!" the statue suddenly shrieks, the upturned palm curled into a fist, a fist like a weapon. "And you think it's as easy as that, do you?"

McGahee stops cold, hovering over the tiny effigy like a giant, a troglodyte, a naked barbarian. Three feet high, grotesque, shaking its fists up at him, the thing changes before his eyes. Gone is the beatific smile, gone the grace of the eyes and the faintly mad and indulgent look of the transported saint. The face is a gargoyle's, a shrew's, and the voice, sharpening, probing like a dental tool, suddenly bears an uncanny resemblance to his ex-wife's. "Sinner!" the gargoyle hisses. "Fall on your knees!"

The crowd gasps. McGahee, his bowels turned to ice, pitches forward into the turf. "No, no, no!" he cries, clutching at the grass and squeezing his eyes shut. "Hush," a new voice whispers in his ear, "look. You must look." There's a hand on his neck, bony and cold. He winks open an eye. The statue is gone and Nuala Nolan leans over him, her hair gone in patches, the death's-head of her face and suffering eyes, her breath like the loam of the grave. "Look, up there," she whispers.

High above them, receding into the heavens like a kite loosed from a string, is the statue. Its voice comes to him faint and distant—"Behold . . . now . . . your sins . . . and excesses . . ."—and then it dwindles away like a fading echo.

Suddenly, behind the naked pedestal, a bright sunlit vista appears, grapevines marshaled in rows, fields of barley, corn, and hops, and then, falling from the sky with thunderous crashes, a succession of vats, kegs, hogsheads, and buckets mounting up in the foreground as if on some phantom pier piled high with freight. *Boom, boom, ka-boom, boom,* down they come till the vista is obscured and the kegs mount to the tops of the trees. McGahee pushes himself up to his knees and looks around him. The crowd is regarding him steadily, jaws set, the inclemency of the hanging judge sunk into their eyes. McCarey, kneeling too now and looking as if he's just lurched up out of a drunken snooze to find himself on a subway car on another planet, has gone steely-eyed with the rest of them. And Nuala Nolan, poised over him, grins till the long naked roots of her teeth gleam beneath the skirts of her rotten gums.

"Your drinking!" shrieks a voice from the back of the throng, his wife's voice, and there she is, Fredda, barefoot and in a snotgreen robe and hood, wafting her way through the crowd and pointing her long accusatory finger at his poor miserable shrinking self. "Every drop," she booms, and the vasty array of vats and kegs and tumblers swivels to reveal the signs hung from their sweating slats—GIN, BOURBON, BEER, WHISKEY, SCHNAPPS, PERNOD—and the crowd lets out a long exhalation of shock and lament.

The keg of gin. Tall it is and huge, its contents vaguely sloshing. You could throw cars into it, buses, tractor trailers. But no, never, he couldn't have drunk that much gin, no man could. And beside it the beer, frothy and bubbling, a cauldron the size of a rest home. "No!" he cries in protest. "I don't even like the taste of the stuff."

"Yes, yes, yes," chants a voice beside him. The statue is back,

Fredda gone. It speaks in a voice he recognizes, though the wheezy, rheumy deathbed rasp of it has been wiped clean. "Ma?" he says, turning to the thing.

Three feet tall, slick as a seal, the robes flowing like the sea, the effigy looks up at him out of his mother's face drawn in miniature. "I warned you," the voice leaps out at him, high and querulous, "out behind the 7-11 with Ricky Reitbauer and that criminal Tommy Capistrano, cheap wine and all the rest."

"But Mom, *Pernod?*" He peers into the little pot of it, a pot so small you couldn't boil a good Safeway chicken in it. There it is. Pernod. Milky and unclean. It turns his stomach even to look at it.

"Your liver, son," the statue murmurs with a resignation that brings tears to his eyes, "just look at it."

He feels a prick in his side and there it is, his liver—a poor piece of cheesy meat, stippled and striped and purple—dangling from the plaster fingers. "God," he moans, "God Almighty."

"Rotten as your soul," the statue says.

McGahee, still on his knees, begins to blubber. Meaningless slips of apology issue from his lips—"I didn't mean . . . it wasn't . . . how could I know?"—when all of a sudden the statue shouts "Drugs!" with a voice of iron.

Immediately the scene changes. The vats are gone, replaced with bales of marijuana, jars of pills in every color imaginable, big, overbrimming tureens of white powder, a drugstore display of airplane glue. In the background, grinning Laotians, Peruvian peasants with hundreds of scrawny children propped like puppets on their shoulders.

"But, but—" McGahee stutters, rising to his feet to protest, but the statue doesn't give him a chance, won't, can't, and the stentorian voice—his wife's, his mother's, no one's and everyone's, he even detects a trace of his high-school principal's in there—the stentorian voice booms: "Sins of the Flesh!"

He blinks his eyes and the Turks and their bales are gone. The backdrop now is foggy and obscure, dim as the mists of

memory. The statue is silent. Gradually the poor sinner becomes
aware of a salacious murmur, an undercurrent of moaning and
panting, and the lubricious thwack and whap of the act itself.
"Davey," a girl's voice calls, tender, pubescent, "I'm scared."
And then his own voice, bland and reassuring: "I won't stick it
in, Cindy, I won't, I swear . . . or maybe, maybe just . . . just
an inch. . . ."

The mist lifts and there they are, in teddies and negligees, in
garter belts and sweat socks, naked and wet and kneading their
breasts like dough. "Davey," they moan, "oh, Davey, fuck me,
fuck me, fuck me," and he knows them all, from Cindy Lou
Harris and Betsy Butler in the twelfth grade to Fredda in her
youth and the sad and ugly faces of his one-night stands and
chance encounters, right on up to the bug-eyed woman with
the doleful breasts he'd diddled in the rest room on the way out
from Kennedy. And worse. Behind them, milling around in a
mob that stretches to the horizon, are all the women and girls
he'd ever lusted after, even for a second, the twitching behinds
and airy bosoms he'd stopped to admire on the street, the legs
he'd wanted to stroke and lips to press to his own. McCarey's
wife, Beatrice, is there and Fred Dolby's thirteen-year-old
daughter, the woman with the freckled bosom who used to
sunbathe in the tiger-skin bikini next door when they lived in
Irvington, the girl from the typing pool, and the outrageous
little shaven-headed vixen from Domino's Pizza. And as if that
weren't enough, there's the crowd from books and films too.
Linda Lovelace, Sophia Loren, Emma Bovary, the Sabine women
and Lot's wife, even Virginia Woolf with her puckered foxy
face and the eyes that seem to beg for a good slap on the bottom.
It's too much—all of them murmuring his name like a crazed
chorus of Molly Blooms, and yes, she's there too—and the mob
behind him hissing, hissing.

He glances at the statue. The plaster lip curls in disgust, the
adamantine hand rises and falls, and the women vanish. "Glut-
tony!" howls the Virgin and all at once he's surrounded by

forlornly mooing herds of cattle, sad-eyed pigs and sheep, fu-
nereal geese and clucking ducks, a spill of scuttling crabs and
claw-waving lobsters, even the odd dog or two he'd inadver-
tently wolfed down in Tijuana burritos and Cantonese stir-fry.
And the scales—scales the size of the Washington Monument—
sunk under pyramids of ketchup, peanut butter, tortilla chips,
truckloads of potatoes, onions, avocados, peppermint candies
and after-dinner mints, half-eaten burgers and fork-scattered
peas, the whole slithering wasteful cornucopia of his secret and
public devouring. "Moooooo," accuse the cows. "Stinker!" "Pig!"
"Glutton!" cry voices from the crowd.

Prostrate now, the cattle hanging over him, letting loose with
their streams of urine and clots of dung, McGahee shoves his
fists into his eyes and cries out for mercy. But there is no mercy.
The statue, wicked and glittering, its tiny twisted features
clenching and unclenching like the balls of its fists, announces
one after another the unremitting parade of his sins: "Insults to
Humanity, False Idols, Sloth, Unclean Thoughts, The Kicking
of Dogs and Cheating at Cards!"

His head reels. He won't look. The voices cry out in hurt and
laceration and he feels the very ground give way beneath him.
The rest, mercifully, is a blank.

When he comes to, muttering in protest—"False idols, I mean
like an autographed picture of Mickey Mantle, for christ's sake?"—
he finds himself in a cramped mud-and-wattle hut that reeks
of goat dung and incense. By the flickering glow of a bank of
votary candles, he can make out the bowed and patchy head of
Nuala Nolan. Outside it is dark and the rain drives down with
a hiss. For a long moment, McGahee lies there, studying the
fleshless form of the girl, her bones sharp and sepulchral in the
quavering light. He feels used up, burned out, feels as if he's
been cored like an apple. His head screams. His throat is dry.
His bladder is bursting.

He pushes himself up and the bony demi-saint levels her tranced gaze on him. "Hush," she says, and the memory of all that's happened washes over him like a typhoon.

"How long have I—?"

"Two days." Her voice is a reverent whisper, the murmur of the acolyte, the apostle. "They say the Pope himself is on the way."

"The Pope?" McGahee feels a long shiver run through him. Nods the balding death's-head. The voice is dry as husks, wheezy, but a girl's voice all the same, and an enthusiast's. "They say it's the greatest vision vouchsafed to man since the time of Christ. Two hundred and fifteen people witnessed it, every glorious moment, from the cask of gin to the furtive masturbation to the ace up the sleeve." She's leaning over him now, inching forward on all fours, her breath like chopped meat gone bad in the refrigerator; he can see, through the tattered shirt, where her breasts used to be. "Look," she whispers, gesturing toward the hunched low entranceway.

He looks and the sudden light dazzles him. Blinking in wonder, he creeps to the crude doorway and peers out. Immediately a murmur goes up from the crowd—hundreds upon hundreds of them gathered in the rain on their knees—and an explosion of flash cameras blinds him. Beyond the crowd he can make out a police cordon, vans and video cameras, CBS, BBC, KDOG, and NPR, a face above a trenchcoat that could only belong to Dan Rather himself. "Holy of holies!" cries a voice from the front of the mob—he knows that voice—and the crowd takes it up in a chant that breaks off into the Lord's Prayer. Stupefied, he wriggles out of the hut and stands, bathed in light. It's McCarey there before him, reaching out with a hundred others to embrace his ankles, kiss his feet, tear with trembling devoted fingers at his Levi's and Taiwanese tweed—Michael McCarey, adulterer, gambler, drunk and atheist, cheater of the IRS and bane of the Major Deegan—hunkered down in the rain like a holy supplicant. And there, not thirty feet away, is the statue, lit like Betelgeuse and as inanimate and snotgreen as a stone of the sea.

Rain pelts McGahee's bare head and the chill seizes him like a claw jerking hard and sudden at the ruined ancient priest-ridden superstitious root of him. The flashbulbs pop in his face, a murmur of Latin assaults his ears, Sister Mary Magdalen's unyielding face rises before him out of the dim mists of eighth-grade math . . . and then the sudden imperious call of nature blinds him to all wonder and he's staggering round back of the hut to relieve himself of his two days' accumulation of salts and uric acid and dregs of whiskey. Stumbling, fumbling for his zipper, the twin pains in his groin like arrows driven through him, he jerks out his poor pud and lets fly.

"Piss!" roars a voice behind him, and he swivels his head in fright, helpless before the stream that issues from him like a torrent. The crowd falls prostrate in the mud, cameras whir, voices cry out. It is the statue, of course, livid, jerking its limbs and racking its body like the image of the Führer in his maddest denunciation. "Piss on sacred ground, will you," rage the plaster lips in the voice of his own father, that mild and pacifistic man, "you unholy insect, you whited sepulcher, you speck of dust in the eye of your Lord and maker!"

What can he do? He clutches himself, flooding the ground, dissolving the hut, befouling the bony scrag of the anchorite herself.

"Unregenerate!" shrieks the Virgin. "Unrepentant! Sinner to the core!"

And then it comes.

The skies part, the rain turns to popcorn, marshmallows, English muffins, the light of seven suns scorches down on that humble crowd gathered on the sward, and all the visions of that first terrible day crash over them in hellish simulcast. The great vats of beer and gin and whiskey fall to pieces and the sea of booze floats them, the cattle bellowing and kicking, sheep bleating and dogs barking, despoiled girls and hardened women clutching for the shoulders of the panicked communicants as for sticks of wood awash in the sea, Sophia Loren herself and Virginia Woolf, Fredda, Cindy Lou Harris, and McCarey's wife swept by in a blur, the TV vans overturned, the trenchcoat torn from Dan Rather's back, and the gardai sent sprawling—"Thank God he didn't eat rattlesnake," someone cries—and then it's over. Night returns. Rain falls. The booze sinks softly into the earth, food lies rotting in clumps. A drumbeat of hoofs thunders off into the dark while fish wriggle and escargots creep, and Fredda, McCarey, the shaven-headed pizza vixen, and all the gap-toothed countrymen and farmwives and palsied children pick themselves up from the ground amid the curses of the men cheated at cards, the lament of the fallen women, and the mad frenzied chorus of prayer that speaks over it all in the tongue of terror and astonishment.

But oh, sad wonder, McGahee is gone.

Today the site remains as it was that night, fenced off from the merely curious, combed over inch by inch by priests and para-psychologists, blessed by the Pope, a shrine as reverenced as Lourdes and the Holy See itself. The cattle were sold off at auction after intensive study proved them ordinary enough, though brands were traced to Montana, Texas, and the Swiss Alps, and the food—burgers and snowcones, rib roasts, fig new-tons, extra dill pickles, and all the rest—was left where it fell, to feed the birds and fertilize the soil. The odd rib or T-bone, picked clean and bleached by the elements, still lies there on the ground in mute testimony to those three days of tumult. Fredda McGahee Meyerowitz, Herb Bucknell and others cheated at cards, the girl from the pizza parlor and the rest were sent home via Aer Lingus, compliments of the Irish government. What became of Virginia Woolf, dead forty years prior to these events, is not known, nor the fate of Emma Bovary either, though one need only refer to Flaubert for the best clue to this mystery. And of course, there are the tourism figures—up a whopping 672 percent since the miracle.

McCarey has joined an order of Franciscan monks, and Nuala

Nolan, piqued no doubt by her supporting role in the unfolding of the miracle, has taken a job in a pastry shop, where she eats by day and prays for forgiveness by night. As for Davey McGahee himself, the prime mover and motivator of all these enduring mysteries, here the lenses of history and of myth and miracology grow obscure. Some say he descended into a black hole of the earth, others that he evaporated, while still others insist that he ascended to heaven in a blaze of light, Saint of the Common Sinner.

For who hasn't lusted after woman or man or drunk his booze and laid to rest whole herds to feed his greedy gullet? Who hasn't watched them starve by the roadside in the hollows and waste places of the world and who among us hasn't scoffed at the credulous and ignored the miracle we see outside the window every day of our lives? Ask not for whom the bell tolls—unless perhaps you take the flight to Cork City, and the bus or rented Nissan out to Ballinspittle by the Sea, and gaze on the halfsize snotgreen statue of the Virgin, mute and unmoving all these many years.

Zapatos

*T*HERE IS, essentially, one city in our country. It is a city in which everyone wears a hat, works in an office, jogs, and eats simply but elegantly, a city, above all, in which everyone covets shoes. Italian shoes, in particular. Oh, you can get by with a pair of domestically made pumps or cordovans of the supplest sheepskin, or even, in the languid days of summer, with huaraches or Chinese slippers made of silk or even nylon. There are those who claim to prefer running shoes—Puma, Nike, Saucony—winter and summer. But the truth is, what everyone wants—for the status, the cachet, the charm and refinement— are the Italian loafers and ankle boots, hand-stitched and with a grain as soft and rich as, well—is this the place to talk of the private parts of girls still in school?

My uncle—call him Dagoberto—imports shoes. From Italy. And yet, until recently, he himself could barely afford a pair. It's the government, of course. Our country—the longest and leanest in the world—is hemmed in by the ocean on one side, the desert and mountains on the other, and the government has leached and pounded it dry till sometimes I think we live atop a stupendous, three-thousand-mile-long strip of jerky. There are duties—prohibitive duties—on everything. Or, rather, on everything we want. Cocktail napkins, Band-Aids, Tupperware, crescent wrenches, and kimchi come in practically for nothing. But the things we really crave—microwaves, Lean

186

Cuisine, CDs, leisure suits, and above all, Italian shoes—carry a duty of two and sometimes three hundred percent. The government is unfriendly. We are born, we die, it rains, it clears, the government is unfriendly. Facts of life.

Uncle Dagoberto is no revolutionary—none of us are; let's face it, we manage—but the shoe situation was killing him. He'd bring his shoes in, arrange them seductively in the windows of his three downtown shops, and there they'd languish, despite a markup so small he'd have to sell a hundred pairs just to take his shopgirls out to lunch. It was intolerable. And what made it worse was that the good citizens of our city, vain and covetous as they are, paraded up and down in front of his very windows in shoes identical to those he was selling—shoes for which they'd paid half price or less. And how were these shoes getting through customs and finding their way to the dark little no-name shops in the ill-lit vacancies of waterfront warehouses? Ask the Black Hand, Los Dedos Muertos, the fat and corrupt Minister of Commerce.

For months, poor Uncle Dagoberto brooded over the situation, while his wife (my mother's sister, Carmen, a merciless woman) and his six daughters screamed for the laser facials, cellular phones, and Fila sweats he could no longer provide for them. He is a heavyset man, my uncle, and balding, and he seemed to grow heavier and balder during those months of commercial despair. But one morning, as he came down to breakfast in the gleaming, tiled expanse of the kitchen our families share in the big venerable old mansion on La Calle Verdad, there was a spring in his step and a look on his face that, well—there is a little shark in the waters here, capable of smelling out one part of blood in a million parts of water, and when he does smell out that impossible single molecule of blood, I imagine he must have a look like that of Uncle Dagoberto on that sunstruck morning on La Calle Verdad.

"Tomás," he said to me, rubbing his hands over his Bran Chex, Metamusil, and decaffeinated coffee, "we're in business."

The kitchen was deserted at that hour. My aunts and sisters were off jogging, Dagoberto's daughters at the beach, my mother busy with aerobics, and my father—my late, lamented father—lying quiet in his grave. I didn't understand. I looked up at him blankly from my plate of microwave waffles.

His eyes darted round the room. There was a sheen of sweat on his massive, close-shaven jowls. He began to whistle—a tune my mother used to sing me, by Grandmaster Flash—and then he broke off and gave me a gold-capped smile. "The shoe business," he said. "There's fifteen hundred in it for you."

I was at the university at the time, studying semantics, hermeneutics, and the deconstruction of deconstruction. I myself owned two sleek pairs of Italian loafers, in ecru and rust. Still, I wasn't working, and I could have used the money. "I'm listening," I said.

What he wanted me to do was simple—simple, but potentially dangerous. He wanted me to spend two days in the north, in El Puerto Libre—Freeport. There are two free ports in our country, separated by nearly twenty-five hundred miles of terrain that looks from the air like the spine of some antediluvian monster. The southern port is called Calidad, or Quality. Both are what I imagine the great bazaars of Northern Africa and the Middle East to have been in the time of Marco Polo or Rommel, percolating cauldrons of sin and plenty, where anything known to man could be had for the price of a haggle. But there was a catch, of course. While you could purchase anything you liked in El Puerto Libre or Calidad, to bring it back to the city you had to pay duty—the same stultifying duty merchants like Uncle Dagoberto were obliged to pay. And why then had the government set up the free ports in the first place? In order to make digital audio tape and microwaves available to themselves, of course, and to set up discreet banking enterprises for foreigners, by way of generating cash flow—and ultimately, I think, to frustrate the citizenry. To keep us in our place. To remind us that government is unfriendly.

At any rate, I was to go north on the afternoon plane, take a room under the name "Chilly Buttons," and await Uncle Dagoberto's instructions. Fine. For me, the trip was nothing. I relaxed with a Glenlivet and Derrida, the film was *Death Wish VII*, and the flight attendants small in front and, well, substantial behind, just the way I like them. On arriving, I checked into the hotel he'd arranged for me—the girl behind the desk had eyes and shoulders like one of the amazons of the North American cinema, but she tittered and showed off her orthodontia when I signed "Chilly Buttons" in the register—and I went straight up to my room to await Uncle Dagoberto's call. Oh, yes, I nearly forgot: he'd given me an attaché case in which there were five hundred huevos—our national currency—and a thousand black-market dollars. "I don't anticipate any problems," he'd told me as he handed me onto the plane, "but you never know, eh?"

I ate veal medallions and a dry spinach salad at a brasserie frequented by British rock stars and North American drug agents, and then sat up late in my room, watching a rerun of the world cockfighting championships. I was just dozing off when the phone rang. "Bueno," I said, snatching up the receiver.

"Tomás?" It was Uncle Dagoberto.

"Yes," I said.

His voice was pinched with secrecy, a whisper, a rasp. "I want you to go to the customs warehouse on La Avenida Democracia at ten A.M. sharp." He was breathing heavily. I could barely hear him. "There are shoes there," he said. "Italian shoes. Thirty thousand shoes, wrapped in tissue paper. No one has claimed them and they're to be auctioned first thing in the morning." He paused and I listened to the empty hiss of the land breathing through the wires that separated us. "I want you to bid nothing for them. A hundred huevos. Two. But I want you to buy. Buy them or die." And he hung up.

At quarter of ten the next morning, I stood outside the warehouse, the attaché case clutched in my hand. Somewhere a cock crowed. It was cold, but the sun warmed the back of my neck. Half a dozen hastily shaven men in sagging suits and battered domestically made oxfords gathered beside me.

I was puzzled. How did Uncle Dagoberto expect me to buy thirty thousand Italian shoes for two hundred huevos, when a single pair sold for twice that? I understood that the black-market dollars were to be offered as needed, but even so, how could I buy more than a few dozen pairs? I shrugged it off and buried my nose in Derrida.

It was past twelve when an old man in the uniform of the customs police hobbled up the street as if his legs were made of stone, produced a set of keys, and threw open the huge hammered-steel doors of the warehouse. We shuffled in, blinking against the darkness. When my eyes became accustomed to the light, the mounds of unclaimed goods piled up on pallets around me began to take on form. There were crates of crescent wrenches, boxes of Tupperware, a bin of door stoppers. I saw bicycle horns—thousands of them, black and bulbous as the noses of monkeys—and jars of kimchi stacked up to the steel crossbeams of the ceiling. And then I saw the shoes. They were heaped up in a small mountain, individually wrapped in tissue paper. Just as Uncle Dagoberto had said. The others ignored them. They read the description the customs man provided, unwrapped the odd shoe, and went on to the bins of churchkey openers and chutney. I was dazed. It was like stumbling across the treasure of the Incas, the Golden City itself, and yet having no one recognize it.

With trembling fingers, I unwrapped first one shoe, then another. I saw patent leather, suede, the sensuous ripple of alligator; my nostrils filled with the rich and unmistakable bouquet of newly tanned leather. The shoes were perfect, insuperable, the very latest styles, au courant, à la mode, and exciting. Why had the others turned away? It was then that I read the customs declaration: *Thirty thousand leather shoes*, it read, *imported from the Republic of Italy, port of Livorno. Unclaimed after thirty days. To be sold at auction to the highest bidder*. Beside the declaration, in a handscrawl that betrayed bureaucratic impatience—disgust, even—of the highest order, was this further notation: *Left feet only*.

It took me a moment. I bent to the mountain of shoes and began tearing at the tissue paper. I tore through women's pumps, stiletto heels, tooled boots, wing tips, deck shoes, and patent-leather loafers—and every single one, every one of those thirty thousand shoes, was half a pair. Uncle Dagoberto, I thought, you are a genius.

The auction was nothing. I waited through a dozen lots of number-two pencils, Cabbage Patch Dolls, and soft-white light-bulbs, and then I placed the sole bid on the thirty thousand left-footed shoes. One hundred huevos and they were mine. Later, I took the young amazon up to my room and showed her what a man with a name like Chilly Buttons can do in a sphere that, well—is this the place to gloat? We were sharing a cigarette when Uncle Dagoberto called. "Did you get them?" he shouted over the line.

"One hundred huevos," I said.

"Good boy," he crooned, "good boy." He paused a moment to catch his breath. "And do you know where I'm calling from?" he asked, struggling to keep down the effervescence in his voice.

I reached out to stroke the amazon's breasts—her name was Linda, by the way, and she was a student of cosmetology. "I think I can guess," I said. "Calidad?"

"Funny thing," Uncle Dagoberto said, "there are some shoes here, in the customs warehouse—fine Italian shoes, the finest, thirty thousand in a single lot—and no one has claimed them. Can you imagine that?"

There was such joy in his tone that I couldn't resist playing out the game with him. "There must be something wrong with them," I said.

I could picture his grin. "Nothing, nothing at all. If you're one-legged."

That was two years ago.

Today, Uncle Dagoberto is the undisputed shoe king of our city. He made such a killing on that one deal that he was able to buy his way into the cartel that "advises" the government. He has a title now—Undersecretary for International Trade— and a vast, brightly lit office in the President's palace.

I've changed too, though I still live with my mother on La Calle Verdad and I still attend the university. My shoes—I have some thirty pairs now, in every style and color those clever Italians have been able to devise—are the envy of all, and no small attraction to the nubile and status-hungry young women of the city. I no longer study semantics, hermeneutics, and the deconstruction of deconstruction, but have instead been pursuing a degree in business. It only makes sense. After all, the government doesn't seem half so unfriendly these days.

THE APE LADY IN RETIREMENT

SOMEHOW, she found herself backed up against the artichoke display in the fruit-and-vegetable department at Waldbaum's, feeling as lost and hopeless as an orphan. She was wearing her dun safari shorts and matching workshirt; the rhino-hide sandals she'd worn at the Makoua Reserve clung to the soles of her pale splayed tired old feet. Outside the big plate-glass windows, a sullen, grainy snow had begun to fall.

Maybe that was it, the snow. She was fretting over the vegetables, fumbling with her purse, the grocery list, the keys to the rheumatic Lincoln her sister had left her, when she glanced up and saw it, this wonder, this phenomenon, this dishwater turned to stone, and for the life of her she didn't know what it was. And then it came to her, the word chipped from the recesses of her memory like an old bone dug from the sediment: *snow*. Snow. What had it been—forty years?

She gazed out past the racks of diet cola and facial cream, past the soap-powder display and the thousand garish colors of the products she couldn't use and didn't want, and she was lost in a reminiscence so sharp and sudden it was like a blow. She saw her sister's eyes peering out from beneath the hood of her snow-suit, the drifts piled high over their heads, hot chocolate in a decorated mug, her father cursing as he bent to wrap the chains round the rear wheels of the car . . . and then the murmur of the market brought her back, the muted din concentrated now in a single voice, and she was aware that someone was addressing her. "Excuse me," the voice was saying, "excuse me."

She turned, and the voice took on form. A young man—a boy, really—short, massive across the shoulders, his dead-black hair cut close in a flattop, was standing before her. And what was that in his hand? A sausage of some sort, pepperoni, yes, and another word came back to her. "Excuse me," he repeated, "but aren't you Beatrice Umbo?"

She was. Oh, yes, she was—Beatrice Umbo, the celebrated ape lady, the world's foremost authority on the behavior of chimpanzees in the wild, Beatrice Umbo, come home to Connecticut to retire. She gave him a faint, distant smile of recognition. "Yes," she said softly, with a trace of the lisp that had clung to her since childhood, "and it's just terrible."

"Terrible?" he echoed, and she could see the hesitation in his eyes. "I'm sorry," he said, grinning unsteadily and thumping the pepperoni against his thigh, "but we read about you in school, in college, I mean. I even read your books, the first one, anyway—*Jungle Dawn?*"

She couldn't respond. It was his grin, the way his upper lip pulled back from his teeth and folded over his incisors. He was Agassiz, the very picture of Agassiz, and all of a sudden she was back in the world of leaves, back in the Makoua Reserve, crouched in a huddle of chimps. "Are you all right?" he asked.

"Of course I'm all right," she snapped, and at that moment she caught a glimpse of herself in the mirror behind the halved cantaloupes. The whites of her eyes were stippled with yellow, her hair was like a fright wig, her face as rutted and seamed as an old saddlebag. Even worse, her skin had the oddest citrus cast to it, a color about midway between the hue of a grapefruit and an orange. She didn't look well, she knew it. But then what could they expect of a woman who'd devoted her life to science and survived dysentery, malaria, schistosomiasis, hepatitis, and sleeping sickness in the process, not to mention the little things like the chiggers that burrow beneath your toenails to lay their eggs. "I mean the fruit," she said, trying to bite back the lisp. "The fruit is terrible. No yim-yim," she sighed, gesturing toward the bins of tangerines, kumquats, and pale seedless grapes. "No wild custard apple or tiger peach. They haven't even got passionfruit."

The boy glanced down at her cart. There were fifty yams—she'd counted them out herself—six gallons of full-fat milk, and a five-pound block of cheese buried in its depths. All the bananas she could find, ranging in color from burnished green to putrescent black, were piled on top in a great towering pyramid that threatened to drop the bottom out of the thing. "They've got Italian chestnuts," he offered, looking up again and showing off his teeth in that big tentative grin. "And in a month or so they'll get those little torpedo-shaped things that come off the cactuses out west—prickly pear, that's what they call them."

She cocked her head to give him an appreciative look. "You're very sweet," she said, the lisp creeping back into her voice. "But you don't understand—I've got a visitor coming. A permanent visitor. And he's very particular about what he eats."

"I'm Howie Kantner," he said suddenly. "My father and me run Kantner Construction?"

She'd been in town less than a week, haunting the chilly cavernous house her mother had left her sister and her sister had left her. She'd never heard of Kantner Construction.

The boy ducked his head as if he were genuflecting, told her how thrilled he was to meet her, and turned to go—but then he swung back round impulsively. "Couldn't you . . . I mean, do you think you'll need some help with all those bananas?"

She pursed her lips.

"I just thought . . . the boxboys are the pits here and you're so . . . casually dressed for the weather and all. . . ."

"Yes," she said slowly, "yes, that would be very nice," and she smiled. She was pleased, terribly pleased. A moment earlier she'd felt depressed, out of place, an alien in her own hometown, and now she'd made a friend. He waited for her behind the checkout counter, this hulking, earnest college boy, this big post-adolescent male with the clipped brow and squared shoulders, and she beamed at him till her gums ached, wondering what he'd think if she told him he reminded her of a chimp.

Konrad was late. They'd told her three, but it was past five already and there was no sign of him. She huddled by the fire, draped in an afghan she'd found in a trunk in the basement, and listened to the clank and wheeze of the decrepit old oil burner as it switched itself fitfully on and off. It was still snowing, snow like a curse, and she wished she were back in her hut at Makoua with the monsoon hammering at the roof. She looked out the window and thought she was on the moon.

It was close to seven when the knock at the door finally came. She'd been dozing, the notes for her lecture series scattered like refuse at her feet, the afghan drawn up tight around her throat. Clutching the title page as if it were a lifejacket tossed her on a stormy sea, she rose from the chair with a click of her arthritic knees and crossed the room to the door.

Though she'd swept the porch three times, the wind kept defeating her efforts, and when she'd pulled back the door she found Konrad standing in a drift up to his knees. He was huge—far bigger than she'd expected—and the heavy jacket, scarf, and gloves exaggerated the effect. His trainer or keeper or whatever she was stood behind him, grinning weirdly, her arms laden with groceries. Konrad was grinning too, giving her the low closed grin she'd been the first to describe in the wild: it meant he was agitated but not yet stoked to the point of violence. His high-pitched squeals—*eeeee! eeeee! eeeee!*—filled the hallway.

"Miss Umbo?" the girl said, as Konrad, disdaining introductions, flung his knuckles down on the hardwood floor and scampered for the fire. "I'm Jill," the girl said, trying simultaneously to shake hands, pass through the doorframe, and juggle the bags of groceries.

Beatrice was still trying to get over the shock of seeing a chimpanzee in human dress—and one so huge: he must have stood better than four and a half feet and weighed close to 180— and it was a moment before she could murmur a greeting and offer to take one of the bags of groceries. The door slammed shut and the girl followed her into the kitchen while Konrad slapped his shoulders and stamped round the fireplace.

"He's so . . . so big," Beatrice said, depositing the bag on the oak table in the kitchen.

"I guess," the girl said, setting her bags down with a shrug.

"And what is all this?" Beatrice gestured at the groceries. She caught a glance of Konrad through the archway that led into the living room: he'd settled into her armchair and was studiously bent over her notes, tearing the pages into thin white strips with the delicate tips of his black leather fingers.

"Oh, this," the girl said, brightening. "This is the stuff he likes to eat," dipping into the near bag and extracting one box after another as if they were exhibits at a trial, "Carnation Instant Breakfast, cheese nachos, Fruit Roll-Ups, Sugar Daffies. . . ."

"Are you—?" Beatrice hesitated, wondering how to phrase the question. "What I mean is, you're his trainer, I take it?"

The girl must have been in her mid-twenties, though she looked fourteen. Her hair was limp and blond, her eyes too big for her face. She was wearing faded jeans, a puffy down vest over a flannel shirt, and a pair of two-hundred-dollar hiking boots. "Me?" she squealed, and then she blushed. Her voice dropped till it was nearly inaudible: "I'm just the person that cleans up his cage and all and I've always had this like way with animals. . . ."

Beatrice was shocked. Shocked and disgusted. It was worse than she'd suspected. When she agreed to take Konrad, she knew she'd be saving him from the sterility of a cage, from the anomie and humiliation of the zoo. And those were the very terms— "anomie" and "humiliation"—she'd used on the phone with his former trainer, with the zookeeper himself. For Konrad was no run-of-the-mill chimp snatched from the jungle and caged for the pleasure of the big bland white apes who lined up to gawk at him and make their little jokes at the expense of his dignity—though that would have been crime enough—no, he was special, extraordinary, a chimp made after the image of man.

Raised as a human, in one of those late-sixties experiments Beatrice deplored, he'd been bathed, dressed, and pampered, taught to use cutlery and sit at a table, and he'd mastered 350 of the hand signals that constituted American Sign Language. (This last especially appalled her—at one time he could actually converse, or so they said.) But when he grew into puberty at the age of seven, when he developed the iron musculature and crackling sinews of the adolescent male who could reduce a room of furniture to detritus in minutes or snap the femur of a line-backer as if it were tinder, it was abruptly decided that he could be human no more. They took away his trousers and shoes, his stuffed toys and his color TV, and the overseers of the experiment made a quiet move to shift him to the medical laboratories for another, more sinister, sort of research. But he was famous by then and the public outcry landed him in the zoo instead, where they made a sort of clown of him, isolating him from the other chimps and dressing him up like something in a toy-store window. There he'd languished for twenty-five years, neither chimp nor man.

Twenty-five years. And with people like this moon-eyed incompetent to look after him. It *was* a shock. "You mean to tell me you've had no training?" Beatrice demanded, the outrage constricting her throat till she could barely choke out the words. "None at all?"

The girl gave her a meek smile and a shrug of the shoulders.

"You've had nutritional training, certainly—you must have studied the dietary needs of the wild chimpanzee, at the very least . . ." and she gestured disdainfully at the bags of junk food, of salt and fat and empty calories.

The girl murmured something, some sort of excuse or melioration, but Beatrice never heard it. A sudden movement from the front room caught her eye, and all at once she remembered Konrad. She turned away from the girl as if she didn't exist and focused her bright narrow eyes on him, the eyes that had captured every least secret of his wild cousins, the rapt unblinking eyes of the professional voyeur.

The first thing she noticed was that he'd finished with her notes, the remnants of which lay strewn about the room like confetti. She saw too that he was calm now, at home already, sniffing at the afghan as if he'd known it all his life. Oblivious to her, he settled into the armchair, draped the afghan over his knees, and began fumbling through the pockets of his overcoat like an absent-minded commuter. And then, while her mouth fell open and her eyes narrowed to pinpricks, he produced a cigar—a fine, green, tightly rolled panatela—struck a match to light it, and lounged back in an aureole of smoke, his feet, bereft now of the plastic galoshes, propped up luxuriously on the coffee table.

It was a night of stinging cold and subarctic wind, but though the panes rattled in their frames, the old house retained its heat. Beatrice had set the thermostat in the high eighties and she'd built the fire up beneath a cauldron of water that steamed the walls and windows till they dripped like the myriad leaves of the rain forest. Konrad was naked, as nature and evolution had meant him to be, and Beatrice was in the clean, starched khakis she'd worn in the bush for the past forty years. Potted plants—cane, ficus, and dieffenbachia—crowded the hallway, spilled from the windowsills, and softened the corners of each of the downstairs rooms. In the living room, the TV roared at full volume, and Konrad stood before it, excited, signing at the screen and emitting a rising series of pant hoots: *"Hoo-hoo, hoo-ah-hoo-ah-hoo!"*

Watching from the kitchen, Beatrice felt her face pucker with disapproval. This TV business was no good, she thought, languidly stirring vegetables into a pot of chicken broth. Chimps had an innate dignity, an eloquence that had nothing to do with sign language, gabardine, color TV, or nacho chips, and she was determined to restore it to him. The junk food was in the trash, where it belonged, along with the obscene little suits of clothes the girl had foisted on him, and she'd tried unplugging the TV set, but Konrad was too smart for her. Within thirty seconds he'd got it squawking again.

"*Eee-eee!*" he shouted now, slapping his palms rhythmically on the hardwood floor.

"Awright," the TV said in its stentorian voice, "take the dirty little stool pigeon out back and extoiminate him."

It was an unfortunate thing for the TV to say, because it provoked in Konrad a reaction that could only be described as a frenzy. Whereas before he'd been excited, now he was enraged. "*Wraaaaa!*" he screamed in a pitch no mere human could duplicate, and he charged the screen with a stick of firewood, every hair on his body sprung instantly erect. Good, she thought, stirring her soup as he flailed at the oak-veneer cabinet and choked the voice out of it, good, good, good, as he backed away and bounced round the room like a huge India-rubber ball, the stick slapping behind him, his face contorted in a full open grin of incendiary excitement. Twice over the sofa, once up the banister, and then he charged again, the stick beating jerkily at the floor. The crash of the screen came almost as a relief to her— at least there'd be no more of that. What puzzled her, though, what arrested her hand in mid-stir, was Konrad's reaction. He stood stock-still a moment, then backed off, pouting and tugging at his lower lip, the screams tapering to a series of squeaks and whimpers of regret.

The moment the noise died, Beatrice became aware of another sound, low-pitched and regular, a signal it took her a moment to identify: someone was knocking at the door. Konrad must have heard it too. He looked up from the shattered cabinet and grunted softly. "*Urk*, he said, "*urk, urk*," and lifted his eyes to Beatrice's as she backed away from the stove and wiped her hands on her apron.

Who could it be, she wondered, and what must they have thought of all that racket? She hung her apron on a hook, smoothed back her hair, and passed into the living room, neatly sidestepping the wreckage of the TV. Konrad's eyes followed her as she stepped into the foyer, flicked on the porch light, and swung back the door.

"Hello? Miss Umbo?"

Two figures stood bathed in yellow light before her, hominids certainly, and wrapped in barbaric bundles of down, fur, and machine-stitched nylon. "Yes?"

"I hope you don't . . . I mean, you probably don't remember me," said the squatter of the two figures, removing his knit cap to reveal the stiff black brush cut beneath, "but we met a couple weeks ago at Waldbaum's? I'm Howie, Howie Kantner?"

Agassiz, she thought, and she saw his unsteady grin replicated on the face of the figure behind him.

"I hope it isn't an imposition, but this is my father, Howard," and the second figure, taller, less bulky in the shoulders, stepped forward with a slouch and an uneasy shift of his eyes that told her he was no longer the dominant male. "Pleased to meet you," he said in a voice ruined by tobacco.

She was aware of Konrad behind her—he'd pulled himself into the precarious nest he'd made in the coat tree of mattress stuffing and strips of carpeting from the downstairs hallway— and her social graces failed her. She didn't think to ask them in out of the cold till Howie spoke again. "I—I was wondering," he stammered, "my father's a big fan of yours, if you would sign a book for him?"

Smile, she told herself, and the command influenced her facial muscles. Ask them to come in. "Come in," she said, "please," and then she made a banal comment about the weather.

In they came, stamping and shaking and picking at their clothing, massive but obsequious, a barrage of apologies—"so late"; "we're not intruding?"; "did she mind?"—exploding around them. They exchanged a glance and wrinkled up their noses at the potent aroma and high visibility of Konrad. Howard Sr. clutched his book, a dog-eared paper edition of *The Wellsprings of Man*. From his coat tree, which Beatrice had secured to the high ceilings with a network of nylon tow rope, Konrad grunted softly. "No, not at all," she heard herself saying, and then she asked them if they'd like a cup of hot chocolate or tea.

Seated in the living room and divested of their impressive coats and ponderous boots, scarves, gloves, and hats, father and son seemed subdued. They tried not to look at the ruined TV or at the coat tree or the ragged section of bare plaster where Konrad had stripped the flowered wallpaper to get at the stale but piquant paste beneath. Howie was having the hot chocolate; Howard Sr., the tea. "So how do you like our little town?" Howard Sr. asked as she settled into the armchair opposite him.

She hadn't uttered a word to a human being since Konrad's companion had left, and she was having difficulty with the amenities expected of her. Set her down amidst a convocation of chimps or even a troop of baboons and she'd never commit a faux pas or gaucherie, but here she felt herself on uncertain ground. "Hate it," she said.

Howard Sr. seemed to mull this over, while unbeknownst to him, Konrad was slipping down from the coat tree and creeping up at his back. "Is it that bad," he said finally, "or is it the difference between Connecticut and the, the—" He was interrupted by the imposition of a long, sinuous, fur-cloaked arm which snaked under his own to deftly snatch a pack of cigarettes from his shirt pocket. Before he could react, the arm was gone. "*Eeeee!*" screamed Konrad, "*eeee-eeee!*," and he retreated to the coat tree with his booty.

Beatrice rose immediately to her feet, ignoring the sharp pain that ground at her kneecaps, and marched across the room. She wouldn't have it, one of *her* chimps indulging a filthy human habit. Give it here, she wanted to say, but then she wouldn't have one of her chimps responding to human language either, as if he were some fawning lapdog or neutered cat. "*Woo-oo-oogh*," she coughed at him.

"*Wraaaaa!*" he screamed back, bouncing down from his perch and careening round the room in a threat display, the cigarettes clutched tightly to his chest. She circled him warily, aware that Howie and his father loomed behind her now, their limbs loose, faces set hard. "Miss Umbo," Howie's voice spoke at her back, "do you need any help there?"

It was then that Konrad tore round the room again—up over the couch, the banister, up the ropes and down—and Howard Sr. made a calculated grab for him. "No!" Beatrice cried, but the warning was superfluous: Konrad effortlessly eluded the old man's clumsy swipe, bounced twice, and was back up in the coat tree before he could blink his eyes.

"Heh, heh," Howard Sr. laughed from the top of his throat, "frisky little fella, isn't he?"

Beatrice stood before him, trying to catch her breath. "You don't," she began, wondering how to put it, "you don't want to, uh, obstruct him when he displays."

Howie, the son, looked bemused.

"You don't, I think, appreciate the strength of this creature. A chimpanzee—a full-grown male, as Konrad is—is at least three times as strong as his human counterpart. Now certainly, I'm sure he wouldn't deliberately hurt anyone—"

"Hurt us?" Howie exclaimed, involuntarily flexing his shoulders. "I mean, he barely comes up to my chest."

A contented grunt escaped Konrad at that moment. He lay sprawled in his nest, the rubbery soles of his prehensile feet blackly dangling. He'd wadded up the entire pack of cigarettes and tucked it beneath his lower lip. Now he extracted the wad of tobacco and paper, sniffed it with an appreciative roll of his eyes, and replaced it between cheek and gum. Beatrice sighed. She looked at Howie, but didn't have the strength to respond.

Later, while Konrad snored blissfully from his perch and the boy and his father had accepted first one bowl of chicken soup and then another, and the conversation drew away from the prosaic details of Beatrice's life in Connecticut—and did she know Tiddy Brohmer and Harriet Dillers?—and veered instead toward Makoua and the Umbo Primate Center, Howard Sr. brought up the subject of airplanes. He flew, and so did his son. He'd heard about the bush pilots in Africa and wondered about her experience of them.

Beatrice was so surprised she had to set down her tea for fear of spilling it. "You fly?" she repeated.

Howard Sr. nodded and leveled his keen glistening gaze on her. "Twenty-two hundred and some-odd hours' worth," he said. "And Howie. He's a regular fanatic. Got his license when he was sixteen, and since we bought the Cessna there's hardly a minute when he's on the ground."

"I love it," Howie asserted, crouched over his massive thighs on the very edge of the chair. "I mean, it's my whole life. When I get out of school I want to restore classic aircraft. I know a guy who's got a Stearman."

Beatrice warmed up her smile. All at once she was back in Africa, 2500 feet up, the land spread out like a mosaic at her feet. Champ, her late husband, had taken to planes like a chimp to trees, and though she'd never learned to fly herself, she'd spent whole days at a time in the air with him, spying out chimp habitat in the rich green forests of Cameroon, the Congo, and Zaire or coasting above the golden veldt to some distant, magical village in the hills. She closed her eyes a moment, overcome with the intensity of the recollection. Champ, Makoua, the storms and sunsets and the close, savage, unimpeachable society of the apes—it was all lost to her, lost forever.

"Miss Umbo?" Howie was peering into her eyes with an expression of concern, the same expression he'd worn that afternoon in Waldbaum's when he'd asked if she needed help with the bananas.

"Miss Umbo," he repeated, "anytime you want to see Connecticut from the air, just you let me know."

"That's very kind of you," she said.

"Really," and he grinned Agassiz's grin, "it'd be a pleasure."

Things were sprouting from the dead dun earth—crocuses, daffodils, nameless buds, and strange pale fingertips of vegetation— by the time the first of her scheduled lectures came round. It was an evening lecture, open to the public, and held in the Buffon Memorial Auditorium of the State University. Her topic was "Tool Modification in the Chimps of the Makoua Reserve," and she'd chosen fifty color slides for illustration. For a while she'd debated wearing one of the crepe-de-chine dresses her sister had left hanging forlornly in the closet, but in the end she decided to stick with the safari shorts.

As the auditorium began to fill, she stood rigid behind the curtain, deaf to the chatter of the young professor who was to introduce her. She watched the crowd gather—blank-faced housewives and their paunchy husbands, bearded professors, breast-thumping students, the stringy, fur-swathed women of the Anthropology Club—watched them command their space, choose their seats, pick at themselves, and wriggle in their clothing. "I'll keep it short," the young professor was saying, "some remarks about your career in general and the impact of your first two books, then maybe two minutes on Makoua and the Umbo Primate Center, is that all right?" Beatrice didn't respond. She was absorbed in the dynamics of the crowd, listening to their chatter, observing their neck craning and leg crossing, watching the furtive plumbing of nostrils and sniffing of armpits, the obsessive fussing with hair and jewelry. Howie and his father were in the second row. By the time she began, it was standing room only.

It went quite well at first—she had that impression, anyway. She was talking of what she knew better than anyone else alive, and she spoke with a fluency and grace she couldn't seem to summon at Waldbaum's or the local Exxon station. She watched them—fidgeting, certainly, but patient and intelligent, all their primal needs—their sexual urges, the necessity of relieving themselves and eating to exhaustion—sublimated beneath the spell of her words. Agassiz, she told them about Agassiz, the first of the wild apes to let her groom him, dead twenty years now. She told them of Spenser and Leakey and Darwin, of Lula, Pout, and Chrysalis. She described how Agassiz had fished for termites with the stem of a plant he'd stripped of leaves, how Lula had used a stick to force open the concrete bunkers in which the bananas were stored, and how Clint, the dominant male, had used a wad of leaves as a sponge to dip the brains from the shattered skull of a baby baboon.

The problem arose when she began the slide show. For some reason, perhaps because the medium so magnified the size of the chimps and he felt himself wanting in comparison, Konrad threw a fit. (She hadn't wanted to bring him, but the last time she'd left him alone he'd switched on all the burners of the stove, overturned and gutted the refrigerator, and torn the back door from its hinges—all this prior to committing a rash of crimes, ranging from terrorizing Mrs. Binchy's Doberman to crushing and partially eating a still-unidentified angora kitten.) He'd been sitting just behind the podium, slouched in a folding chair around which Doris Beatts, the young professor, had arranged an array of fruit, including a basket of yim-yim flown in for the occasion. "Having him onstage is a terrific idea," she'd gushed, pumping Beatrice's hand and flashing a zealot's smile that showed off her pink and exuberant gums, "what could be better? It'll give the audience a real frisson, having a live chimp sitting there."

Yes, it gave them a frisson, all right.

Konrad had been grunting softly to himself and working his way happily through the yim-yim, but no sooner had the lights been dimmed and the first slide appeared, than he was up off the chair with a shriek of outrage. Puffed to twice his size, he swayed toward the screen on his hind legs, displaying at the gigantic chimp that had suddenly materialized out of the darkness. "*Wraaaaa!*" he screamed, dashing the chair to pieces and snatching up one of its jagged legs to whirl over his head like a club. There was movement in the front row. A murmur of concern—concern, not yet fear—washed through the crowd. "*Woo-oo-oogh*," Beatrice crooned, trying to calm him. "It's all right," she heard herself saying through the speakers that boomed her voice out over the auditorium. But it wasn't all right. She snapped to the next slide, a close-up of Clint sucking termites from a bit of straw, and Konrad lost control, throwing himself at the screen with a screech that brought the audience to its feet.

Up went the lights. To an individual, the audience was standing. Beatrice didn't have time to catalogue their facial expressions, but they ran the gamut from amusement to shock, terror, and beyond. One woman—heavyset, with arms like Christmas turkeys and black little deepset eyes—actually cried out as if King Kong himself had broken loose. And Konrad? He stood bewildered amidst the white tatters of the screen, his fur gone limp again, his knuckles on the floor. For a moment, Beatrice actually thought he looked embarrassed.

Later, at the reception, people crowded round him and he took advantage of the attention to shamelessly cadge cigarettes, plunder the canape trays, and guzzle Coca-Cola as if it were spring water. Beatrice wanted to put a stop to it—he was demeaning himself, the clown in the funny suit with his upturned palm thrust through the bars of his cage—but the press around her was terrific. Students and scholars, a man from the local paper, Doris Beatts and her neurasthenic husband, the Kantners, father and son, all bombarding her with questions: Would she go back? Was it for health reasons she'd retired? Did she believe in UFOs? Reincarnation? The New York Yankees? How did it feel having a full-grown chimp in the house? Did she know Vlastos Reizek's monograph on the seed content of baboon feces in the Kalahari? It was almost ten o'clock before Konrad turned away to vomit noisily in the corner and Howie Kantner, beaming sunnily and balancing half a plastic cup of warm white wine on the palm of one hand, asked her when they were going to go flying,

"Soon," she said, watching the crowd part as Konrad, a perplexed look on his face, bent to lap up the sour overflow of his digestive tract.

"How about tomorrow?" Howie said.

"Tomorrow," Beatrice repeated, struck suddenly with the scent of the rain forest, her ears ringing with the call of shrike and locust and tree toad. "Yes," she lisped, "that would be nice."

Konrad was subdued the next day. He spent the early morning halfheartedly tearing up the carpet in the guest room, then brooded over his nuts and bananas, all the while pinning Beatrice with an accusatory look, a look that had nacho chips and Fruit Roll-Ups written all over it. Around noon, he dragged himself across the floor like a hundred-year-old man and climbed wearily into his nest. Beatrice felt bad, but she wasn't about to give in. They'd made him schizophrenic—neither chimp nor man—and if there was pain involved in reacquainting him with his roots, with his true identity, there was nothing she could do about it. Besides, she was feeling schizophrenic herself. Konrad was a big help—the smell of him, the silken texture of his fur as she groomed him, the way he scratched around in the basement when he did his business—but still she felt out of place, still she missed Makoua with an ache that wouldn't go away, and as the days accumulated like withered leaves at her feet, she found herself wishing she'd stayed on there to die.

Howie appeared at ten of three, his rust-eaten Datsun rumbling at the curb, the omnipresent grin on his lips. It was unseasonally warm for mid-April and he wore a red T-shirt that showed off the extraordinary development of his pectorals, deltoids, and biceps; a blue windbreaker was flung casually over one shoulder. "Miss Umbo," he boomed as she answered the door, "it's one perfect day for flying. Visibility's got to be twenty-five miles or more. You ready?"

She was. She'd been looking forward to it, in fact. "I hope you don't mind if I bring Konrad along," she said.

Howie's smile faded for just an instant. Konrad stood at her side, his lower lip unfurled in a pout. "*Hoo-hoo*," he murmured, eyes meek and round. Howie regarded him dubiously a moment, and then the grin came back. "Sure," he said, shrugging, "I don't see why not."

It was a twenty-minute ride to the airport. Beatrice stared out the window at shopping centers, car lots, Burger King and Stereo City, at cemeteries that stretched as far as she could see. Konrad sat in back, absorbed in plucking cigarette butts from the rear ashtray and making a neat little pile of them on the seat beside him. Howie was oblivious. He kept up a steady stream of chatter the whole way, talking about airplanes mostly, but shading into his coursework at school and how flipped out his Anthro prof would be when she heard he was taking Beatrice flying. For her part, Beatrice was content to let the countryside flash by, murmuring an occasional "yes" or "uh huh" when Howie paused for breath.

The airport was tiny, two macadam strips in a grassy field, thirty or forty airplanes lined up in ragged rows, a cement-block building the size of her basement. A sign over the door welcomed them to Arkbelt Airport. Howie pushed the plane out onto the runway himself and helped Beatrice negotiate the high step up into the cockpit. Konrad clambered into the back and allowed Beatrice to fasten his seatbelt. For a long while they sat on the ground, as Howie, grinning mechanically, revved the engine and checked this gauge or that.

The plane was a Cessna 182, painted a generic orange and white and equipped with dual controls, autopilot, a storm scope, and four cramped vinyl seats. It was about what she'd ex-

pected—a little shinier and less battered than Champ's Piper,
but no less noisy or bone-rattling. Howie gunned the engine
and the plane jolted down the runway with an apocalyptic roar,
Beatrice clinging to the plastic handgrip till she could taste her
breakfast in the back of her throat. But then they lifted off like
gods, liberated from the grip of the earth, and Connecticut
swelled beneath them, revealing the drift and flow of its topol-
ogy and the hidden patterns of its dismemberment.

"Beautiful," she screamed over the whine of the engine.

Howie worked the flaps and drew the yoke toward him. They
banked right and rose steadily. "See that out there?" he shouted,
pointing out her window to where the ocean threw the sky back
at them. "Long Island Sound."

From just behind her, Konrad said: "*Wow-wow, er-er-er-er!*"
The smell of him, in so small a confine, was staggering.

"You want to sightsee here," Howie shouted, "maybe go
over town and look for your house and the university and all,
or do you want to go out over the Island a ways and then circle
back?"

She was dazzled, high in the empyrean, blue above, blue
below. "The Island," she shouted, exhilarated, really exhilarated, for the first time since she'd left Africa.

Howie leveled off the plane and the tan lump of Long Island
loomed ahead of them. "Great, huh?" he shouted, gesturing
toward the day like an impresario, like the man who'd made it.
Beatrice beamed at him. "Woooo!" Howie said, pinching his
nostrils and making an antic face. "He's ripe today, Konrad,
isn't he?"

"Forty years," Beatrice laughed, proud of Konrad, proud of
the stink, proud of every chimp she'd ever known, and proud
of this boy Howie too—why, he was nothing but a big chimp
himself. It was then—while she was laughing, while Howie
mugged for her and she began to feel almost whole for the first
time since she'd left Makoua—that the trouble began. Like most

trouble, it arose out of a misunderstanding. Apparently, Konrad had saved one of the butts from Howie's car, and when he reached out nimbly to depress the cigarette lighter, Howie, poor Howie, thought he was going for the controls and grabbed his wrist.

A mistake.

"No!" Beatrice cried, and immediately the tug of war spilled over into her lap. "Let go of him!"

"*Eeeee! Eeeee!*" Konrad shrieked, his face distended in the full open grin of high excitement, already stoked to violence. She felt the plane dip out from under her as Howie, his own face gone red with the rush of blood, struggled to keep it on course with one hand while fighting back Konrad with the other. It was no contest. Konrad slipped Howie's grasp and then grabbed *his* wrist, as if to say, "How do you like it?"

"Get off me, goddamnit!" Howie bellowed, but Konrad didn't respond. Instead, he jerked Howie's arm back so swiftly and suddenly it might have been the lever of a slot machine; even above the noise of the engine, Beatrice could hear the shoulder give, and then Howie's bright high yelp of pain filled the compartment. In the next instant Konrad was in front, in the cockpit, dancing from Beatrice's lap to Howie's and back again, jerking at the controls, gibbering and hooting and loosing his bowels in a frenzy like nothing she'd ever seen.

"Son of a bitch!" Howie was working up a frenzy of his own, the plane leaping and bucking as he punched in the autopilot and hammered at the chimp with his left hand, the right dangling uselessly, his eyes peeled back in terror. "*Hoo-ah-hoo-ah-hoo!*" Konrad hooted, spewing excrement and springing into Beatrice's lap. For an instant he paused to shoot Howie a mocking glance and then he snatched the yoke to his chest and the plane shot up with a clattering howl while Howie flailed at him with the heavy meat of his fist.

Konrad took the first two blows as if he didn't notice them, then abruptly dropped the yoke, the autopilot kicking in to level them off. Howie hit him again and Beatrice knew she was going to die. "*Er-er,*" Konrad croaked experimentally, and Howie, panic in his face, hit him again. And then, as casually as he might have reached out for a yam or banana, Konrad returned the blow and the plane jerked with the force of it. "*Wraaaaa!*" Konrad screamed, but Howie didn't hear him. Howie was unconscious. Unconscious, and smeared with shit. And now, delivering the coup de grace, Konrad sprang to his chest, snatched up his left hand—the hand that had pummeled him—and bit off the thumb. A snap of the jaws and it was gone. Howie's heart pumped blood to the wound.

In that moment—the moment of Howie's disfigurement—Beatrice's own heart turned over in her chest. She looked at Konrad, perched atop poor Howie, and at Howie, who even in repose managed to favor Agassiz. They were beyond Long Island now, headed out to sea, high over the Atlantic. Champ had tried to teach her to fly, but she'd had no interest in it. She looked at the instrument panel and saw nothing. For a moment the idea of switching on the radio came into her head, but then she glanced at Konrad and thought better of it.

Konrad was looking into her eyes. The engine hummed, Howie's head fell against the door, the smell of Konrad—his body, his shit—filled her nostrils. They had five hours' flying time, give or take a few minutes, that much she knew. She looked out over the nose of the plane to where the sea swallowed up the rim of the world. Africa was out there, distant and serene, somewhere beyond the night that fell like an axe across the horizon. She could almost taste it.

"*Urk,*" Konrad said, and he was still looking at her. His eyes were soft now, his breathing regular. He sat atop Howie in a forlorn slouch, the cigarette forgotten, the controls irrelevant, nothing at all. "*Urk,*" he repeated, and she knew what he wanted, knew in a rush of comprehension that took her all the way back to Makoua and that first, long-ago touch of Agassiz's strange spidery fingers.

She held his eyes. The engine droned. The sea beneath them seemed so still you could walk on it, so soft you could wrap yourself up in it. She reached out and touched his hand. "*Urk*," she said.

IF THE RIVER WAS WHISKEY

THE WATER WAS a heartbeat, a pulse, it stole the heat from his body and pumped it to his brain. Beneath the surface, magnified through the shimmering lens of his face mask, were silver shoals of fish, forests of weed, a silence broken only by the distant throbbing hum of an outboard. Above, there was the sun, the white flash of a faraway sailboat, the weatherbeaten dock with its weatherbeaten rowboat, his mother in her deck chair, and the vast depthless green of the world beyond.

He surfaced like a dolphin, spewing water from the vent of his snorkel, and sliced back to the dock. The lake came with him, two bony arms and the wedge of a foot, the great heaving splash of himself flat out on the dock like something thrown up in a storm. And then, without pausing even to snatch up a towel, he had the spinning rod in hand and the silver lure was sizzling out over the water, breaking the surface just above the shadowy arena he'd fixed in his mind. His mother looked up at the splash. "Tiller," she called, "come get a towel."

His shoulders quaked. He huddled and stamped his feet, but he never took his eyes off the tip of the rod. Twitching it suggestively, he reeled with the jerky, hesitant motion that would drive lunker fish to a frenzy. Or so he'd read, anyway.

"Tilden, do you hear me?"

"I saw a Northern," he said. "A big one. Two feet maybe." The lure was in. A flick of his wrist sent it back. Still reeling, he ducked his head to wipe his nose on his wet shoulder. He could feel the sun on his back now and he envisioned the skirted lure in the water, sinuous, sensual, irresistible, and he waited for the line to quicken with the strike.

*   *   *

The porch smelled of pine—old pine, dried up and dead—and it depressed him. In fact, everything depressed him—especially this vacation. Vacation. It was a joke. Vacation from what?

He poured himself a drink—vodka and soda, tall, from the plastic half-gallon jug. It wasn't noon yet, the breakfast dishes were in the sink, and Tiller and Caroline were down at the lake. He couldn't see them through the screen of trees, but he heard the murmur of their voices against the soughing of the branches and the sadness of the birds. He sat heavily in the creaking wicker chair and looked out on nothing. He didn't feel too hot. In fact, he felt as if he'd been cored and dried, as if somebody had taken a pipe cleaner and run it through his veins. His head ached too, but the vodka would take care of that. When he finished it, he'd have another, and then maybe a grilled swiss on rye. Then he'd start to feel good again.

*   *   *

His father was talking to the man and his mother was talking to the woman. They'd met at the bar about twenty drinks ago and his father was into his could-have-been, should-have-been, way-back-when mode, and the man, bald on top and with a ratty beard and long greasy hair like his father's, was trying to steer the conversation back to building supplies. The woman had whole galaxies of freckles on her chest, and she leaned forward in her sundress and told his mother scandalous stories about people she'd never heard of. Tiller had drunk all the Coke and eaten all the beer nuts he could hold. He watched the Pabst Blue Ribbon sign flash on and off above the bar and he watched the woman's freckles move in and out of the gap between her breasts. Outside it was dark and a cool clean scent came in off the lake.

"Un huh, yeah," his father was saying, "the To the Bone Band. I played rhythm and switched off vocals with Dillie Richards. . . ."

The man had never heard of Dillie Richards.

"Black dude, used to play with Taj Mahal?"

The man had never heard of Taj Mahal.

"Anyway," his father said, "we used to do all this really outrageous stuff by people like Muddy, Howlin' Wolf, Luther Allison—"

"She didn't," his mother said.

The woman threw down her drink and nodded and the front of her dress went crazy. Tiller watched her and felt the skin go tight across his shoulders and the back of his neck, where he'd been burned the first day. He wasn't wearing any underwear, just shorts. He looked away. "Three abortions, two kids," the woman said. "And she never knew who the father of the second one was."

"Drywall isn't worth a damn," the man said. "But what're you going to do?"

"Paneling?" his father offered.

The man cut the air with the flat of his hand. He looked angry. "Don't talk to me about paneling," he said.

*   *   *

Mornings, when his parents were asleep and the lake was still, he would take the rowboat to the reedy cove on the far side of the lake where the big pike lurked. He didn't actually know if they lurked there, but if they lurked anywhere, this would be the place. It looked fishy, mysterious, sunken logs looming up dark from the shadows beneath the boat, mist rising like steam, as if the bottom were boiling with ravenous, cold-eyed, killer pike that could slice through monofilament with a snap of their jaws and bolt ducklings in a gulp. Besides, Joe Matochik, the old man who lived in the cabin next door and could charm frogs by stroking their bellies, had told him that this was where he'd find them.

It was cold at dawn and he'd wear a thick homeknit sweater over his T-shirt and shorts, sometimes pulling the stretched-out hem of it down like a skirt to warm his thighs. He'd take an apple with him or a slice of brown bread and peanut butter. And of course the orange lifejacket his mother insisted on.

When he left the dock he was always wearing the lifejacket—for form's sake and for the extra warmth it gave him against the raw morning air. But when he got there, when he stood in the swaying basin of the boat to cast his Hula Popper or Abu Relfex, it got in the way and he took it off. Later, when the sun ran through him and he didn't need the sweater, he balled it up on the seat beside him, and sometimes, if it was good and hot, he shrugged out of his T-shirt and shorts too. No one could see him in the cove, and it made his breath come quick to be naked like that under the morning sun.

*   *   *

"I heard you," he shouted, and he could feel the veins stand out in his neck, the rage come up in him like something killed and dead and brought back to life. "What kind of thing is that to tell a kid, huh? About his own father?"

She wasn't answering. She'd backed up in a corner of the kitchen and she wasn't answering. And what could she say, the bitch? He'd heard her. Dozing on the trundle bed under the stairs, wanting a drink but too weak to get up and make one, he'd heard voices from the kitchen, her voice and Tiller's. "Get used to it," she said, "he's a drunk, your father's a drunk," and then he was up off the bed as if something had exploded inside of him and he had her by the shoulders—always the shoulders and never the face, that much she'd taught him—and Tiller was gone, out the door and gone. Now, her voice low in her throat, a sick and guilty little smile on her lips, she whispered, "It's true."

"Who are you to talk?—you're shit-faced yourself." She shrank away from him, that sick smile on her lips, her shoulders hunched. He wanted to smash things, kick in the damn stove, make her hurt.

"At least I have a job," she said.

"I'll get another one, don't you worry."

"And what about Tiller? We've been here two weeks and you haven't done one damn thing with him, nothing, zero. You haven't even been down to the lake. Two hundred feet and you haven't even been down there once." She came up out of the corner now, feinting like a boxer, vicious, her sharp little fists balled up to drum on him. She spoke in a snarl. "What kind of father are you?"

He brushed past her, slammed open the cabinet, and grabbed the first bottle he found. It was whiskey, cheap whiskey, Four Roses, the shit she drank. He poured out half a water glass full and drank it down to spite her. "I hate the beach, boats, water, trees. I hate you."

She had her purse and she was halfway out the screen door. She hung there a second, looking as if she'd bitten into something rotten. "The feeling's mutual," she said, and the door banged shut behind her.

*   *   *

There were too many complications, too many things to get between him and the moment, and he tried not to think about them. He tried not to think about his father—or his mother either—in the same way that he tried not to think about the pictures of the bald-headed stick people in Africa or meat in its plastic wrapper and how it got there. But when he did think about his father he thought about the river-was-whiskey day.

It was a Tuesday or Wednesday, middle of the week, and when he came home from school the curtains were drawn and his father's car was in the driveway. At the door, he could hear him, the *chunk-chunk* of the chords and the rasping nasal whine that seemed as if it belonged to someone else. His father was sitting in the dark, hair in his face, bent low over the guitar. There was an open bottle of liquor on the coffee table and a clutter of beer bottles. The room stank of smoke.

It was strange, because his father hardly ever played his guitar anymore—he mainly just talked about it. In the past tense. And it was strange too—and bad—because his father wasn't at work. Tiller dropped his bookbag on the telephone stand. "Hi, Dad," he said.

His father didn't answer. Just bent over the guitar and played the same song, over and over, as if it were the only song he knew. Tiller sat on the sofa and listened. There was a verse— one verse—and his father repeated it three or four times before he broke off and slurred the words into a sort of chant or hum, and then he went back to the words again. After the fourth repetition, Tiller heard it:

> *If the river was whiskey,*
> *And I was a divin' duck,*
> *I'd swim to the bottom,*
> *Drink myself back up.*

For half an hour his father played that song, played it till anything else would have sounded strange. He reached for the bottle when he finally stopped, and that was when he noticed Tiller. He looked surprised. Looked as if he'd just woke up. "Hey, ladykiller Tiller," he said, and took a drink from the mouth of the bottle.

Tiller blushed. There'd been a Sadie Hawkins dance at school and Janet Rumery had picked him for her partner. Ever since, his father had called him ladykiller, and though he wasn't exactly sure what it meant, it made him blush anyway, just from the tone of it. Secretly, it pleased him. "I really liked the song, Dad," he said.

"Yeah?" His father lifted his eyebrows and made a face. "Well, come home to Mama, doggie-o. Here," he said, and he held out an open beer. "You ever have one of these, ladykiller Tiller?" He was grinning. The sleeve of his shirt was torn and his elbow was raw and there was a hard little clot of blood over his shirt pocket. "With your sixth-grade buddies out behind the handball court, maybe? No?"

Tiller shook his head.

"You want one? Go ahead, take a hit."

Tiller took the bottle and sipped tentatively. The taste wasn't much. He looked up at his father. "What does it mean?" he said. "The song, I mean—the one you were singing. About the whiskey and all."

His father gave him a long slow grin and took a drink from the big bottle of clear liquor. "I don't know," he said finally, grinning wider to show his tobacco-stained teeth. "I guess he just liked whiskey, that's all." He picked up a cigarette, made as if to light it, and then put it down again. "Hey," he said, "you want to sing it with me?"

*   *   *

All right, she'd hounded him and she'd threatened him and she was going to leave him, he could see that clear as day. But he was going to show her. And the kid too. He wasn't drinking. Not today. Not a drop.

He stood on the dock with his hands in his pockets while Tiller scrambled around with the fishing poles and oars and the rest of it. Birds were screeching in the trees and there was a smell of diesel fuel on the air. The sun cut into his head like a knife. He was sick already.

"I'm giving you the big pole, Dad, and you can row if you want."

He eased himself into the boat and it fell away beneath him like the mouth of a bottomless pit.

"I made us egg salad, Dad, your favorite. And I brought some birch beer."

He was rowing. The lake was churning underneath him, the wind was up and reeking of things washed up on the shore, and the damn oars kept slipping out of the oarlocks, and he was rowing. At the last minute he'd wanted to go back for a quick drink, but he didn't, and now he was rowing.

"We're going to catch a pike," Tiller said, hunched like a spider in the stern.

There was spray off the water. He was rowing. He felt sick. Sick and depressed.

"We're going to catch a pike, I can feel it. I know we are," Tiller said, "I know it. I just know it."

*   *   *

It was too much for him all at once—the sun, the breeze that was so sweet he could taste it, the novelty of his father rowing, pale arms and a dead cigarette clenched between his teeth, the boat rocking, and the birds whispering—and he closed his eyes a minute, just to keep from going dizzy with the joy of it. They were in deep water already. Tiller was trolling with a plastic worm and spinner, just in case, but he didn't have much faith in catching anything out here. He was taking his father to the cove with the submerged logs and beds of weed—that's where they'd connect, that's where they'd catch pike.

"Jesus," his father said when Tiller spelled him at the oars. Hands shaking, he crouched in the stern and tried to light a cigarette. His face was gray and the hair beat crazily around his face. He went through half a book of matches and then threw the cigarette in the water. "Where are you taking us, anyway," he said, "—the Indian Ocean?"

"The pike place," Tiller told him. "You'll like it, you'll see."

The sun was dropping behind the hills when they got there, and the water went from blue to gray. There was no wind in the cove. Tiller let the boat glide out across the still surface while his father finally got a cigarette lit, and then he dropped anchor. He was excited. Swallows dove at the surface, bullfrogs burped from the reeds. It was the perfect time to fish, the hour when the big lunker pike would cruise among the sunken logs, hunting.

"All right," his father said, "I'm going to catch the biggest damn fish in the lake," and he jerked back his arm and let fly with the heaviest sinker in the tackle box dangling from the end of the rod. The line hissed through the guys and there was a thunderous splash that probably terrified every pike within half a mile. Tiller looked over his shoulder as he reeled in his silver spoon. His father winked at him, but he looked grim.

It was getting dark, his father was out of cigarettes, and Tiller had cast the spoon so many times his arm was sore, when suddenly the big rod began to buck. "Dad! Dad!" Tiller shouted, and his father lurched up as if he'd been stabbed. He'd been dozing, the rod propped against the gunwale, and Tiller had been studying the long suffering-lines in his father's face, the grooves in his forehead, and the puffy discolored flesh beneath his eyes. With his beard and long hair and with the crumpled suffering look on his face, he was the picture of the crucified Christ Tiller had contemplated a hundred times at church. But now the rod was bucking and his father had hold of it and he was playing a fish, a big fish, the tip of the rod dipping all the way down to the surface.

"It's a pike, Dad, it's a pike!"

His father strained at the pole. His only response was a grunt, but Tiller saw something in his eyes he hardly recognized anymore, a connection, a charge, as if the fish were sending a current up the line, through the pole, and into his hands and body and brain. For a full three minutes he played the fish, his slack biceps gone rigid, the cigarette clamped in his mouth, while Tiller hovered over him with the landing net. There was a surge, a splash, and the thing was in the net, and Tiller had it over the side and into the boat. "It's a pike," his father said, "goddamnit, look at the thing, look at the size of it."

It wasn't a pike. Tiller had watched Joe Matochik catch one off the dock one night. Joe's pike had been dangerous, full of teeth, a long, lean, tapering strip of muscle and pounding life. This was no pike. It was a carp. A fat, pouty, stinking, ugly mud carp. Trash fish. They shot them with arrows and threw them up on the shore to rot. Tiller looked at his father and felt like crying.

"It's a pike," his father said, and already the thing in his eyes was gone, already it was over, "it's a pike. Isn't it?"

*   *   *

It was late—past two, anyway—and he was drunk. Or no, he was beyond drunk. He'd been drinking since morning, one tall vodka and soda after another, and he didn't feel a thing. He sat on the porch in the dark and he couldn't see the lake, couldn't hear it, couldn't even smell it. Caroline and Tiller were asleep. The house was dead silent.

Caroline was leaving him, which meant that Tiller was leaving him. He knew it. He could see it in her eyes and he heard it in her voice. She was soft once, his soft-eyed lover, and now she was hard, unyielding, now she was his worst enemy. They'd had the couple from the roadhouse in for drinks and burgers earlier that night and he'd leaned over the table to tell the guy something—Ed, his name was—joking really, nothing serious, just making conversation. "Vodka and soda," he said, "that's my drink. I used to drink vodka and grapefruit juice, but it tore the lining out of my stomach." And then Caroline, who wasn't even listening, stepped in and said, "Yeah, and that"—pointing to the glass—"tore the lining out of your brain." He looked up at her. She wasn't smiling.

All right. That was how it was. What did he care? He hadn't wanted to come up here anyway—it was her father's idea. Take the cabin for a month, the old man had said, pushing, pushing in that way he had, and get yourself turned around. Well, he wasn't turning around, and they could all go to hell.

After a while the chill got to him and he pushed himself up from the chair and went to bed. Caroline said something in her sleep and pulled away from him as he lifted the covers and slid in. He was awake for a minute or two, feeling depressed, so depressed he wished somebody would come in and shoot him, and then he was asleep.

In his dream, he was out in the boat with Tiller. The wind was blowing, his hands were shaking, he couldn't light a cigarette. Tiller was watching him. He pulled at the oars and nothing happened. Then all of a sudden they were going down, the boat sucked out from under them, the water icy and black, beating in on them as if it were alive. Tiller called out to him. He saw his son's face, saw him going down, and there was nothing he could do.

FOR THE BEST IN PAPERBACKS, LOOK FOR THE

In every corner of the world, on every subject under the sun, Penguin represents quality and variety—the very best in publishing today.

For complete information about books available from Penguin—including Pelicans, Puffins, Peregrines, and Penguin Classics—and how to order them, write to us at the appropriate address below. Please note that for copyright reasons the selection of books varies from country to country.

In the United Kingdom: For a complete list of books available from Penguin in the U.K., please write to *Dept E.P., Penguin Books Ltd, Harmondsworth, Middlesex, UB7 0DA*.

In the United States: For a complete list of books available from Penguin in the U.S., please write to *Dept BA, Penguin*, Box 120, Bergenfield, New Jersey 07621-0120.

In Canada: For a complete list of books available from Penguin in Canada, please write to *Penguin Books Ltd, 2801 John Street, Markham, Ontario L3R 1B4*.

In Australia: For a complete list of books available from Penguin in Australia, please write to the *Marketing Department, Penguin Books Ltd, P.O. Box 257, Ringwood, Victoria 3134*.

In New Zealand: For a complete list of books available from Penguin in New Zealand, please write to the *Marketing Department, Penguin Books (NZ) Ltd, Private Bag, Takapuna, Auckland 9*.

In India: For a complete list of books available from Penguin, please write to *Penguin Overseas Ltd, 706 Eros Apartments, 56 Nehru Place, New Delhi, 110019*.

In Holland: For a complete list of books available from Penguin in Holland, please write to *Penguin Books Nederland B.V., Postbus 195, NL-1380AD Weesp, Netherlands*.

In Germany: For a complete list of books available from Penguin, please write to *Penguin Books Ltd, Friedrichstrasse 10-12, D-6000 Frankfurt Main I, Federal Republic of Germany*.

In Spain: For a complete list of books available from Penguin in Spain, please write to *Longman, Penguin España, Calle San Nicolas 15, E-28013 Madrid, Spain*.

In Japan: For a complete list of books available from Penguin in Japan, please write to *Longman Penguin Japan Co Ltd, Yamaguchi Building, 2-12-9 Kanda Jimbocho, Chiyoda-Ku, Tokyo 101, Japan*.

FOR THE BEST IN CONTEMPORARY AMERICAN FICTION ℗

☐ **THE WOMEN OF BREWSTER PLACE**
A Novel in Seven Stories
Gloria Naylor

Winner of the American Book Award, this is the story of seven survivors of an urban housing project — a blind alley feeding into a dead end. From a variety of backgrounds, they experience, fight against, and sometimes transcend the fate of black women in America today.
192 pages   ISBN: 0-14-006690-X   **$5.95**

☐ **STONES FOR IBARRA**
Harriet Doerr

An American couple comes to the small Mexican village of Ibarra to reopen a copper mine, learning much about life and death from the deeply faithful villagers.
214 pages   ISBN: 0-14-007562-3   **$5.95**

☐ **WORLD'S END**
T. Coraghessan Boyle

"Boyle has emerged as one of the most inventive and verbally exuberant writers of his generation," writes *The New York Times*. Here he tells the story of Walter Van Brunt, who collides with early American history while searching for his lost father.
456 pages   ISBN: 0-14-009760-0   **$8.95**

☐ **THE WHISPER OF THE RIVER**
Ferrol Sams

The story of Porter Osborn, Jr., who, in 1938, leaves his rural Georgia home to face the world at Willingham University, *The Whisper of the River* is peppered with memorable characters and resonates with the details of place and time. Ferrol Sams's writing is regional fiction at its best.
528 pages   ISBN: 0-14-008387-1   **$6.95**

☐ **ENGLISH CREEK**
Ivan Doig

Drawing on the same heritage he celebrated in *This House of Sky,* Ivan Doig creates a rich and varied tapestry of northern Montana and of our country in the late 1930s.
338 pages   ISBN: 0-14-008442-8   **$6.95**

☐ **THE YEAR OF SILENCE**
Madison Smartt Bell

A penetrating look at the varied reactions to a young woman's suicide exactly one year later, *The Year of Silence* "captures vividly and poignantly the chancy dance of life." (*The New York Times Book Review*)
208 pages   ISBN: 0-14-011533-1   **$6.95**